The Assassin's Tear

KIRALYNN EPICS

Books by Karen L Azinger
The Silk & Steel Saga

Book One: *The Steel Queen*
Book Two: *The Flame Priest*

Forthcoming books

Book Three: *The Skeleton King*
Book Four: *The Poison Priestess*
Book Five: *The Battle Immortal*

THE ASSASSIN'S TEAR

A COLLECTION OF SHORT STORIES BY
THE AUTHOR OF

THE SILK & STEEL SAGA

Karen L. Azinger

KIRALYNN EPICS

Published by Kiralynn Epics L.P. 2011

Copyright © Karen L. Azinger 2011

First published in the United States of America by
Kiralynn Epics 2011

Cover Artwork by Peggy Lowe

Celtic Lettering used with permission of Alfred M
Graphics Art Studio

ISBN 978-0-9835160-3-3

Library of Congress Control Number: 2011961451

ACKNOWEDGEMENTS

It takes a lot of people to make the dream of a book come true. First and foremost, to my husband Rick, who is always keen for the next adventure and always believes no matter the odds. To my best friend and first reader, Danae Powers, who listened to every story. To my writer friend, Peggy Lowe, a critique circle of one. To my alpha readers, Mike D, Nick K, Diane C, Mary G, Christine M, Glenda N, Nicki B and Mary V, your feedback and enthusiasm keeps me going. To Cynthia Whitcomb for her feedback on *The God Planet*. To Peggy Lowe, graphic artist extraordinaire, for the front cover and the back cover and the logo, well done! To my readers who are avidly following *The Silk & Steel Saga,* thanks for your enthusiasm and support and please tell your friends! And to my mom, for everything, I so hope you know.

CONTENTS

Introduction-Inspiration

Welcome to a collection of my best short stories written over the last ten years, a mixture of fantasy, science fiction, and forgotten truths. The two signature stories, *Prophecy's Twist* and *The Assassin's Tear,* are set in the medieval fantasy world of *The Silk & Steel Saga.* These two stories give my saga readers a chance to glimpse the kingdoms of Erdhe from a completely different perspective, answering questions that are not explored in the saga itself. If you are not yet a reader of *The Silk & Steel Saga,* then these stories will give you an introduction to the kingdoms of Erdhe.

Prophecy's Twist was inspired by one of my alpha readers. Mary G. wanted to know what the kingdoms of Erdhe were like before the War of Wizards. Her questions sparked a cascade of thoughts from which this story was born. A thousand years before *The Steel Queen,* magic flourished in the lands of Erdhe and women held power equal to men, ruling great city-states. This story takes you to the very cusp of the War of Wizards, to the deceit that started the war, forever changing the kingdoms of Erdhe.

The Assassin's Tear is the second story set in the world of Erdhe. This story occurs at roughly the same time as the prologue to *The Steel Queen.* The inspiration for this story is the Dark Citadel, the stronghold of the Mordant. In the third book of the saga, *The Skeleton King,* the characters travel to the Dark Citadel, but the readers only get to experience the citadel from a ruler's perspective. One of a writer's most powerful tools is the choice of point-of-view. I wrote this story to give my readers a chance to experience the Mordant's domain from the bottom of the social ladder. By following the exploits of a petty thief, the reader gains a unique insight into the malevolent genius of the Mordant.

The Emperor's Shadow is an archeological thriller in the style of Indiana Jones. The inspiration for this story came from a series of shows on the History Channel. I've always been intrigued by the mystery of China's first emperor, by the riddle of his unopened tomb and the curse protecting it, so I followed my curiosity, doing extensive research on the emperor's life, his tomb, his historian, and other tombs of the era. Once the research was done, I let my imagination run wild, filling in all the blanks left unanswered by history. *The Emperor's Shadow* is an international thriller that combines the power of superstition with archeology in a desperate attempt to end a World War.

A Man's World is my homage to post apocalyptic stories. As a writer, I find post apocalyptic stories fascinating because the setting is always so familiar but all the rules are completely changed. This story was inspired by a Science Channel show that talked about extinction events. I instantly knew the story had to be set in Wollongong Australia. This setting perfectly fits the needs of the story, and also works well for me since I was lucky enough to live in Wollongong for three years and worked as a general manager for the nearby coal mines. So this story is grounded in reality, but it quickly becomes a nightmare as the miners emerge to discover the world is forever changed.

Pieces of the Truth is another story inspired by the rich treasure trove of history. A show on the Biography channel snared my imagination, revealing a slice of history that I'd never heard before. Intrigued, I did my own research and decided it was a story that needed to be told. All the facts are accurate, yet history is often incomplete, leaving much to the imagination. *Pieces of the Truth* is a time travel story where a young physicist journeys to a bygone era to discover a forgotten truth.

Snakes and Ladders evolved from a writing challenge in my first critique group. Eric Witchey asked us to chose three cards from three different decks, and then write a story using the images on the cards. By the luck of the draw, I got an image of a full moon, a tarot card, and the photo of a woman's high-heeled shoe. Once I saw the tarot card, I knew the story had to be set in New Orleans, a city of mystery steeped in the supernatural. Mixing fantasy with reality, I drew on my experience working in the oil industry. In *Snakes and Ladders,* Lynn Gallant sets out to shatter the glass ceiling by taking a walk to the dark side of New Orleans.

And finally I had to include at least one story set in deep space. *The God Planet* was initially inspired by an old cult-classic science fiction horror movie, *Galaxy of Terror,* but of course, my story is very different. Originally written as a short story, I then converted it to a screenplay call *The Seekers*, and then converted it back into the story published in this collection. *The God Planet* is a science fiction thriller set at the farthest reaches of the universe. The Big Dark is a true enigma to modern astronomers, a gaping emptiness at the edge of the cosmos, a perfect setting for a deep space thriller. "Legends say even light cannot survive the Big Dark. A vacuum waiting to suck my soul dry, yet there's something fascinating about the dark, compelling on a primordial level, a vast stretch of midnight that confounds scientists, taunts explorers, and sends the religious into a worshipful frenzy." In *The God Planet,* universal dreams spark a religious frenzy, summoning humanoid kind to a riddle on the edge of Dark Space.

Welcome to my short stories. I hope you find this collection fun, interesting, and entertaining...but I also hope these stories will make you think. Enjoy.

Karen Azinger

Prophecy's Twist
A tale of Erdhe

Smoke stung his eyes and ash clogged his nose as he reached the city gates. A sinister cloud overshadowed the city. Dark and unnatural and reeking of burnt flesh, it cast an eerie twilight despite the noon sun. Tyock shuddered, making the hand sign against evil. He'd come for the mighty cloud, lured from his mountain perch by a prophecy sprung to life, but he wished it wasn't so. For nigh on two years he'd kept watch over the great city of Azreal, waiting for a sign or a dark portent, but in his worst nightmares he never imagined anything so malevolent.

His footsteps slowed to a crawl. The gates gaped open like the maw of a hungry beast, but Tyock saw no sign of any people, no carts drawn to market, no guards at the gate. All his senses screamed in warning, the very air reeking of forbidden magic, but duty called him forward. Drawing his robes close, Tyock passed beneath the gates, needing to witness the awful truth.

Such a terrible stillness, the ash fell like snow, creating a fearful hush. He stayed on the main thoroughfare, broad and straight and paved with marble. Slender spires and graceful towers rose on either side, all blackened to ash, but where were the people? The city felt like a tomb, cold and dark and silent. And then he saw them, figures in the gloom...except none of them moved.

"Greetings of the Light." His words found no reply, swallowed by the falling ash.

Tyock ventured forward, peering through the dimness till the details became clear, and then he staggered to a stop, stifling a gasp. A mother cradled a child to her breast, both blackened to char, forever locked in a fearful embrace. Stunned, he backed away, gaping in horror. Something nudged his shoulder. He whirled to find another charcoal statue, a tall man held in place by dark magic. Everywhere he looked, he saw more figures. Corpses blackened to statues, but the metamorphous was incomplete. Blackened fissures bled a foul pink fluid, proof of the flesh within. A shudder ran through him, acid rising like bile in his throat. He bent forward, heaving the contents of his stomach into the ashes. Clammy with sweat, he leaned against a marble pillar, surrounded by death.

He'd stumbled into a nightmare. Too late to shut his eyes against the horror, for he had the god-given gift of perfect remembering, but on this day his memory felt like a curse. Hardening his resolve, he kept walking, forcing himself to study the details. Even in death, the city had a story to tell, a lesson to learn, a truth waiting to be revealed. As a sworn monk of the Kiralynn Order, he'd come for the truth, for clues to the prophecy.

Each footfall raised a dark cloud of ash, the great city reduced to a crematorium. So many dead, yet he knew it was only the beginning, the first doom of a prophecy long foretold. If only they'd listened. A tear slid down his cheek. A tear for the dead, a tear for himself, wishing he'd lived in a different era, but the gods had their reasons, no matter how murky.

Ash oozed between his sandals, cold and repulsive. He gathered his midnight-blue robes and pressed on, making his way to the heart of the once-great city. Everything was blackened and burned. Mounds of ash buried the sculpted white marble, nothing left but the city's bones.

The thoroughfare widened, spilling into a square. The dead multiplied. He'd reached the great market. Blackened figures crowded the square, locked in a hideous mockery of life. A foul stench hovered over the market, the putrid smell of death mingled with burnt flesh. Holding his sleeve to his nose, he pressed on, desperate for answers.

"*Caw!*" A single cry cut the gloom. And then he saw them. Ravens and crows, too many to count, sharp beaks scavenging the dead, digging for flesh beneath the char.

The grisly feast roused his anger. "*Be gone!*" His shout echoed against the ruins. Raising his arms, he flapped his dark robes like a specter of the living. His stride lengthened to a run and found he couldn't stop. A scream burst out of him, full of rage and frustration. "*Be gone!*"

The ravens took flight, a thousand wings stirring the gloom.

He ran amongst them, dodging birds and bodies, hurling across the great square. Somewhere in the middle his scream changed to "*Why? Why didn't you listen?*"

A rush of dark feathers beat against him, like running through a whirlwind...and then they were gone. A sudden stillness returned, as grim as a gravestone.

He slowed to a walk, alone with the dead.

The great amphitheater loomed in front of him, the heart of the city. Slender columns and high archways marked the entrance, grace wrought into stone, but everything was blackened to ash, like a penitent stained with sins. He leaned against a column, dizzy with dread, yet this was his life's work. He'd come to bear witness to the prophecy. Taking a shallow breath of ash-laden air, he made the hand sign against evil and entered the amphitheater.

Tiered seats of white marble rose like a crescent moon, disappearing into the gloom. Most of the seats were full. Not with bodies turned to charred statues, no these corpses were worse, far worse. Melted, misshapen lumps of horror filled the seats, the blasted remains of the wizards of Azreal. So destroyed he could not discern men from women. Tyock closed his eyes but the image remained graven on his mind. Sick with loss, he struggled to still his mind, and then he realized what was missing. So close, he should have felt the Heartstone, should have been comforted by its pulsing power, but all he felt was a cold dead void.

Chilled with dread, he opened his eyes and stared down at the center of the amphitheater. Every great city had a focus of power, a beacon of light. For Azreal it was the Heartstone, a great monolith of white marble veined with gold and quartz, a remnant from a distant land imbued with boundless magic. It should have stood at the heart of the city, enshrined in the amphitheater, but all he saw was rubble. His vision blurred. For half a heartbeat his perfect memory played a trick on him, showing him the Heartstone whole and unbroken, pulsing with light, a boon to its people. But the moment passed and the truth hit hard.

Dark.

Broken.

Destroyed.

The great stone lay dim and dark and inert, sundered to a dozen pieces, all the majesty and magic snuffed out, drained away, blasted to ruin. *"Noooo!"* The scream keened out of him. *"It cannot be!"* A cold chill swept across him and he bent double, gasping for breath as if he'd been punched. The stone's death confirmed his worst fears; the Orb's most dire prophecy was upon them.

He stumbled down the ramp, and then he saw a slender form crumpled amongst the broken stones. Only this corpse was different from all the others. The skin was blistered and burned but it was still flesh, still a woman. The body lay twisted amongst the rubble, the head and torso hidden behind a lump of Heartstone, but one hand was flung backward, palm out toward him, as if beckoning him forward. And in that hand, a speck of emerald green gleamed bright. A memory gem!

He knelt by the body, reverently lifting the gem. Bright as an emerald, yet it had the crystalline form of quartz. Memory gems were rare. Few beyond the Order used them. He'd not expected to find one here. Perhaps the gem held the truth he sought. Like a gift from the gods, he lifted it to the heavens in thanks. "Seek knowledge, Protect knowledge, Share knowledge." He whispered the oath of his Order and then pressed the gem to his forehead, opening his mind to the magic.

Wings beat against his mind and somewhere a chime sounded. A green flash filled his vision, like an exploding star. He tumbled into the gem, sliding along the crystalline planes, pulled by the light. And then he was through, thrust into an altered existence. Dizzy and disoriented, it seemed as if he saw through a tunnel, through two sets of eyes, one looking through another. Tyock struggled to bring the world into sharp relief. Desperate for an anchor, he stared down at his hands, but they were not his own. Instead, he saw a woman's hands, bejeweled with many rings. His gaze latched onto the rings. *The great seal of Azreal.* Only one woman wore that ring. He'd entered the memories of Emrath, the Enchantress of Azreal.

Another chime sounded and he was sucked deeper into the gem. Images flooded his mind, pulling him into a glowing whirlpool of green. Caught in the undertow, his breath exploded outward. Memories poured in his mouth, rushing down his throat, drowning him in otherness. Pinned to the bottom of a deep green well, his mind was not his own, submersed beneath another consciousness. A chime sounded and the transfer was complete. The spinning stopped and he saw the world through a single pair of eyes.

Emrath leaned on the balcony, staring down at her city. *Her city,* Azreal on the edge of the forest, a city of light and life and laughter spread below her tower. The song of a flute drifted upward, underscored by the murmur of conversation. The great market teamed with people, a surging tide of sound and color. Caravan masters hawked their wares while citizens haggled for bargains. So many wonders to choose from; shimmering bolts of cloud-silk from distant

Trajen, pyramids of succulent spice-melon from the Grey Isle, casks of frost wine from the Tearen Mountains, and bins of rare spices from Athalgar. Goods from every corner of Erdhe poured into the city, merchants come to barter their wares for a wizard's boon. Commerce was the lifeblood of the city-states and none prospered more than Azreal. The sight of the great market normally brought a smile to her face, but not today. Mired in worry, she wrestled with thoughts of war.

A knock at the door interrupted her thoughts.

"Come."

Her seneschal, Garret entered, a tall dark-haired man with wisps of gray at his temples. Cloaked in somber robes of black, he gave her a half bow, his face carefully neutral. "The Cynod is convened."

She glanced at the sky, noting the first hint of sunset, a glint of pale pink among the golden clouds. "Yes, it is time. Perhaps past time," yet she lingered on the balcony, fingering the great gold amulet nestled between her breasts. She hesitated, but some things could not be delayed. Emrath felt his gaze bore into her and knew what he saw; a tall spare woman cloaked in pale blue cloud-silk, the severity of her figure softened by the fall of auburn curls reaching halfway down her back. "You don't agree?"

"You know my thoughts."

He'd served as her seneschal her for nigh on twenty years, never once overstepping his office. She turned to face him. "Delay invites attack."

"Perhaps." He gave her that much but no more, as if he was done arguing.

"You've heard the Councilor's testimony."

"He's very persuasive."

"But you still don't believe."

A shrug was his only answer.

"And the people?" She gestured toward the market, a flash of light reflecting off her jeweled hands.

"Rumors abound. The people are worried but they trust their Enchantress to protect them."

And that was it. In just one sentence he uttered the reason that spurred her forward, the single argument that trumped all others. She nodded, her voice stiff with resolve. "Mine to protect."

He bowed then, his eyes glinting with compassion, as if he understood all the burdens she carried. "You'll want your staff."

"Yes." It was only a symbol, a slender rod of white ash filigreed with silver, devoid of magic, yet symbols had their own sort of power. She accepted the staff, resisting the urge to lean on it. "Time to go."

He nodded, taking his place at her left shoulder.

A rush of footsteps clattered up the stairwell, Emrath hesitated, sensing ill news.

"I'll see to it." Garret stepped beyond the double doors.

She waited, a pool of stillness, regal in her robes of cloud-silk.

Garret returned alone, closing the doors behind him, his face set in a pale mask. "Another basket left at the city gates."

A chill shivered down her spine. "Who is it this time?"

Garret blanched. "Lord Childriss."

"*No!*" Her beloved uncle. Emrath clutched her staff, fighting for composure. A wave of grief swamped her but she choked it back. "Show me."

"My lady, there is no need for you to see."

"*I* sent him. It is my duty to see." Her tone was iron-hard.

He bowed and opened the doors, ushering a single guard inside. Pale-faced and shaking, the guard dropped to his knee, a wicker basket clutched to his chest. "We found this at the west gate, m'lady."

"Show me."

The guard removed the lid, lifting the severed head by the hair. A ripe stench filled the chamber, the sickening smell of decay. Already long dead, the skin was a putrid gray, the mouth set in a grimace, yet she knew him. Such a barbaric way to die, his severed throat was jagged and raw, as if sawed not cleanly cut. The gruesome detail scorched her mind, proof of the cruelty of the north. She clutched her staff, grief warring with outrage.

"Enough." Garret gestured and the guard returned the grisly head to the basket.

Emrath found her voice. "Clean the head and present it the priests for burial. Lord Childriss will be buried with all the honors of a fallen warrior."

The guard saluted, his head bowed.

"And you will speak of this to no one." Her voice hardened to marble. "The enemy uses brutality like a weapon to sow fear among us. I will not permit it to infect the city."

The guard bowed. "As you command." Garret showed him to the door.

Emrath turned, staring out the window, but she saw nothing, her mind roiling with grief and anger.

Soft footsteps returned. "Perhaps we should delay the Cynod for another day."

"There will be no delay."

"But my Lady..."

She whirled on him, her voice a lash of anger. "I will not let his death go unpunished." She pointed toward the open window. "Rumors of another basket will spread despite my order. I will not let this city descend into fear."

He bowed then, his gaze full of compassion. "Yours to command."

She swept passed him, out of the chamber and down the spiral staircase, eight turns to reach the bottom, her black-robed seneschal following like a shadow. A pair of guards with silver crescents embroidered on their sky-blue livery, leaped to open the tower doors. And then she was out amongst her people, surrounded by the bustle of the marketplace. Her presence drew stares but not surprise. Most offered smiles or nods of reverence, a balm to her heart. She wandered the market place, breathing deep the scents of cinnamon and ginger mixed with the honest sweat of people and horses, so different from the rarefied air of her tower.

Waving her guards away, she wove a path through the stalls, accepting the greetings of her people. Most were polite; their greetings full of deference, but then a silver-haired grandmother drew near, her voice low and urgent. "Lady, will there be war?" Like the first stone tumbling down a cliff, the old woman's fear released an avalanche of questions.

"Will the beast-men attack?"

"Can nothing stop the war?"

"What will the Cynod do?"

"When will a decision be made?"

"Can the evil be defeated?"

Questions beat against her like a rain of hail. Garret moved to intervene but she stopped him with a glance. Raising her hands against the tumult, she kept her face solemn, a pillar of calm against the storm.

The crowd stilled to a hush, a thousand stares turned in her direction.

She took her time, surveying her people, sensing the depth of their concern. Standing tall and regal, she pitched her voice to carry. "Magic is the sword and shield of the city-states," she filled her voice with steel, "and no city is greater in magic than Azreal. I swear by the Light, this city *will* be protected."

A sigh rippled through the crowd, as if a burden lifted from their shoulders. Murmurs of conversation resumed and people began to drift away as the great market swirled back to life, but Emrath sensed a hidden tension lurking just beneath the surface.

Knowing the crowd watched, she resumed her pace, keeping her face carefully closed. Garret stayed one step behind, his voice pitched for her ears alone. "Well done, my Lady. Fear left unchecked can lead to panic."

Annoyed, she waved him to silence. Consumed by her own thoughts, she studied the crowd as she walked. Small details became important, things she'd overlooked before. Many wore charms against evil and more than a few wore swords belted beneath their tunics. *Swords worn in the market,* her people felt threatened. Anger boiled within her, stiffening her resolve.

A ripple of unexpected laughter pierced the crowd. The people nearest to her parted and a flutter of golden wings soared in her direction, a dozen Tamara songbirds trilling in unison. Bright and cheerful, they circled her head like a golden crown, trilling a sweet serenade. Such a simple pleasure, their evening song coaxed a smile to her face, a soothing balm against the horror of her uncle's death. Three times the birds circled her head, a crown of golden feathers and cheerful tweets. Chirping a final melody, they winged a path back down a side aisle, alighting on the shoulders of a mud-spattered urchin-lad. The lad flashed her a gap-toothed grin, offering an exaggerated bow as the songbirds fluttered to his shoulders.

Emrath clapped in appreciation. "I see the market has a new performer." She tossed a gold coin to the lad. "A small token for the pleasure of your songbirds."

The boy caught the coin in his cap, a gleam of thanks in his dark eyes. The crowd murmured their approval, a shower of coins falling in the lad's direction.

Emrath gestured to her seneschal, drawing him close. "The caravans bring more than just goods to our fair city. That lad has a touch of beastmaster about him. See to it he is given a place at the school. Magic, no matter how low-born, should never be wasted."

"As you wish." Garret turned and threaded his way back toward the boy, a somber note in a sea of bright silks.

Emrath resumed her walk across the great square. The amphitheater loomed ahead, white marble fashioned by magic into slender arches, the meeting place for the Cynod.

A loud crash disturbed the peace of the market, a cloud of dust rising to the left. A woman screamed and the crowd began to roil. Emrath turned toward the disturbance. "Let me through."

The crowd parted. Melting away on either side, they opened a path to a collapsed wagon, a load of spice-melons spilled across the paving, a young child trapped beneath the rear axle. A grieving woman knelt over the child. "Somebody help her, please help her. Somebody help my daughter."

Emrath laid a gentle hand on the woman's shoulder. "Does she live?"

Startled, the woman gasped, a sudden gleam of hope in her tear-streaked face. "Enchantress! Her heart still beats but her leg is trapped. Please help her."

Emrath gestured to a pair of brawny men standing in the crowd. "Lift the wagon. I can do nothing till she is free."

The men sprang to do her bidding, using a pole to lift the collapsed wagon, while a third man pulled the child from the wreckage. Pale and still, the dark-haired girl lay twisted and broken, her face glazed with shock. So small and innocent, nothing touched Emrath more than the plight of a hurt child. The Enchantress knelt by the girl, her robes of cloud-silk forming a blue puddle on the paving. "What is her name?"

"Tabetha." The mother's breath caught. "Can you save her?"

"Tabetha, such a lovely name." Emrath examined the girl with gentle hands. The child still lived, her breathing slow and labored, but her right knee was crushed, the leg twisted to an unnatural angle. As the master healer of Azreal, Emrath had seen far worse, but she knew time was of the essence. She reached for the golden amulet dangling from a chain at her neck, the Amulet of Healing, the greatest of all her focuses. Closing her eyes, she sought the magic within. Warmth flooded through her, a surge of golden power, and with that power came the knowledge of sinew and bone, of flesh and blood. Endowed with a type of second-sight, she peered within the wound, mentally sorting through broken flesh and shattered bone. Such a terrible fracture, so many bits of bone, she strained to find each fragment, using her magic to fit them back together like a well-known puzzle. Power flared from her fingertips, fusing bone to bone, repairing the damage. Satisfied, she turned her attention to twisted sinew and torn flesh. More power poured from her amulet, answering her call. Beneath her glowing hands, the girl's leg straightened and pale pink skin closed across the wound. Looking deep within the flesh, Emrath saw that it was good.

As if the Amulet knew the healing was complete, it withdrew its power from her like a tide returning to the sea. Suddenly weak with dizziness, Emrath slumped to the ground, limp as a rag doll.

Strong arms caught her from behind.

Emrath fought the waves of dizziness, the devastating lack of magic. Like a god struck down from the heavens, she felt stunned by her own weakness, forced to become suddenly mortal. Refusing to succumb, she reached for the third ring on her right hand, tapping a small store of power. Magic poured through her like the elixir of life. The dizziness receded and the world came back into sharp focus. Emrath gazed down at the sleeping child. Her eyes were closed, her breathing regular, a pale blush of pink in her cheeks. "The child will be fine."

A cheer erupted from the people.

The tear-streaked mother grasped her hand. "A thousand thanks, mistress! A thousand thanks!"

Emrath got to her feet, brushing the dirt from her robes. Someone retrieved her ash staff, handing it to her with a reverent bow. The people pulled back, as if suddenly shy. Magic was common in Azreal but public healings were not. Awed to silence, they cleared a path around her, more than one making the hand sign of the Light.

She turned to leave, expecting Garret to stand behind her, but it was someone else, someone with dark eyes and a ruggedly handsome face. *"Braith!"* She made the name a curse.

The dark-robed monk had the grace to flush.

"What are you doing here? I thought you and your brethren were long gone from the city gates."

"The others are five days gone, but I chose to stay, hoping to change your mind."

"Then you waste your time." She turned away, setting a brisk pace toward the amphitheater.

Ever the stubborn one, he fell into step beside her. "This is wrong and you know it."

Anger pulsed within her. "I've heard enough. You and your blue-robed Order are nothing but a pack of doomsayers."

"Our magic is subtle but never underestimate its power. You dismiss the Order's warnings at your peril." His voice held a dangerous edge. "The Orb foretells a terrible future, the destruction of all magic, the downfall of our cities, chaos and death spread like a plague across every land, a great triumph for the Dark."

"And so you would have us do nothing? Let evil go unpunished?"

"Perhaps this evil is not yours to punish. Give the Star Knights a chance. Let the knights enforce the Great Compact."

"Trust swords instead of magic? How archaic."

"Is your way any better? Magic," he shook his head in dismay, "we're drunk on too much power. Magic will be our undoing."

She scoffed at his words. "Another one of your prophecies?" She raked him with a scathing stare. "What would you have us do? Abandon magic? Leave our great cities and go back to living in caves? Should we turn our backs on magic and become savages once more?"

"No, but man was not meant to wield the power of the gods. We don't have the wisdom." He stared at her, dark eyes in a disturbingly handsome face, eyes that always seemed to see too much. "Emrath, do not do this."

"It's too late."

The monk's voice dropped to a harsh whisper. "I fear for your people, for your great city...I fear for you."

For half a heartbeat, his sincerity pierced her heart, but then she remembered her uncle, and the fear infecting her people, and her resolve hardened. "You've heard the testimony of the Counselor, how the north is perverting magic to build an army of beast-men."

"Yes," his face twisted to a grimace, "I've heard the Counselor speak, a gifted orator, but I do not trust him. The Mordant is too sly by half. I fear he sets city against city, a great dark divide."

The accusation shocked her. "But he took a truth-oath upon the Heartstone, swearing testimony to the army of beast-men. None can tell a falsehood with their hand upon the stone."

"You forget I was there the day he took the oath. I heard his words but I did not believe them."

She gave him a piercing look. "You and Garret."

"Your seneschal? Then trust Garret if you will not trust me."

She refused to answer, hastening her steps.

"My lady, please listen." He kept pace beside her. "I cannot explain it, but something feels wrong, as if some great power works against us. I beg you to wait, to gain more proof."

"More proof!" Her anger exploded. "Every emissary sent north is returned with their heads in a basket! We cannot afford more proof."

"Do not trust the Mordant."

"Shadow and plots, that's all you and your brethren ever see." She increased her pace, hoping to leave him in the crowd. But the monk was nothing if not persistent. He grabbed her arm. "Listen to me!"

She whirled, a flash of magic rising to her hand.

He retreated a step, his hands raised in supplication. "For the sake of your city."

It was the one argument she could not refuse. Quelling her anger, she said, "Walk with me."

He stayed by her side, like a dark shadow dogging her steps. For three strides, nothing was said, and then he whispered. "Offense or defense?"

His words made no sense. "What?"

"You're planning to use the Heartstone."

A pointed glance was her only reply.

"The stone can be used for either offense or defense, but it cannot be used for both. If you unleash the magic, your city will be vulnerable to attack. I would not see Azreal fall."

"We shall only be vulnerable for a short time, a matter of days at most till the stone regains its power, and meanwhile our enemy will be destroyed."

"Not if others strike while the Heartstone is drained."

His reply slowed her steps, making her doubt.

"Who else knows your plans?"

"A mere handful, only those I most trust."

"Is the Counselor among them? He's conveniently gone from the city."

Her voice bristled with outrage. "It's because of your rantings that I made him swear his testimony on the Heartstone."

"Then why is he gone?"

A splinter of doubt pierced her heart, but she burnt it away with anger. "Why do you hate him so? Is it because I chose him for my lover instead of you?"

He staggered backwards as if slapped.

His reaction said much. "So you did not know." She took small satisfaction in knowing her household could keep a secret. "I thought your Order knew everything."

His voice sounded hollow, like it came from the grave. "Mock me if you wish, but heed the Order. Our prophecies are not to be taken lightly."

"Prophecies are never believed until they come true."

Something hardened in his face, like a statue chiseled from stone. "If you must do this, then I beg you to delay for a day or two and see if evil dares to strike. Do not leave your city unprotected."

"It has gone too far to turn back now."

His face turned ghost-pale. "Then I offer you a gift and hope it is not the last." Reaching within the pocket of his midnight-blue robe, he withdrew a small crystalline shard, dark green in color.

"A memory gem?"

He nodded. "To record the day, for better or for worse." Lifting her hand, he nestled the gem in her upturned palm. "I pray to the Light that I am wrong." Closing her fingers on the gem, he kissed her hand in farewell, as gentle as a windborne leaf.

She watched him leave, disappearing into the crowd. For half a heartbeat, she was tempted to call him back, but then Garret appeared, striding to her side. "The Cynod awaits."

"Yes." She closed her fist on the gem and slipped it into her pocket. "Yes, it is past time for justice to be done." Pushing all doubt aside, she turned and entered the amphitheater.

Guards in the sky-blue livery of the city, snapped to attention, spears held rigid in salute. She passed between them with nary a glance, feeling the call of the Heartstone. Magic washed across her, warm and welcoming, a beacon of light in the dark. She followed the throbbing pulse through the colonnade and down the ramp to the center of the amphitheater.

The Heartstone waited for her, a great monolith, more than thrice the height of a tall man. White marble veined with streaks of gold and pockets of quartz, it pulsed with light and magic, the heartbeat of the city. Her footsteps quickened, needing to touch the stone. Gentle as a lover, she laid her hand upon the warm marble. Power surged into her, forging an instant connection. The Heartstone called to her, ancient magic thrumming through her fingertips. She swelled with purpose. This was her destiny, to protect and serve her city.

A gong sounded. "All rise for the Enchantress of Azreal!"

The herald's cry pulled her back from the stone's depths. She stared up at the tiered seats rising to a graceful crescent of dazzling white marble. Men and women filled the amphitheater, more than eight hundred adorned in robes of bright silks and glittering jewels, the most powerful wizards of Azreal. Her gaze roamed the colorful assembly, acknowledging familiar faces, friends and mentors, staunch supporters and bitter rivals, adversaries and critics. She welcomed them all, their very diversity lending strength to the magic. For this great undertaking, she would need every one.

Taking a deep breath, she raised her arms to the Cynod. "We meet on a matter of grave importance." Her voice rang with power, gathering the gaze of everyone in the amphitheater. "You have all heard the testimony of the Counselor. Our sister city in the north has broken the Great Compact. Soul magic is being twisted to its darkest form, creating an army of beast-men, malformed creatures designed for war."

Anger rumbled through the assembly. More than one muttered the word, "Abomination."

She raised her voice above the tumult. "The Law is clear. According to the Great Compact, any city engaging in Dark magic is subject to annihilation. It is time to bring justice to the north and end this foul threat." The assembly fell silent, like water dowsing flames.

One man rose in protest, Thaddeus, a tall white-haired wizard in robes of autumn brown, the leader of the opposition. "We need more proof. Who among us has seen these beast-men, these abominations? How do we know this threat is real?"

Emrath answered before doubt could spread. "The truth has been staring at us with dead eyes. This Cynod has sent more than a dozen delegates into the north, all of them seeking the truth. Every one has been brutally murdered, their heads returned in a basket. How many more lives must be lost before we acknowledge the truth and end this threat?"

Her supporters rallied to her words. "It's true! No more deaths! Stop the evil!"

Thaddeus stood his ground. "At least wait till Lord Childriss returns."

"He has returned," a hush stilled the amphitheater, "the same as the others."

"*No!*" Grief ran rampant through the Cynod; Lord Childriss was much loved by both lords and commoners alike.

She gave them a moment to mourn and then raised her voice above the tumult. "There will be a time for grief later, a time to remember the honored dead, but now is the time for duty." Emrath pointed to the Heartstone. "You've already heard the truth. The Counselor came before this very Cynod and gave testimony with his hand upon the Heartstone. Locked in a truth-trance, he described in great detail the legion of beast-men being created in the north, a foul army waiting to strike. What greater proof do we need?"

More than a hundred shouted their support, raising a thunder of agreement.

Thaddeus stood, waiting for a break in the thunder. "We are talking about the annihilation of a city!"

"And the protection of our own!" Rage boiled through her. "Will you wait till an army comes to our very gates?" She pointed toward the market. "I have walked in the marketplace and seen the look of fear on the faces of our people, the very people we are sworn to protect! As the Light is my witness, I shall not fail them."

A roar erupted from the assembly. Thaddeus sank into his seat, a look of defeat on his face.

Emrath waited for the roar to subside, her gaze roving the tiers, taking the pulse of the assembly. When quiet returned, she spoke calm and clear. "I call upon the Cynod to decide this issue."

The sound of the great gong shimmered through the amphitheater, emphasizing the solemnity of her words.

"Stand if you agree to support the Great Compact, to bring justice to the northern city of Seanth."

More than three hundred surged to their feet. Others rose more slowly, their faces mired in worry. One at a time they stood, till only a handful remained seated, a small island of dissenters clustered around Thaddeus. The decision was overwhelming, no need for a count. The old wizard had the grace to concede. "It seems you have won the consent of the Cynod."

She nodded but there was no joy in the victory, just a grim determination to protect her city. "As Enchantress of Azreal, I choose to act *now*, so that fear will no longer plague this great city."

A murmur of surprise swept through the assembly.

Thaddeus gaped. "No need to be hasty!"

Emrath raised her hands, gaining a measure of quiet. "We dare not delay lest the enemy learn of our decision. In a battle of wizards, timing is everything. The first to strike is most oft the victor. I will see this done *now*, ending the abomination of the north." Her words rang with conviction.

Ripples of agreement ran through the tiers.

"Then let us begin." Taking a deep breath, she placed her left hand on the Heartstone, tapping into a wellspring of magic. Power thrummed through her like waves lapping at the ocean shore. The Heartstone began to glow, brighter than a full moon in winter. Light flowed up her arm, creating a nimbus around her body. More than mortal, she became a vessel of power, but such power was unstable without the consent of many. "The magic of the Cynod is summoned." She raised her right hand toward the assembly, demanding their support.

The gong sounded again, a deep solemn sound.

One by one, the wizards of the Cynod brought their power to a glow. Threads of light shot from their hands to hers. Emrath gathered every strand, like a spider at the heart of a web, binding them together. With each link she felt a jolt of strength, a jolt of human will. Emrath became the fulcrum, balancing the will of the many with the strength of the Heartstone. So much raw power, she thought her skin would ignite. Magic claimed her, too much for a mere mortal. A scream rode her lips. Her head jerked backward, her auburn hair trailing down her back. Caught in a mixture of pain and rapture, she began to burn from within, glowing like a captured star. Ancient words sprang to her lips. *"Tazreal Tamoth An! Let my will be done!"*

Loosed from her earthly bonds, she exploded upward, a spirit-phoenix riding on wings of magic. Like a comet she soared northward, streaking across the sky. All emotions, all humanity, burned away, leaving nothing but pure purpose fueled by awesome power. Higher and faster, she blazed a glowing trail above a range of snowcapped mountains, soaring out over an endless expanse of rippling grass. Moonlight silvered the land but she saw none of the beauty. Cold air buffeted against her but she did not slow. Neither beauty nor obstacles could deter her. Emrath was gone, burned away, replaced by pure purpose, a doom loosed upon the wicked.

Light glowed in the north, the towers of a city lit by magic.

The purpose that was Emrath latched onto its goal, the city of the enemy, the city of abominations. Her power formed a giant fist of air. Like the hand of a god, she streaked towards the enemy.

Details became clear, towers and palaces, lights glowing in glass-paned windows. She half expected some resistance, a magical shield or a barrage of fireballs, but there was nothing, only the chill of the night, only the calm before the storm. For a fleeting moment, puzzlement pricked her conscious with a splinter of doubt, but her purpose dominated her will, eliminating the glimmer of hesitation. Unprotected, the city laid spread before her, the enemy sleeping unawares within her grasp.

Like the fist of an avenging god, she plunged downward. In one fell strike she smote the city, crushing towers and leveling buildings, smashing the city to bedrock. A great boom shook the air, like the sound of a thousand thunderclaps. In the blink of an eye, she obliterated the city, but her rage burned on, hurling her forward. Crushing the city to bedrock was not enough, not nearly enough. She hammered deep into the earth, pounding a grave for the city, leaving nothing behind but a gaping hole. Her power flared, melting rock to glass, crushing everything in her path. Half a league down, her power began to wane, her will finally sated.

Her purpose was spent, the enemy destroyed.

Something snapped inside and her conscious re-emerged. Empty of power, the spirit-phoenix hovered over the floor of a great pit. Dark smoke billowed around her, the city obliterated to heat and ash. Earthen walls glowed red and angry, heated to molten glass, a smoking pit of ruin. *"It is done."* The words sounded in her mind, full of smug triumph, but the voice was not her own, a voice she dared not acknowledge.

Something tugged at her soul.

A thin strand of light connected her spirit back to her body. Depleted of power, the connection grew dim. Such a fragile thread, if it snapped, her body would die, her spirit lost to the in-between. The Heartstone called her home, tugging on her soul. Upwards she sped, pulled by a desperate urgency. Like the faintest of shooting stars, she followed the thread home, soaring back across the steppes and over the mountains, to the great city of gleaming white marble nestled by the forest's edge.

A roaring sound filled her ears, and then she was back, a mortal soul trapped once more within a frail body of flesh and bone. Reality crushed her. So hard to be merely mortal, she lay on the cold hard ground like a useless worm, the stars spinning overhead. Small and insignificant, she moaned for all that was lost.

"My Lady?" Garret was at her side, helping her sit. Not just her seneschal, he was also her Taramour, her hidden strength. A minor magician, he poured his power back into her. Magic flowed through her like a sweet elixir.

She felt her strength return. "It is done." For a moment the words seemed like they belonged to someone else, but the memory was fleeting, like an itch at the back of her mind.

Garret helped her stand.

Emrath smoothed her cloud-silk robes and accepted her staff. Still weak, she leaned on the slender length of white ash. All through the amphitheater, Taramours attended their wizards, restoring strength to the members of the Cynod, but Emrath's concern was drawn toward the Heartstone. Drained to the limit, the great stone appeared dormant. So faint, she could barely feel the magic of the great monolith. Fear spiked through her, she'd never seen the stone this weak. She stumbled forward, placing her hand on the Heartstone, searching for the magic within. Buried deep inside, she found a faint glimmer. So slow, the pulse of the great white monolith was like a sleeping heartbeat; its light dimmed to the brightness of a single candle, like the last embers of a great bonfire.

Dim but not extinguished.

She sighed in relief. Given time, the magic would rekindle, recharging the great stone. Emrath leaned against the Heartstone, seeking succor.

The Cynod stirred. Wizards stood in the tiers as if summoned back to life. Questions rumbled through the amphitheater, calling the Enchantress back to her duties.

Emrath leaned on her staff, staring up at the rows of wizards, at friends and colleagues, at critics and opponents, all awaiting her word. She raised her staff and the amphitheater stilled to a hush. A wane smile crossed her face. "It is done." Taking a deep breath, she searched for the right words. Images of the smoking pit filled her mind and she wondered why she'd felt the need to obliterate the enemy so completely, but she kept her doubts to herself. "The city of Seanth is no more. The Great Compact has been upheld. The abominations are destroyed and the threat to Azreal is forever ended."

A ragged cheer rose from the tiers. Some wizards shook hands while others sagged down into their seats, exhausted by the ordeal.

Emrath studied her colleagues. Most were flooded with relief, slumped in their seats, weary from the magic. A few glowed in triumph, celebrating a great victory, but Emrath stood alone, empty and devoid of all emotions. Perhaps it was the aftereffects of the great working. Magic had a way of exacting its own price.

"My Lady, look!"

Her skin prickled in warning. Staring skyward, she stifled a gasp. A great fireball roared through the sky, descending toward her. Vast as a falling sun, it threatened to incinerate the entire city.

"No." She tried to deny her sight, but her heart knew the truth. *"We are betrayed!"*

Panic erupted in the tiers, but Emrath stayed by the Heartstone, her voice rising above the tumult. "Rally to me! We must shield the city!"

Most of the wizards quelled their fear, refusing to flee. Standing in the tiers, they summoned their magic, sending faint tendrils of light toward their Enchantress.

Emrath kept one hand on the Heartstone, raising the other toward the Cynod, invoking their magic in defense of the city. Balancing the two forces, she gathered the power, but the gossamer tendrils were too few and too weak. Needing more, she pulled deep on the Heartstone, but it was like sucking on an empty well. Too much had already been drained, leaving little left for defense. Desperate, she reached deeper, coaxing flames from the embers, summoning every glimmer of magic.

Slow and sluggish the Heartstone responded. Magic coalesced within her. Gathering her strength, she cast her power outward, raising a shimmering shield, a crescent of light. Gossamer thin, it arched upward, a slender shell of magic capping the amphitheater, but it was not large enough to protect the city. *Not enough,* she called on the Heartstone, her need laced with panic. Desperate, she draw from the stone, but the well was dry.

A cry escaped her. "Give me more!" She reached toward the Cynod.

Her colleagues answered. Magic poured into her.

She pushed outward, desperate to lend protection to the city. Stretched thin, the magic shield arched over the amphitheater like a net of stars, but it did not grow. Panic beat against her, she was going to watch her city die! She emptied all of her rings and bracelets, drawing on every store of magic, frantic to enhance the shield.

Overhead, the sky grew blindingly bright. Heat and light leached through the shield, scorching the air in the amphitheater. And then the fireball struck, slamming the shield with the force of a falling sun.

Explosions boomed through the city and light flared overhead. The shield shimmered and sparked, magic colliding with magic. For half a heartbeat the shield held but then it began to shrink.

"No!" She rallied her magic, reaching deep within the Heartstone. For precious minutes, the shield held aloft, but then the fireball bore down, forcing the shield to slowly collapse. She watched in horror as heat reached the top tiers, melting friends and colleagues, turning them to twisted lumps of char.

Tears streamed down her face as she fought to reinforce the shield, but it was no use, her magic was spent. Like a relentless hand, the fireball pressed down, consuming each tier of wizards till none stood alive save her. A sob escaped her; she'd failed her city and her people. Her own words came back to haunt her; *timing was everything.* The enemy knew just when to strike. She'd been betrayed. Sick at heart, she dropped her hands, resigned to her fate...*but the shield still held!*

The Heartstone glowed like a distant star, maintaining the shield around her. She stood within the sheltering sphere, watching the fireball consume everything she loved.

But the destruction of the city was not enough. The malevolent force attacked the Heartstone, as if determined to destroy the very essence of her people. Burning with a savage intensity, the fireball glowed like an angry sun, encircling the Heartstone. Heat blistered around her, fierce enough to melt flesh from bone, but the Heartstone resisted. Pulsing with magic, the great stone fought back, maintaining the shield.

But then the stone began to keen, releasing a piercing wail as if it suffered, and then the great stone shattered. *The Heartstone shattered!*

Emrath was blown backwards, landing hard on the marble paving.

The fireball pounced like a hungry beast. Heat beat against her, scorching her hair and skin, trying to reduce her to ash, but something kept her alive. At her breast, the Amulet of Healing glowed, rebuilding everything the fireball destroyed, keeping flesh on bone, keeping her alive. Trapped in hell, Emrath writhed in pain. Her body burned and was rebuilt, an endless torture of destruction and repair, an agony of pain making her long for death.

Time seemed to stretch to forever, caught in one long searing torment, but then the fireball died, suddenly extinguished, as if snuffed out by a giant hand. A hush descended on the city and ash began to fall, big black flakes falling like a grim mockery of a snow. And through it all, Emrath still lived.

"Why?" The word was a harsh croak forced from blackened lips. Trapped between life and death, she had one shining moment of

clarity. She recognized the taunting voice in her mind, the one that said *it is done.* It was the voice of the betrayer, the voice of a deceiver; the one who named himself Counselor...it was the voice of the Mordant. Pain pierced her heart, betrayed by her own lover. So many mistakes but perhaps she could make amends.

She rolled on her side, her fingers probing the mounds of ash. Her robes were gone, burnt to char, but perhaps the gem survived. Amidst the ash, she found the memory gem, the last gift from the monk. Whole and unbroken, she pressed the crystalline shard to her forehead. *"Remember!"*

A nimbus of green light surrounded her. Into the gem, she poured her memories. Not just memories of the battle, but memories of her city, alive and whole, a beacon of light on the edge of the forest. *"Remember!"* Her memories blazed into the gem, revealing the truth of the conflict. And then it was done.

Empty of thought, she collapsed to the ground, the gem glowing bright like an emerald. She wondered if it would ever be found.

Exhausted, she lay in the ash, a battered remnant of burnt flesh kept alive by magic.

A single thought pierced her pain, the Heartstone...*she should have felt the Heartstone.* She rolled on her side and stared toward the center of the amphitheater. The destruction was devastating. The Cynod was dead, melted to lumps of char. And at the heart, the great stone lay shattered in a dozen pieces. A sob escaped her, but then she saw it. Amongst the ruins, one fragment of Heartstone still glowed. The magic was faint, weak as a candle buffeted by a storm, but it was not extinguished.

Her breath caught, as long as the Heartstone survived, a remnant of her city still lived. Desperate for the stone to endure, she crawled toward it. Burnt skin sloughed from her hands and knees, but she did not falter. Collapsing next to the fragment, she laid a gentle hand against the wounded marble. With her other hand, she reached for the Amulet of Healing, her last store of magic. Thrumming with power, the Amulet fought to save her life, but Emrath exerted her will, turning the healing power toward the Heartstone. Magic poured into marble, but stone is not flesh and she had no way to direct the power. For a moment, nothing happened, but then light blazed to life in the depths of the stone. Like a captured star, the stone fragment burned bright, filling her heart with hope.

A sixth sense warned her that something had changed; something was different, as if another power meddled with the stone.

A tremor passed through her. The ground began to rumble and quake. A great crack appeared in the paving, a fissure running through the marble floor. More cracks shattered the paving, each one radiating from the fractured Heartstone. Magic coursed through the ground like a strange power awakening.

The last fragment of Heartstone blazed bright, but then it split as if struck by lightning, sundered into three large pieces.

"*No!*" Her cry rent the gloom.

The stone fragments turn dark and inert, devoid of magic, the final death knell of her city. A cry keened out of her, but then a strange magic prickled her skin. Something stirred in the ashes, in the very place where the Heartstone had stood. From deep within the cracked marble, a sapling emerged, a sprig of green shooting upward. Like magic, the sapling grew before her eyes. Only as tall as a sword, yet it was perfectly formed, sprigs of green needles and a reddish trunk, releasing a scent of evergreen.

Emrath stared in wonder, for this was something far beyond the ken of her magic, as if the gods themselves interfered, offering life to a city of death.

Pain beat against her. Her strength began to fail, the last of her magic exhausted, yet she reached for the sapling. "My life for yours." She plunged her hand into the crack, into the moist earth beneath the paving, her words like a prayer. "Let my magic join to yours. Let the Light triumph over the Dark. *Remember!*" With death hovering at her shoulder, she thrust her hand deep into the soil, a last offering to the gods. In her dying moments, she felt a gentle touch. Roots of the sapling entwined around her fingers, claiming her rings, her bracelets, and her memories. Succumbing to death, Emrath closed her eyes, satisfied that her offering was accepted.

#

"*No!*" Tyock howled in pain, clawing his way out of memory, refusing to be trapped in Emrath's death. Like a drowning man, he struggled against an ocean of darkness. *I will not succumb. I will not die.* Death-agonies were never embedded in memory gems, lest they turn the gem into a lethal trap. Frantic with fear, he fought to reclaim his own life. *My name is Tyock and I walk in the Light.* Over and over, he screamed the words, fighting to hold onto a thin thread of consciousness. Oblivion tugged at his heels, but he clawed his way upward, fleeing the death of the Enchantress. Memories of his identity became his only shield, his only lifeline. *My name is Tyock, I am a monk of the Kiralynn Order, and I walk in the Light.* Like a chant, he repeated the words, howling them into the dark. He fought for his life, refusing to die. Green light flared around him, blindingly bright, and then a chime sounded and he was through.

Released from the gem, he gasped for breath.

Exhausted, he lay sprawled on his back like a shipwrecked sailor tossed on a strange shore. Ash-laden air filled his lungs, but he still lived. Tyock coughed and sputtered, as understanding slowly returned. He gazed up at the gloom, at the ash-strewn amphitheater. Slowly he tested each of his fingers, moving his hands, his feet, relieved to discover he inhabited his own body. Sitting up, he found the shattered gem held in his fist. Dark and lusterless, the gem was destroyed but the memories remained fixed in his mind. He stared at Emrath's corpse. Blackened and burned, the body of the Enchantress lay twisted among the Heartstone's shattered fragments. So it was all true. His vision blurred. For half a heartbeat he thought his own body lay ruined amongst the stones, but then the world came back into sharp focus, and he saw with his own eyes.

He stayed still, sorting through his newfound memories, trying to absorb the lessons learned. Understanding struck with relentless clarity. Empowered by the Heartstone, Emrath had hurtled north to stop an abomination, but she never met any resistance. The north never intended to invade. It was all a web of lies. Yet for the sake of her city, she was goaded to attack. Magic of such power dictated that the winner strike first, annihilating the loser, yet the war was only a ruse, a great dark deceit.

The truth hit hard, making him retch. His stomach convulsed trying to disgorge all of his nightmares, but prophecies are not so easily denied. Sodden with sweat, he wiped his mouth, staring up at the ruined amphitheater. Every portent, no matter how dire, had come to pass. Two great cities felled in one day, just as the Orb predicted, the start of a bitter war. "So the doom is upon us. The darkest prophecy unfolds."

Tyock staggered to his feet, needing to see it all.

Bowing to the Enchantress, he stepped around her body. Between the lumps of fractured Heartstone, he saw it, a glimmer of green amongst the ash. The sapling was real. No taller than a sword, yet it stood perfectly formed, sprigs of green on the slender trunk of a noble redwood. The Enchantress lay next to the sapling, her left arm thrust deep into the soil.

Tyock knelt beside her. "Your city will be remembered and the Deceiver's name will be known." He made the sign of the Light over her and then reached for the gold chain around her neck, the Amulet of Healing, too potent a magic to be left to scavengers. Cold to the touch, it felt dead in his hands, but he'd trust the Kiralynn masters to find a way to waken it. Placing the Amulet in his pocket, he reached for her other hand, for the gleaming rings and bracelets of power worn by an enchantress, but before he could remove the rings, a tendril of root shot from the ground, twinning around her fingers.

Tyock staggered backwards. He'd never seen anything like it, as if the sapling was sentient. More roots erupted from the ground, weaving a fine blanket across the body of the Enchantress, as if the tree claimed her for its own.

Stunned, he watched in amazement, realizing he witnessed the birth of a new power, something wondrous and unexpected. Bowing toward the sapling, he turned and trudged from the amphitheater, anxious to return to the monastery. He had much to report to the Grand Master. He carried a tale of two cities, a story of preemptive magic and unexpected endings. Dark times were upon them, the start of the war of wizards, the start of dire prophecies, but amidst all the death and destruction, it seemed the gods had not abandoned them. Among the ruins, he'd found a fresh hope. The prophecy was fulfilled, but the gods had added a new twist. And for that, he was deeply grateful. Only time would tell how it would all unfold.

The Assassin's Tear
A tale of Erdhe

*G*ood things come to those who wait, at least that's what everyone in the ninth tier always said but Dolf didn't believe it. Waiting never got him anything. By craft or by filch, if you wanted something you had to get it yourself. So Dolf steeled his courage and started asking questions in all the shadowy places. Three bribes and two promised favors later, he finally learned the secret behind the rumors.

He waited till midnight, the thieves' hour, before turning down the alley. A putrid stench hit him like a slap. Something dead rotted in the alleyway, a not-so-subtle warning to keep out, but Dolf refused to turn away. Quiet as a shadow, he slipped down the alley till he found the metal door. Chains bound the door handle to the stone wall, a massive lock embedded in the metal. Rumors said the lock was impossible to pick, unless you knew the secret. So simple yet so clever, he'd bought the truth with a favor, learning the lock and the chains were both a ruse. Pull on the handle and the door would never open, regardless of the lock. The secret was reversed hinges. Dolf slipped his knife from his belt, running the tip along the "hinged" side till he found the narrow space beneath the door. Sliding the thin blade beneath the metal, he angled the knife. The door whispered open.

Nothing but darkness inside, Dolf crouched at the doorway, stretching his senses. A slight scuffing sound came from the left. It could be a rat...or something else. His eyes adjusted to the gloom. Crates lined the far wall, but otherwise the large room looked empty...but looks could be deceiving. Gripping his knife, he dared to enter.

Six paces forward, three left, two forward, seven right, one backward...he followed the instructions, praying he got them right. Twice the floor boards squeaked beneath his bare feet. Dolf winced, feeling like a fumble-footed novice, but it couldn't be helped. He finished the pattern and found himself stranded near the middle. Kneeling, he felt along the gritty floorboards till he found the lip of a trapdoor. Relief washed through him; so far his bribes were well spent.

Using the hilt of his dagger, Dolf tapped the code.

The trapdoor swung upwards, a blare of light from below.

Dolf squinted against the brightness.

A gruff voice said, "Drop your metal. All of it, if you want to come below."

Metal? The order puzzled Dolf and then he realized almost anything metal could be used as a weapon. Fear pricked the back of his neck, wondering if he risked too much.

The bearded man said, "Decide."

He'd come this far, he wouldn't give up now. Dolf lowered his knife to the floor and then he emptied his pockets, even the secret ones sewn along the seams. One knife, two iron lock picks, one copper ring, and a pitifully thin coin purse.

The big man scooped everything into a leather bag. "Stay peaceable and you'll get it all back." Tossing the bag down through the trapdoor, he stepped toward Dolf. "I need to search you."

Dolf hated to be touched, but he remained statue-still. The big man had surprisingly light hands, deftly finding all of Dolf's hidden pockets, but nothing metal remained.

"You're clean. You can go below."

Dolf entered the trapdoor, descending a steep set of stairs. The room below was surprisingly warm and clean. A charcoal brazier gave off light and heat. Two men sat at a round table, dice and coins strewn across the tabletop. Big and burly, they bristled with weapons...not what Dolf was expecting.

One of the men grinned. "We got us a fresh fish."

The other one said, "First time?"

Dolf nodded.

"Look behind you."

Dolf turned and found a closed door inset in the far wall.

"Knock first. Ain't good to surprise him."

Dolf knocked.

"Come."

Dolf opened the door and stepped into luxury. A soft wool rug covered the floor, a roaring fireplace filled the far corner, but it was the smell of roast chicken that nearly made him swoon. A small wiry man sat at a table feasting on a whole chicken. Crispy and golden, the chicken sat on a platter next to a mound of buttered leeks and pan-fired potatoes, a meal worthy of the Mordant himself.

"Did you come for the chicken or did you have something else in mind?"

Dolf tore his gaze away from a juicy drumstick and really looked at the man. Small and slight with graying hair, at first glance he almost looked frail...but Dolf sensed a feral stillness in the man, as if danger lurked beneath a false exterior. "I've come to find the rune forger."

The man grinned, leaning back in the chair. "Takes guts to seek me out."

Dolf waited.

"But guts will only get you so far. You'll have to meet my price."

There was always a price in the Citadel, always, but Dolf was half afraid to ask. "How much?"

"Fifty silvers for the eighth rune, two hundred for the seventh."

Fifty, Dolf struggled not to gape. He'd thieved the ninth tier for most of his fourteen years and rarely found silver in a mark's purse. "Too much."

"Not from where I'm sitting."

Dolf waited. In the ninth tier, bargaining was a way of life.

The rune forger laughed, but the sound held no mirth. "No bargaining, no deals. Pay the fee if you want the rune."

Dolf bit his lip, stalling, but in truth he had nothing to bargain with. "For so much, I need proof."

"Of course." The forger rolled up his left sleeve and extended his arm. Three tattooed runes marked his forearm, dark black ink on pale white skin.

Dolf stared. "So it's true!" Hope leaped within him, proof he could climb beyond the ninth tier.

"Like you, I was born to the ninth. The eighth and the seventh are my own handiwork."

Dolf dared a question. "If your work is so good, why stop at the seventh?"

The forger gave him a stony look. "The higher tiers are protected by more than mere guards."

The priests, Dolf shuddered with understanding. "I'm just seeking the eighth."

"Smart," the forger lowered his sleeve. "Climb one tier at a time, else you'll look out of place. Plenty of ways to die in the Citadel if you don't belong." He gnawed on a chicken leg. "I like you, boy, but the price remains the same. Bring your silvers when you have them and my men will keep a running tally. Make the price and you'll get the mark."

"I'll be back."

The rune forger chuckled, "I bet you will. My men will be waiting. In the meantime, keep your mouth shut, or you'll find your throat slit for the telling. Now be gone, and let no one see you leave."

Dolf collected his belongs and then slipped back up the trapdoor and out into the alleyway. The price was high, nigh on impossible, but so was the prize. *A chance to live in the eighth tier, to move up in the world.* Spurred by hope, Dolf quickened his pace. By craft or by filch, he'd find a way to make the forger's price.

#

Stretching for the next handhold, Dolf wedged his fingers into a gap and reached for the roof. Gripping the edge, he pulled up. *Crack!* The roof tile gave way, tumbling to shatter on the street below. Dolf slammed against the wall, swinging by one hand. His breath rushed out of him, but he did not let go. Hanging by his fingertips, Dolf scrabbled for a second handhold. Fingernails scrapping against stone, his left hand caught a crack. He jammed his fingers deep. His arms straining, he smeared his bare feet across the wall, desperate for purchase. His right foot found the slightest bulge. Pushing off, he lunged for the roof, praying the tile would hold. His fingers curled around the lip and he swung himself onto the roof.

Gasping for breath, Dolf lay flat on the night-cooled tiles, looking back down over the edge. Smooth as a pigeon's egg, the thirty-foot wall was a challenge, the hairline-cracks small and subtle. None of the other boys in his gang could have made the climb. Flushed with victory, he scrambled up the tiles to the ridge. Sitting cross-legged on the rooftop like a gargoyle, he pulled a half-eaten onion from his pocket and watched the sun rise over the Citadel.

Dark walls soared toward the clouds. Thrust up from the flat grasslands like a mailed fist, the Dark Citadel was truly a wonder. Nine tiers of city streets wrapped around a central monolithic boulder, a stone beehive of servants, soldiers, craftsmen, and priests. Dolf leaned back and stared at the upper tiers, hoping for a glimpse of the golden palace crowning the top...but a low cloud obscured his view. He took another bite of onion, imagining the pleasures above. He'd heard a rumor about something called marmalade, a sweet fruit-paste smeared on fresh white bread. *Marmalade,* the name itself was enough to make his mouth water. If he ever got to the upper tiers he'd break his fast with marmalade every morning. And at supper there'd always be meat, perhaps lamb roasted on a spit with garlic or maybe he'd order his servants to roast a fine young duckling. But he would never again eat pigeon, or rat, and he'd never, ever, have to settle for the tasteless gruel of the ninth tier.

His stomach rumbled with hunger, banishing his daydream. Sitting up, he munched on the onion and pulled up his left sleeve. The rune of the ninth tier stared back at him. Black ink etched into his forearm at birth, he traced the rune with his finger, so much power in a single symbol. He knew he was lucky, at least the priests always said so. The rune marked him as a citizen of the Citadel, granting him all the privileges of the ninth tier...but he wanted more. By craft and by filch, he'd finally found a way. Tonight he'd dare to change his fate.

Finishing the onion, he ran across the roof tiles. Laughing, he balanced on one foot, the king of the rooftops. A gust of wind beat against his face, tugging at his unruly black hair, but the wind could not shake his balance. Pushing the hair out of his eyes, he scrambled along the ridge to the nearest chimney. Just as he suspected, a pigeon's nest perched on top. Standing on tiptoes, he deftly plucked a pair of small white eggs from the nest and tucked them into his belt-pouch, plunder for the mid-day meal.

A warning pricked at the back of his neck.

Dolf melted into the shadows. Hiding behind the chimney, he remained stature-still, staring out across the rooftops. Every shadow held a possible threat, but he found nothing. His gaze turned to the dark wall looming over the rooftops, the stone divide between the eighth and ninth tier. He searched the battlement for the glint of burnished steel; the telltale sign of soldiers, but the guards must be patrolling elsewhere. Still, it paid to be cautious; patience was a large part of the craft. Dolf kept watch till his left leg began to cramp. Finely deciding it was safe, he slithered down the roof and climbed to the streets below.

Sunrise brought the ninth tier to life. Citizens in a thousand shades of dingy brown wool and faded leather jostled in the street, making their way toward the higher tiers. Lean and hungry, they all looked alike...till you met their eyes. Most had given up, especially the older ones, but a few were determined, and fare-few more were desperate to the point of being dangerous. Dolf made sure to stay away from the dangerous ones.

Sidestepping a puddle of piss, he melted into the throng, just another street-urchin looking for a meal. Normally he worked the crowd, taking advantage of a bulging pocket or a dangling purse, but not this morning. Today he'd save his luck and his skill for bigger risks.

Dolf walked against the crowd, making his way downhill, a lone fish swimming against the tide of early-morning risers. The ritual migration started every morning, hungry citizens all making their way to the eighth tier gate, hoping for day-work in the wealthier tiers above. He'd tried it a few times himself, before he'd come to the craft, but skinny lads like him only got work cleaning chimneys or mucking privies. The hard work wasn't worth the overseer's measly copper.

"Porridge for a copper!" A gruel-monger pushed his cart into the crowd, singing for patrons.

Dolf moved to the far side of the street, his stomach roiling at the sour smell.

The crowd thinned to a trickle, the stragglers looking defeated before the day even began. Dolf ignored them. Taking the last turn of the wide cobblestone street, he reached the great gatehouse, the entrance to the Citadel. Dark stones crowned by crenelated battlements, the gates marked the separation between citizens and slaves. Soldiers in black and gold armor clustered around the open gate, watching as a team of oxen struggled to pull a wain laden with grain. Peering past the wain, Dolf caught a glimpse of the land beyond the gates, flat farmland edged by cliffs that fell away to a turbulent sea. He shuddered at the sight, pitying the poor rune-less bastards born beyond the largess of the Citadel.

The farmer yanked on the reins, slowing the oxen to a stop. Four soldiers swarmed onto the back and began thrusting spears deep into the grain, checking for anyone bold enough to sneak into the Citadel.

Dolf seized the moment to slip to the far side of the street, making his way to the small statue carved into the side of the gatehouse. The statue was an oddity of the ninth tier, a rare ornament of unknown origins. Three creatures sat carved in a row, rounded ears, pushed-in faces, long tails wrapped around their skinny legs, but despite their strangeness, the animals all had very human expressions. The first covered his mouth, the second hid his eyes, and the third stopped his ears. Rumors said the statue was carved as a lesson from the priests, a warning to avoid all evil. But whatever the truth behind the rumors, the brethren of the craft claimed the statue as their own, a good luck charm, a patron saint of thieves. Given his plans for tonight, Dolf needed all the luck he could get.

"Ho, boy!" The shout echoed across the street.

Dolf froze, hoping to avoid notice.

"You there, do you belong?"

The question drilled into Dolf's spine like a spear. He turned to find a grim-faced guard striding toward him.

"Yes, you. Prove you belong."

Dolf rolled up his left sleeve and extended his forearm. "I'm a citizen of the ninth."

The soldier grabbed his arm, studying the rune. "So you are." Growling, he pushed Dolf away. "Then don't be loitering around the gate. Those who work get fed." The soldier turned away, striding back to his post.

Relieved, Dolf's first instinct was to slink away, but he still needed to claim his luck. He ran to the statue, reaching up to touch the polished hands of the second creature. Making his words a whisper, he begged three wishes of the Three. "*Let me slip through the city unseen. Let my footsteps go unheard. Grant me invisibility for a night and a day.*" Finished, he sped away, eager to be gone.

Dolf ran as if the very shadows chased him. The cobblestone street curved upwards, obscuring the gate. Slowing to a walk, he thrust his hands in his pockets and kicked a pebble uphill, just another urchin-lad with nothing to do. After the morning rush, the ninth tier was nearly empty. Only the beggars remained, sitting forlorn on the side of the street.

A warning pricked at the back of his neck, the same feeling he'd had on the rooftop. Dolf kicked the pebble sideways, making excuses to suddenly turn...but he never glimpsed the watcher. He wondered if one of the forger's men tracked him, but he dismissed the thought. The feeling gradually faded but he couldn't afford to be followed. Slipping into a narrow alleyway, he sat cross-legged, his back pressed to the stone wall. He kept vigil till the shadows were consumed by the midday sun.

Satisfied he'd outlasted any watcher, he set off at a run. Dolf sprinted through the back alleyways, twisting and turning through narrow gaps, threading his way to the secret meeting place. Kneeling by the weathered sideboard, he knocked three times. Hearing no reply, he twisted the board and slipped into the basement's cool darkness.

A single candle lit the far corner. Benny, Sam, Neffer and Carmack sat cross-legged in the circle of light. Dolf flashed his gang a grin.

"You're late." Carmack was the second in command, a mop of red hair framing a freckled face.

Dolf nodded. "Needed to see the Three." He joined the others, sitting cross-legged around the candle stub. Thin and wiry, dressed in threadbare clothes, they all looked younger than their age. Dolf was the oldest at fourteen but he knew he only looked nine, a clear advantage for a pickpocket thief. "What's the score for the morning?"

They turned out their pockets, depositing their spoils in a dented metal pot. A half-loaf of brown bread, a bracelet carved of bone, three copper coins, a small pouch stuffed full of grain, and a spoon with a fancy handle. Dolf contributed two pigeon eggs and a copper ring he'd filched the day before. Benny, the youngest, added two dead pigeons freshly plucked.

"Not pigeon again." Carmack groaned. "Bloody rats with wings."

Dolf silently agreed, but he nudged Carmack with an elbow. "Better than no meat at all." He flashed the youngest boy an encouraging grin. "Did you get them with your sling or your hands?"

Benny turned beet-red and picked at a hole in his tunic. "The sling."

"Good shooting, but next time use your hands. It's good practice for the craft."

Benny gave a sheepish-nod and Dolf got back to business. Picking up the bracelet, he inspected the carving. "The details are nice. Too bad it's not ivory." He tossed the bracelet to the brown-haired lad with the pug nose and crocked smile. "Neffer, you'll see to the fence?"

"Always do." The bracelet disappeared into one of Neffer's many pockets along with the ring and the fancy spoon.

Sam gathered up the food. "I'll take these down to Gwen's cook-pot. She's throwing in free salt for the day."

The lads all laughed, nothing was ever *free* in the Dark Citadel.

Sam turned bright red. "Don't laugh if you buggers want stew. I'll be back in the turn of an hour." He rose to go, but Dolf pulled him down. "Stay, we've business to discuss."

The mood turned somber. Dolf stared at his gang. "Who's with me tonight?"

Carmack looked away and Benny worried the hole in his tunic.

"We've talked about this before." Dolf met the stares of his crew. "It's our best chance at a better life."

Sam mumbled, "Life's not so bad here."

Dolf exploded. "Not so bad! We grub for food every day; eating pigeon stew when we're lucky and gruel when we're not." He swallowed his anger, his voice going cold. "We've all stood in line, taking day-work in the higher tiers. You've seen how they live." He pinned them with his stare. "Have you forgotten the smell of roast lamb? Or the soft sheen of silk the priests and nobles wear? Yet you want to live like this?" He gestured to the dank basement. "There's a world of pleasure above us...if we dare to reach for it."

Neffer shrugged. "We do better than most." He danced a copper coin between his fingers. "We have the craft."

Quick as lightning, Dolf snatched the coin from Neffer's fingers. "And it's the craft that'll get us out of here." He tossed the coin back, the copper gleaming in the candlelight. "But it'll never happen if we only work the ninth tier. It'll take much more than a fist full of coppers to pay the rune forger's fee."

The coin disappeared into Neffer's pocket, but he did not meet Dolf's stare. None of them did. Dolf shook his head, wondering where their courage had fled. "I thought we'd agreed?"

Carmack scowled. "Maybe you didn't hear about this morning's scuffle at the eighth tier gate." His voice dropped to harsh whisper. "They caught Squib trying to sneak through without a work-marker."

Dolf's breath caught, he hadn't heard the news.

"Word on the street says the guards will shorten Squib by a head at sunset."

Sam's voice broke. "A bad way to die." He stared at Dolf. "I'll not risk my life for a handful of silvers."

For half a heartbeat Dolf agreed, but then a deep-seated anger boiled inside him. The ninth tier was not enough. "Filth flows downhill." He stared at his friends, his voice hard. "I'm sick of living in the filth of the upper tiers, eating their slop, and pretending to be grateful for the privilege."

Sam shook his head. "It's not worth the risk, Dolf."

"It's not the same risk. Everyone knows it's stupid to try and sneak through a gate. The guards catch everyone who tries." The lads began to nod, swayed by the truth. "Squib's a third-rate cutpurse with pigeon feathers for brains. He took a stupid risk and got caught...but *we* have a *plan*." Dolf leaned forward, putting steel in his voice. "I've found the perfect place to crossover. A few weeks working the eighth tier and we'll make the forger's fee. Once the eighth rune is tattooed on our arms then no one can say we don't belong." He snapped his fingers. "And just like that, we're out of the ninth tier and moving up in the world."

Carmack grinned. "You make it sound easy."

Dolf smiled. "It's a good plan."

Sam shook his head. "I don't know. The jump still seems too far to me."

"The jump's the only hard part." Dolf stood and moved to the far side of the basement. Pacing the distance, he marked two lines in the dirty grit. "We spend the afternoon practicing. Anyone who can't make the jump stays home tonight."

Carmack nodded and Neffer grinned, but Sam still seemed reluctant.

Knowing they needed reassurance, Dolf turned and took two running strides. He leaped the marks, clearing the second by half a foot. "See, it's easy."

Sam scowled. "Easy for you, but I'm not taking the risk." He looked away, refusing to meet Dolf's stare. "Besides, I have supper to cook." He grabbed the dented cook-pot and slipped out the door.

Silence reigned in the basement.

Dolf nodded, trying to hide his disappointment. "It's all right. Each to his own fate." He gave them a devil-may-care grin, his voice full of confidence. "Who's with me? Who'll dare the eighth tier?"

Carmack grinned. "Count me in."

Neffer gave a solemn nod, but Benny seemed the most enthusiastic, a touch of hero-worship on the youngest boy's face. "I'm with you, Dolf."

Dolf nodded. "Then let's get to work." They took turns at the jump, working for the better part of the afternoon. Carmack and Neffer cleared the marks every time but Benny struggled. A full head shorter than the other lads, Benny missed the mark more often than he made it, but he refused to give up, showing the same dogged determination that had earned him a spot in the gang.

Three knocks on the door.

Dolf reached for his knife.

The boards swung back and Sam scrambled into the basement, carrying the dented cook-pot like a rare prize. "A damned-big black dog kept following me. Must have liked the stew's smell."

Carmack muttered, "Must have been a desperate dog."

Sam ignored the barb and settled the pot on the floor. Sitting in a circle, they tore off chunks of brown bread, sopping up the stew. Thin and watery-brown, the stew smelled like pigeon and tasted worse but at least it was still warm. They ate without talking, hungry enough to scrape the last morsel from the bottom. When the pot ran dry the silence thickened, as if Sam had added a dollop of doubt to the stew.

"Everyone's talking about it." Sam stared into the empty pot, his voice a low mumble. "They're saying the guards'll make a show of Squib's death, an example to us all."

Annoyed, Dolf sought the gaze of Carmack and Neffer. "We'll make the jump at the thieves' hour." He grabbed his cloak, a worn-weave of dull brown that also served as a blanket, and settled it across his shoulders. "I'll meet you on the rooftops at midnight. Make sure you're not followed."

He peered through the slit in the loose board and then stepped out into the alleyway. A rat scurried across his path but otherwise the alley was empty. Needing to walk, he threaded his way to the main street, pulled by the murmur of voices. The street pulsed with life, people looking for a meal or trading stories about the day. He'd heard rumors the upper tiers had places called 'taverns' where people met for a meal or a mug of mead but there was nothing like that here. In the ninth tier, the central street served as the main meeting place. Charcoal braziers set on corners heated communal cook-pots. Pockets of people gathered around the braziers, trying to survive. The mass mingling made it easy for a thief...if only the pickings weren't so lean.

The sun dipped toward the horizon, a blaze of red sinking into the west. Dolf left the crowd, making his way to the inner alley ring. The ring was a type of no-man's-land. Six feet wide, the alley served as a moat of air, separating the ninth-tier houses from the long dark wall. Dolf stood in the shadows, studying the dark divide. Looming overhead like a black-toothed monster, the crenellated battlements stood stark against the twilight sky. A flash of burnished steel revealed the soldiers patrolling the battlements, spears and crossbows protecting the citizens of the eighth from the rabble of the ninth. But tonight, that would change. He'd searched the length of the wall to find the one place where the alley narrowed to five feet, a place where a daring thief might jump from the rooftops and breach the dark divide.

Dolf scanned the battlement. Honed smooth by master stonemasons the dark wall looked impossible to climb, but the stone houses lining the alleyway offered a way up. Poorly kept, the houses showed their age, subtle cracks veining their outer walls, plenty of handholds for a nimble thief. Dolf moved to the nearest house and reached for the first handhold. His fingertips found every crack and cranny, making quick work of the forty-foot climb. Pulling himself up onto the sun-warmed tiles, he lay flat, gazing across at the wall. The rooftop gave him a birds-eye view, the only place in all the ninth that looked down on the dark wall. Lying still beneath his cloak, he studied the battlement, counting the time between patrols.

Stars appeared in the sky, the Big Ladle rising in the east. A stiff breeze blew from the west, carrying the salty scent of the sea and the mournful cries of gulls. The sky darkened and the air grew cold. Dolf huddled beneath his cloak, marking the movements of the guards.

"Whoo-hoo-who-ho-oo." The cooing of a dove came from the alleyway below.

Dolf gave the answering signal. "Who-hoo-ho."

Ten minutes later, Carmack and Benny scrambled up onto the rooftop.

Dolf kept his voice a whisper. "Where's Neffer?"

Carmack shook his head. "Not coming."

"Why not?"

Benny answered. "We went to see Squib watch his last sunset." His voice broke. "It was awful."

Carmack finished the tale. "The bloody guards must have used a blunt axe. Took three chops to take the poor bugger's head off."

Dolf shook his head, dispelling the gruesome image. "So Neffer's not coming."

"None of us are."

Dolf swallowed his disappointment. Somehow he'd always known he'd do this alone. "So be it then." He extended his hand toward Carmack. "Wish me luck."

They brushed fingertips in the manner of thieves. "Luck."

Dolf checked the stars. The Big Ladle had traveled halfway across the starry vault. "Time to go."

"Wait." It was Benny's voice. "I'll go with you, Dolf."

The boy's bravery warmed him to the core. "We'd make a great team, Benny, you diverting their eyes while I divert their coins...but I can't let you risk the jump." He gave the younger boy's hair an affectionate ruffle. "Another year and you'll be ready."

Benny nodded. "The luck of the Three go with you."

Dolf smiled. "I'll see you tomorrow night. We'll sip a flagon of mead and count the riches of the eighth tier." He bid them farewell and moved down to the edge of the roof.

A patrol had just passed; he'd have half the turn of an hourglass before the next. Time waited for no man, and neither did opportunity. Dolf crouched on the roof, trying to ignore the forty-foot drop. Whispering a quick prayer to the Three, he took two running strides and leaped. Arms outstretched, he lunged across the gap, an eternity hanging in a heartbeat. The wall rushed towards him. He fell hard against the dark stone, hands scrabbling for a hold. His right hand gripped the top of a merlon. He hugged the smooth stone, pulling himself over the battlement. Crouching low, he caught his breath. A rush of exhilaration ran through him, *he'd done it!*

Dolf crossed the battlement and slipped into the eighth tier. The far side held no challenges, just a short five-foot drop to a rooftop. Space was valuable in the Dark Citadel. In the eighth tier, houses abutted the dark wall, proving no one ever sought to escape the upper tiers. Dolf slunk across the rooftop and dropped to the inky-darkness below.

Crouching on the cobbled street, he listened. Somewhere in the city a dog barked and a baby cried...but there was no shout of alarm. A slow smile spread across his face, he'd gained the eighth tier.

Dolf set out to explore. Night hung like a shroud over the city. Most windows were dark and shuttered, only a rare few glowing by candlelight. Dolf slipped through the back ways, startling a hunting cat and sidestepping a sleeping beggar. For the most part, the alleys were empty, but a warning prickled at the back of his neck. Nagged by a feeling of unease, he kept glancing over his shoulder, but there was never anyone there. He walked for the better part of an hour, meandering left and then right, eventually choosing an empty alley near the main street. Pulling his cloak tight, he sat with his back to the wall, willing himself to sleep.

He woke with a start, sunlight warming his face. The unease of the night vanished, replaced by excitement. Opportunity waited in the eighth tier streets, a chance to gain the rune forger's fee. Standing, he stretched, working his fingers though a series of exercises, needing to be limber. He took a piss against the wall and then made his way to the main street.

The street thrummed with citizens making their way toward the seventh tier gate. Like birds following the summer sun, the whole city flocked upwards every morning. Dolf joined the migration, slipping into the crowd.

Just another urchin-lad, he followed the stream, wending his way toward tight clusters of people, choosing folks distracted by their own conversations. Distraction was ever a thief's best friend. While the sheep bleated, the wolf went to work. Lightning-quick, his hands sought dangling purses and bulging pockets. Sometimes he feigned a slip, falling into his victims. Other times, it was all about speed, dipping into a pocket unnoticed, or cutting the strings of a purse. Quick and nibble, he worked the crowd, always looking for the richest mark. He often chose his victims by scent, the smell of soap or the faint whiff of rosewater marking a man of means. Luck and the craft were on his side. No one noticed the thief among them.

The wide cobblestone street curved around a bend and Dolf gained a glimpse of the seventh tier gate. Thrice the height of a tall man, the gates gaped open, a hungry mouth in the dark wall. Soldiers in gleaming armor patrolled the gateway, protecting the upper tiers. Citizens of the eighth stood in the gate's shadow, vying for the attention of overseers while priests in black robes wove their way through the crowd. The street became a market, but instead of selling food or goods, people sold their skills, their talents, and their raw muscles. More than a few sold their desperation, willing to undertake any task. He saw an old man kneel to kiss the hem of a silk-robed overseer, begging for work. Disgusted, Dolf turned away, thankful he had the craft to rely on. Threading his way through the crowd, he kept his head down, avoiding the gaze of the overseers. With so many soldiers, the craft became too risky. Deciding he'd done enough, Dolf angled his way towards a side alley.

"Thief! Someone stole my purse!"

The cry echoed through the street but Dolf was already gone. Slipping into an alleyway, he kept walking at the same idle pace, praying the guards did not follow. One step and then another, he wished himself invisible. His heart pounding, he reached a corner and turned into a second alley. The luck of the Three was with him. He strained to listen, but no footsteps gave chase. Fear turned to elation; he'd played the game and won! But the day was not yet done. Without friends, or hiding holes, he couldn't afford to drop his guard.

Dolf headed downhill, meandering through the alleyways, slowly making his way back toward the eighth tier gate. His stomach rumbled with hunger, but he ignored it. He kicked a stone, making a game of it, just an urchin-lad whiling away the hours. Turning a corner, he froze. A squad of soldiers patrolled the alleyway; he'd stumbled on a rune-search. Fear shivered through him, without a work-chit he'd lose his head if the soldiers caught him. Hugging the shadows, Dolf retreated back down the alley.

Deciding it was best to hide in plain sight, he made his way to the main street. Dolf hunched beneath his cloak, trying to look younger than his years. The street was mostly empty, just a few loiterers, a beggar, and a gruel-monger pushing a cart.

"Fish stew! Two coppers for a bowl! Fish stew!"

Hunger pushed Dolf towards the monger. Flashing a smile, he opened his hand, revealing the gleam of copper. "I'll have a serving, sir."

The old man grunted and stopped the cart. "No work fer you today?" He lifted the lid on a cast-iron cauldron, releasing a belch of steam. "Yer lucky I still have some left." Gripping the ladle, he gave the dull-brown stew a stir, a few fish heads floating on top. "Where's yer bowl?"

"Lost it." Dolf sniffed the fishy brew. The salty broth smelled much better than pigeon gruel.

The old man gave him a gap-toothed grin. "Bowl's an extra copper."

It was robbery of another sort, but hunger was hard to deny. He paid the man the extra fee. "But I want a serving from the top," everyone knew the best floated to the top, "and I want one of the fish heads."

"Sure you do," the old man cackled. "Luck of the ladle, boyo. Hungry lads can't be choosers." He stirred the stew, pouring a single ladle's worth into a small iron bowl.

Dolf held his breath, watching. A fish head floated on top, proving luck was on his side. "My lucky day." Dolf slurped a finger's width of the salty broth, carefully carrying the bowl to the side of the street. Sitting cross-legged, he lapped at the stew like a hungry cat, sucking tender morsels from the fish head. He counted himself lucky when two floating lumps turned out to be diced potato. Eighth-tier folks definitely ate better than the ninth, all the more reason to earn the rune forger's fee. He licked the bowl clean and then tucked it into his pouch, one more thing for Neffer to fence.

His stomach silenced, Dolf walked downhill till he found a shadowy corner in an empty alley. Wrapped in his cloak, he sat cross-legged, willing the sky to darken. Curiosity gnawed at his mind, wondering how much he'd filched. He fingered his pockets, hoping the stolen purses held silvers not coppers. His back pressed to the wall, he kept watch for soldiers, waiting for the cloak of night.

The sun crawled across the sky, eventually setting in a blaze of muted gold. Twilight brought the return of the crowds, a dull mummer pressing impatiently at the eighth tier gate. Dolf watched from the shadows. One at a time, they relinquished their work-markers to the overseers for pay and then made their way back home through the gate. Dolf considered working the crowd, but the gleanings would be the same as the ninth tier, not worth the risk.

Night slowly claimed the city, darkening the sky to black. Dolf waited till the Big Ladle rose before making his way to the dark wall. He'd planned to crossover at the same place, but from this side, the houses abutting the wall all looked alike. Cursing his carelessness, he scouted the buildings till he found a spot that seemed familiar. The stone house proved easy to scale. Reaching the roof, he hid behind a chimney, waiting for a patrol to pass.

The soft clank of armor gave the soldiers away. Once the patrol was safely passed, Dolf took a running leap and reached for the battlement. His hands caught a merlon, smooth stone beneath his fingertips. His heart hammering, he pulled himself over and then slunk low. With no soldiers in sight, he crossed to the other side, just a long drop away from safety.

He leaned on the battlement...and stifled a scream. Something sharp pierced his palm. Pulling his hand free, he licked the wound. Blood welled into his mouth. His left hand throbbed, but at least his fingers still worked. Puzzled and more than a little afraid, he studied the battlement, shocked to find obsidian shards embedded in the capstones. Wicked sharp, the shards would shred the rope of a grappling hook...or a climber's hand. Fear shivered down his back. So the wall had teeth...but there'd been no obsidian the other night, otherwise his hands would have been cut to ribbons. Why would obsidian be used on one part of the wall but not another...unless it was some kind of trap. Dolf shrank to the floor, fear gnawing the pit of his stomach. The longer he stayed in the eighth tier, the more likely he'd lose his head. He had to find a way back.

Left or right? He decided to follow the soldiers. His heart thundering, he ran along the battlement, his bare feet whispering on the cold stone. Straining his senses, he listened for the tramp of hobnailed boots while watching the battlements for a break in the obsidian. The wall seemed to stretch to forever...and so did the obsidian shards. Doubt warred with fear. With every stride he wondered if he'd chosen the wrong way. Just when he thought he should turn back, the obsidian came to an abrupt stop. The spiked capstones were gone, the merlons smooth as a pigeon's egg...but it seemed so suspicious.

Crouching low, Dolf peered over the battlement, searching for a gleam of armor in the alley below. If it truly was a trap, he saw no sign of it.

The tramp of soldiers came from behind; he'd run out of time.

Easing over the battlement, he dangled by his fingertips, hoping to lessen the fall. Pushing off from the wall, he let go, his cloak fluttering behind like a broken wing. The cobblestones came up hard, driving his knees to his chin. Rolling forward, he tumbled, coming to a stop at the foot of the wall. Dolf froze, certain the soldiers must be overhead. Breathing hard, he rose to a crouch, ready to run.

"Whoo-hoo-who-ho-oo." The signal-call came from the nearest alley. Dolf shrank against the wall, praying the soldiers would think it just a dove.

Benny stepped from the shadows, a broad smile on his face. *"Dolf, you made..."* The smile changed to fear as the lad stared up at the wall.

"Halt or die!" The command thundered from the battlement.

Dolf couldn't let the boy be caught. He pushed off from the wall and sprinted for the alley, drawing the attention of the soldiers. *"Run Benny!"* Feeling death staring down his back, Dolf dodged left and then right. A crossbow quarrel slammed into the cobblestones, spitting splinters of stone. A chip struck Dolf's forehead, drawing blood. He stumbled and nearly fell. Another quarrel whistled past his head, he wasn't going to make it. Desperate to reach the side alley, he bolted like a frightened rat.

Ahead, Benny raised his slingshot, aiming at the wall. A stone whooshed toward the battlement, proving the boy had more bravery than brains.

A yell rang from the wall; the stone must have found its mark.

Dolf reached the boy and hustled him into the alleyway. *"Run!"* They fled into the shadows, another quarrel nicking the side of the building. Left and then right, they raced into the depths of the ninth tier. Behind them, whistles blew, summoning the night watch.

Sweat drenched Dolf's tunic but he could not afford to slacken the pace. He led the boy deeper into the alleyways, hoping to lose the soldiers in the tangle of streets.

Footsteps echoed from a side alley, hobnailed boots clattering on cobblestones.

"This way!" He steered Benny toward a burnt-out building. *"Give me your slingshot."* Dolf shoved the boy's slingshot into his back pocket and then boosted the boy up through a blackened window. *"Hide in the rubble, I'll draw them away."* For once, the boy did not argue.

Dolf crossed to the opposite building and scaled the wall. He reached the roof just as the soldiers rounded the corner. Staying low, he hugged the tiles, crawling to the roof's spine. Crouching behind a chimney, he watched as the soldiers moved towards the burnt-out building.

Praying Benny stayed silent; Dolf fitted the slingshot with a pebble and took aim at a distant alleyway.

Stone clattered against stone.

The soldiers took the bait, chasing the sound.

Dolf raced along the roofline, jumping from one building to the next, shadowing the soldiers below. He made a game of it, sending the soldiers on a merry chase. Every time they slowed, he fired another pebble, sending them in a new direction. A twist and two turns latter, he let them go, convinced they'd lost the scent.

Grinning, Dolf climbed to the ridge, the king of the rooftops. Sitting cross-legged like a gargoyle, he stared down at the ninth tier. From the rooftops, the city seemed peaceful, all the danger and dinginess cloaked beneath darkness. He fingered the stolen purses tucked deep in his pockets and smiled. A few more fortnights working the eighth tier and he'd have enough silver to pay the rune forger. A smile spread across his face; *he'd done it!* He'd beaten the traps and tricks of the Citadel. Soon the ninth tier would be nothing but a bitter memory. He was moving up in the world. Elation thrummed through him. Dolf felt like shouting but he kept his triumph to himself.

Pulling his cloak tight against the night chill, he sat on the rooftop, content to be alone...till a hand grabbed him from behind. An iron grip held him tight, clamping a bitter cloth against his face. Dolf kicked and bucked, trying to pry the hand from his face but the assailant's grip tightened like a steel band. Dolf struggled to breathe. A bitter smell swamped his senses. His eyes grew tired and his arms weakened. The world faded to black.

#

Dolf woke on his back, lying on a pallet of stale straw. Unsure of his surroundings, he feigned sleep. Taking short shallow breathes, he tested the air. Dank and musty, the air reeked of old piss, not a good sign...but he heard no movement, so perhaps he was alone. Dolf dared a glance through hooded eyes. A low wood-beamed ceiling hung overhead, rough stone walls cloaked in shadow, the only light coming from a barred window in the door. *Bars on the window*...hope sank like a stone in his stomach. So they'd caught him. He slowly sat up and checked his pockets. Everything was gone, his stolen plunder, his knife, his lock picks, even Benny's sling. Caught with so many purses, they'd name him a thief for sure...but perhaps they didn't know he'd crossed into the eighth tier. He'd rather lose a hand than a head, but either way, he didn't relish the punishment. He needed a way out.

Stretching, he got to his feet. Ten paces by ten, the cell was small and spare, shut tight as a tomb. Sturdy stone walls, a piss-bucket in the corner, and a thick oak door, his chances looked bleak. He tried the door but the lock would not budge. Peering out the barred window, he caught a glimpse of a long stone hallway lit by torches, no sign of any guards. Thrusting his arm around the bars, he reached for the lock but his hand fell short. Caged like a rat, he gripped the iron bars, pushing and pulling, all to no avail. A scream lurked at the back of his throat, but Dolf kept silent, knowing it would only hasten his fate.

Taking a deep breath, he tried to swallow his fear. Sitting cross-legged on the bed, he stared at the door, desperate for a way out. The silence seemed to mock him, heavy as a shroud. Dolf thought he was alone...till the shadows moved.

A dark figure dropped from the ceiling. Clothed in black leather, his face and hands blackened with soot, he moved like liquid darkness.

Dolf shrank against the stone wall, his words a whisper. "What are you?"

The figure laughed. "A nightmare, a dark dread, a grim reaper...the Mordant's slayer."

A chill raced down Dolf's back. "Only a legend."

The laughter deepened. "Legends say the slayers shatter at the touch of light. Shall I put the legend to the test?" Moving with the lithe grace of a hunting cat, he stepped into striped light cast through the cell bars.

Dolf held his breath, but nothing happened.

The dark man grinned. Short and spare, he rippled with muscles beneath black leather, a baldric of nine throwing knives slung across his chest. Even the knives were dull black, danger cloaked in darkness. "Now do you believe?"

Dolf sucked air through his teeth. "What do you want?"

The reaper flashed a smile. "Are you a good thief?"

His pride pricked, Dolf raised both hands. "Two hands, tens fingers."

"Yes, you've avoided paying the thief's price...but not the bite of the obsidian shards."

His left hand betrayed him, the wound still bloody from the wall. Dolf balled his fists. Fear settled into the pit of his stomach, knowing the mistake could cost his head. "A cut from a broken roof tile." A thin lie but he had to try.

"A good thief but a bad liar." The reaper flashed a feral grin. "I watched you cross the wall, a brave jump."

"You *watched?*" It came back to him then, that feeling of being followed. "So it was you?"

The reaper nodded, his dark eyes glittering in the torchlight.

"But if you saw me cross the wall, why let me roam the eighth tier?"

"To see if you survived."

"And everything I stole?"

The reaper shrugged. "Wool from the sheep."

Dolf shook his head, struggling to understand. "And what about the obsidian shards? Why were they absent from that stretch of wall? My hands should have been cut to ribbons." He raised his hands as proof, staring at the reaper. "Or was this all just an elaborate trap?"

"Not a trap...*a test.*"

Dolf held his breath, waiting.

"Everything in the Dark Citadel exists for a reason." The reaper moved to the door, a shadow blocking the light. "Even in the ninth tier, there is always a way out, a way to climb the tiers, but only for those rare few who are daring and skilled enough to try."

"But why?"

"To separate the wolves from the sheep. So the best of us can serve the Mordant."

Dolf shook his head, finding it hard to take in.

"The ninth tier is a constant struggle for survival...the perfect breeding ground for assassins."

Dolf gasped. "The whole tier...for one reason?" The thought was staggering.

The reaper nodded. "We all serve the Mordant. The Citadel is his design."

Dolf saw it then, the reaper was small and wiry...like the citizens of the ninth tier. He shivered. "What now?"

"Come with me...if you dare." The reaper reached through the bars. Dolf heard the faint rasp of metal against metal. The lock clicked and the door swung open. The reaper stepped into the hallway, a dark shadow against the light.

The door gaped open, like an invitation...or a trap.

Dolf rose from the pallet and followed, his bare feet soft in the long hallway. He saw no guards, only the black-clad reaper. Silence blanketed the dungeon like a shroud. They passed a dozen cells, but if other prisoners festered behind locked doors, Dolf could not tell.

An ironbound door blocked the end of the hallway. The reaper reached for the lock. Dolf moved to the side to watch, surprised to find that the reaper had no keys, only a simple metal pick.

The lock clicked open.

The door swung in to reveal a den of horrors. Chains dangled from the center of the ceiling, iron manacles waiting to hold the next victim. Instruments gleamed on the walls, knives, axes, prongs, and hooks. A brazier lit the chamber, a pair of tongs glowing in the red coals. The smell was horrendous, the stench of blood and piss choking the chamber with fear.

Dolf shrank against the wall. "Why here?"

The reaper stood in the brazier's red glow. "To give you a choice." He eased a knife from his baldric and cut the leather of his left sleeve, a deft slice running from elbow to hand. "I'm offering you a chance to change your fate." He peeled back the leather, revealing his left forearm.

"*Nine runes!*" Drawn like a puppet on a string, Dolf moved towards the reaper. Awestruck, he studied the dark tattoos. Nine runes filled the reaper's forearm, running from wrist to elbow. "You have all nine," another legend sprung to life.

The reaper nodded. "An assassin of the ninth rank."

Dolf stared in wonder. "How?"

"By passing all the tests." The reaper lowered his arm. "A chance you've earned by daring the eighth tier."

"What must I do?"

The reaper flashed a smile. "Smart enough to know there is always a price." He moved to the back of the chamber, to a door hidden by shadows. "The price of the eighth rune is not measured in silvers...but in blood."

Dolf gasped, feeling naked and exposed. "So you know!"

The reaper nodded. "The rune forger is one of ours, an assassin of the third rank." He gestured toward the door. "This door holds your only path to the eighth rune. Come and see your price." Metal shrieked against metal as the reaper slid open a small grate in the door.

It was only then, that Dolf heard the muffled crying.

The reaper gestured. "Come."

Dolf hesitated.

"Come but do not speak."

Dolf shuffled towards the door, dread weighing his every step.

The reaper studied him, a grim smile on his face.

Shaking, Dolf stepped to the door and peered through the grate. Torches lit the small chamber. A boy sat trussed in a chair, his eyes blindfolded, his left hand splayed on a cutting board. *Benny!*

The reaper slammed the grate closed. "Now you know the price."

"But he's only a boy!"

"There are no children in the ninth tier, only victims and survivors." The reaper's voice was hard. "Will you sink with the victims or rise with the survivors?"

"But he's my friend!"

"He's a thief...and now he'll pay a thief's price."

"*I* taught him to steal." Dolf held up his left hand. "Take my fingers instead."

"You're no use to us maimed." The reaper walked to the wall of instruments and chose a wicked-looking butcher's knife. A quick flick of his hand, and the knife quivered upright in a wooden chopping block. "Take the knife and make the cuts...and the eighth rune will be yours before tomorrow."

Dolf moved to the bloodstained block. He fingered the blade, considering his choices.

The reaper laughed, a low rumble of menace. "You're too smart to try it...not against an assassin of the ninth rank."

Dolf sighed, a sick feeling settling in the pit of his stomach. "Is there no other way?"

The reaper shook his head. "We serve the Mordant, reaping the lives of men, women, and children, killing without question, all part of our lord's grand dark design." He gestured toward the butcher knife. "Blood is part of the test." The reaper grinned. "You'll be well rewarded, gaining a better life in a higher tier." His gaze turned cold. "But someone has to pay the price. It's only a few fingers."

Dolf's stomach churned. "And afterwards?"

"The boy will be released to the ninth tier, believing you're dead. Rumors will say you died under the executioner's axe, shortened by a head for daring to cross the wall." The reaper flashed a feral grin. "Your *death* will be an example to others...while you gain a new life in the eighth tier."

"And then I'll train to be an assassin?"

"Your training has already begun."

A single tear slid down the side of Dolf's face...but he could not say if it was for the boy...or himself. He took the knife and turned towards the door.

The Emperor's Shadow

The map said it all. Red color leached across the western states like a fatal bloodstain. Zebastion stopped and stared at the big screen, stunned to silence by the truth. The war was going badly, worse than the media let on. Everything west of the Rockies was lost, captured by the Chinese. Los Angeles fell first, the bastion of western propaganda silenced by saturation bombing and paratroopers, followed closely by the tech-brains of Silicon Valley and Seattle. At least neither side used nukes, not yet, but America had its back to the wall, anything was possible. Zebastion ground his teeth, staring up at the map. So hard to believe the United States could actually fall, it left a sick feeling in the pit of his stomach, like jumping from an airplane without a parachute.

He stood forgotten in the corner of the concrete bunker, a pair of armed guards at his back, the only civilian in a sea of uniforms. Bird colonels rushed back and forth delivering messages to three and four star generals. Technicians sat in front of keyboards, bathed in the eerie glow of computer screens. Overhead, symbols flashed across the map, air squadrons and infantry groups locked in a death struggle with the enemy.

A student of history, Zebastion memorized every detail. It wasn't often an archeologist got a front row seat on the making of history, especially a world war. *A world at war*, the words thundered through his mind like a death knell. Such wars were supposed to be the stuff of history, or fiction. No one ever expected to be caught in the grip of a real World War, when all the rules were broken, and anything could happen, when death and destruction became the norm. But worst of all was the thought that America could actually lose, defeated by the Chinese dragon. His mouth tasted like ashes.

"Doctor Kole?" A weightlifter in a black pin-stripe suit approached. His blond hair was crew-cut short, a not-so-discrete earplug in his left ear, probably a member of the secret service. "President Anders will see you now."

President Anders! Zebastion stared, slack-mouthed. The last he'd heard, Anders had only been the Vice-President. The rumors of Chinese assassination squads must be true, another victory for the enemy.

"Doctor Kole?" The agent's baritone broke Zebastion's shock. "If you'll follow me, please, the President will see you now."

Gripping the handles of his tattered briefcase, he followed the agent to a side door plated in armor. A pair of armed guards stood at attention. Fingers on triggers, they eyeballed him as he passed through to the bunker's inner sanctum.

The air inside was tense as a drum. The agent cleared his throat and the conversation crashed to a halt. Six men turned his way, like staring into a firing squad. The Joint Chiefs of Staff sat clustered around the far end of a conference table, enough medals gleaming from their uniform jackets to decorate a small army. The only man not in uniform sat at the head of the table, his shirtsleeves rolled up, his tie askew, his gray hair rumpled. President Anders looked like a man who hadn't slept in a month. Deep bags lined his eyes and his mouth tightened to a tense slash, sobering a face normally creased with political laugh lines. "Take a seat, Kole."

"I'd prefer to stand, sir."

"As you wish." The President leaned back in his chair, his right hand cradling a coffee mug embossed with the seal of the United States of America. "You've seen the map." It was a statement not a question.

"Yes, sir."

"Then you know how desperate we are." His cordial southern charm dissolved, replaced by grim expediency. "Desperate enough to try your plan."

The army general intervened. "Sir, once we recall our troops from the Middle East we'll be in a better position to..."

The President cut him off. "Yes, yes, every military measure will be put into play, but as President, I plan to exhaust any and all means to save this country." His gaze raked across his generals. "*Any* means." His voice dropped to a low rasp. "I'll not go down in history as the *last* President of these United States."

The generals looked away, bitter scowls on their faces.

"Good." The President turned his stare back to Zebastion. "My predecessor discarded your proposal as little more than a joke, a delusion fermented by Hollywood. But like you, Doctor Kole, I too am a student of history. And I'm also a politician, so I know the power of propaganda." His voice took on an orator's ring. "History proves that religious relics inspire armies to great victories. The Israelites carried the Arc of the Covenant before them, defeating the armies of the Philistines. The kings of medieval France had the Oriflamme, a silk battle banner fashioned from the robe of St. Martin deTours. And more recently, we have the example of the Spear of Destiny, the spear Longinus used to pierce the side of Jesus during the crucifixion."

"Spears and battle banners," the air force general interrupted, his gruff western twang riddled with sarcasm. "With all due respect, Mr. President, you're talking voodoo and witchcraft when we need to be considering the nuclear option."

A hush settled across the chamber like a tombstone.

"A scorched earth policy." The President shook his head. "Not yet, general, not until we've tried every other option." Weariness flooded the President's voice. "As you can see, my generals think I'm wasting time, but you know differently, don't you, Doctor Kole?" He drilled Zebastion with his stare. "Tell them about the Spear."

"The Spear." Zebastion took a deep breath, stalling for time to get his thoughts in order. "Legends claim that whoever holds the Spear of Destiny holds the fate of the world in his hands. Since the Middle Ages, leaders have sought to wield the Spear in their quest for power. Charlemagne was among the first, crediting the Spear with fifty battle victories in his struggle to create the Holy Roman Empire. Even Napoleon sought the Spear, but men loyal to the Habsburgs smuggled it out of Vienna prior to the Battle of Austerlitz. Most recently, Hitler became obsessed with the Spear, assigning a special SS squad to seek it out. The Spear came into Nazi possession just prior to the first blitzkrieg assault on Poland. Hitler held the Spear for six years, six long years of amazing military victories, until the American army captured it. Within hours of losing the Spear, Hitler committed suicide in his bunker. The American army went on to defeat the Japanese, ending the death and destruction of the Second World War. After the war, Eisenhower returned the Spear to the Royal House of Hapsburg, where it remains in a museum in Austria to this day."

The marine general leaned forward, his voice as rough as gravel. "So we're supposed to steal this spear from a museum, wave it at the Chinese, and hope their army just melts away?"

Gallows laughter circled the table.

"No. Not the spear." Zebastion's answer doused their humor. "The Spear of Destiny is a relic of the West. Steeped in the lore of Christianity, it will have no impact on the Chinese. Relics only hold power over those who believe. Some inspire the ability to heal, like the statue of the Virgin in Guadalupe, while others like the Spear incite feelings of invincibility, leading to wars and bloodshed. It all comes down to the power of belief."

The marine general bit on the argument like a trout snapping at a fly. "So what do the Chinese believe in?"

"Their first emperor."

"What?"

"China, despite all its modern advancements, is still a country obsessed with its own history and the near-religious worship of its ancestors. Even Chairman Mao could not sever the link to the past. Ancestor-worship and a deep-seeded sense of superstition are the real reasons so many tombs of past dynasties remain unopened. And the most famous of these, is the tomb of the first emperor." He fumbled with the buckles on his briefcase, rummaging through papers and maps for a small digital projector. "Almost everyone in the world knows about the tomb, they just don't understand the history behind it." Setting the projector in the center of the table, he flicked the remote. Rows of terra-cotta warriors appeared on the far wall, a clay army standing in battle formation.

"Farmers working in the fields near the city of Xi'an first discovered fragments of terra-cotta warriors while digging a well in 1974. Excavations undertaken by the Chinese government soon unearthed a complete army of terra-cotta warriors. Over seven thousand life-size soldiers, six hundred horses, and one hundred chariots stand in defense of the emperor's tomb." He thumbed the remote and the details became clear, projecting a series of faces sculpted in clay. Each face was eerily unique. Some scowled while others seemed eager for battle, as if the ancient sculptors captured a soul within each statue. Zebastion stared at the images, seduced by the mystery. "Superbly crafted, the incredible detail of each soldier is only outdone by the grand scale of an entire army, an army of soldiers waiting to be woken from two thousand years of slumber." A mixture of awe and excitement rode his voice. "The terra-cotta warriors are one of the greatest archeological discoveries of the modern age."

The air force general interrupted. "But if the tomb's already been excavated, what's the point?"

"That's just it. The tomb's never been opened."

"But what about the army of clay soldiers?"

"Those are only the outlying pits." Zebastion flicked through a series of slides till he found an aerial photo of the site. "You have to understand that the burial site is enormous. According to Sima Qian, the historian of the first emperor, the burial complex mimics the layout of the old imperial capital, complete with a standing army and a replica of the imperial palace." He moved to the wall, pointing to the main sites. "The tomb itself is here, buried under an earthen mound over 47 meters tall. From the surface it doesn't look like much, just a wooded hill in the shape of a truncated pyramid, but the size of the tomb hidden beneath is larger than the Great Pyramid at Giza. Can you imagine the archeological wonders waiting to be discovered? What secrets we could learn about ancient China? This tomb will make King Tut look like a pauper."

The President cleared his voice.

Chagrined, Zebastion bit back his enthusiasm, sticking to the facts. "This photo shows the scale of the site. The first pit of clay warriors discovered by the farmers is here, over a full kilometer away from the emperor's tomb. The tomb complex is enormous, an entire necropolis. Over 80 pits have been excavated, all of them peripheral sites, yielding everything from hay for the emperor's horses, to clay birds and flowers, to the latest discovery of life-sized terra-cotta musicians."

The air force general leaned forward, a look of studied boredom on his face. "I'm sure this is all mighty interesting, but what's the point?"

"The point is, the Chinese refuse to excavate the tomb."

"Why?"

"Because to them it's a sacred site, a symbol of national pride and unity, the tomb of the first emperor of China." He thumbed the remote till the projector showed a painting of a stern-faced older man in classical Chinese robes. "It all started in 245 BC, almost one hundred and fifty years before the birth of Julius Caesar. Prior to the first emperor, the land we now know as China was made up of seven warring kingdoms locked in a brutal battle for dominance." Zebastion gestured to the painting, trying to imagine the convoluted genius behind the bearded face. "The Warring States Period ended with the ascendancy of this man. At the age of 13, Prince Zheng inherited the throne of Qin. A military genius, he reinvented the army based on standardized weapons and training. At the age of 28, the general-king began conquering the surrounding kingdoms using a combination of brute force and intimidation. In less than ten years, he united them for the first time into one vast empire named China." Zebastion clicked to a map faded by age, the borders eerily similar to present-day China. "Like an ancient-day Napoleon, Zheng was part general, part statesman, and all dictator. Upon becoming supreme emperor, he changed his name to Qin Shi Huang Di. Literally translated the name means "the first august god of Qin". As absolute ruler and a god incarnate, the Tiger of Qin dethroned the local aristocracy and ran roughshod over local customs and cultures, imposing a central government. Ruthless in the use of power, he placed unbearable burdens on his people, forcing them to complete the Great Wall and build massive dams and canals on the Yellow River." Zebastion flicked through a series of slides showing the emperor's accomplishments, finally returning to the ancient portrait, to the dark eyes nested in an inscrutable face. "To the Chinese, he is the Uniter, the god-emperor, the man who laid the foundations of China. In so many ways, he truly is the Supreme Ancestor of China."

"So?" The air force general made the single word an insult.

"So, if history isn't enough for you, there's also the legend. Legends say that if the tomb of the first emperor is ever opened, then China will crumble, dissolving back into its many parts."

The general barked a rude laugh. "What a load of bull! You came here to sell us this crap? I don't believe it."

Zebastion hit back. "It doesn't matter if *you* believe. It only matters what the *Chinese* believe."

"And what makes you think they believe it?"

"Actions speak louder than words. The Chinese government refuses to open the tomb, foregoing millions of dollars of increased tourist revenue, not to mention the value of the treasure hidden within. And if money isn't enough of an argument, consider this; the Chinese have run detailed seismograms across the site yet they refuse to make the results public. Any data gathered on the emperor's tomb is guarded like a national secret." Zebastion stared at the generals. "Like I said before, it all comes down to a matter of belief."

The air force general shook his head. "Sounds like a bunch of horse crap to me." But the marine general seemed interested, his chiseled face locked in thought. "So if the tomb is opened, you're saying China will break apart?"

Zebastion nodded. "Legends say it will crumble from within."

President Anders joined the discussion. "And this, gentlemen, is why I'm willing to back Doctor Kole's venture. Modern China is an uneasy sum of its many parts. The Tibetans have been agitating for years and then there's the Uyghurs and a hundred other dissident groups." His stare roved the table, stopping at each general. "We need a way to end this war, and we need it fast. Opening the tomb might be like taking a chisel to a cracked statue. One hit in the right place and the whole thing crumbles to dust."

"But breaking into a tomb?" The air force general scanned the room for support. "No one will even know, let alone care!"

"You underestimate the power of propaganda." The President leaned back in his chair; a politician's smile playing across his face. "We make a vidcast of the whole thing and put it on the web, on the Chinese equivalent of You-tube or other such sites, like launching a virus into the Chinese psych, and then we wait and see if they really believe."

The air force general threw up his hands in disgust. "We're grasping at straws!"

The marine general disagreed. "Yeah, but it's my boys who'll be taking the brunt of the fighting." He gestured to Zebastion. "Screwy as it sounds, if this plan has even a snowball's chance in hell, then I'm all for it."

The President smiled. "A conclusion I came to long ago."

Zebastion's mouth went dry and his mind spun. He gripped the edge of the table, needing an anchor. One of the greatest archeological mysteries of all time might soon be his to explore.

"Well, Doctor Kole, what will you need to complete this mission?"

Zebastion scrambled to organize his thoughts. "First off we'll need to get there. The tomb is in east-central China, near the city of Xi'an."

"Not a problem," the air force general gave him a sadistic smile, "we'll just HALO you and your team in."

"Halo?"

But the President gave him no time for questions. "What else?"

"Archeology is a slow and methodical science, but this," Zebastion shook his head, momentarily overwhelmed by the challenge, "this is going to be a blitzkrieg, a lightning raid, and we only get one shot at it. So we're going to need someone who specializes in traps and tricks, we're going to need an expert thief."

"A thief?"

Zebastion ignored the general's outburst. "The historian, Sima Qian, gives us the best description of the tomb. He describes it as a microcosm of heaven and earth, but amidst all the splendor the ancient architects hid deadly traps and tricks to foil tomb raiders. We'll need a thief to navigate the tomb."

"A thief." The President nodded. "What else?"

"We'll need a linguist."

The air force general interrupted. "But I thought *you* were the expert?"

Zebastion nodded. "Of the period and the emperor's life, yes, I'm your man, but you have to understand that the Chinese language has over forty-seven *thousand* characters. Misinterpreting a single character could put the entire mission in jeopardy." Anger bled into his voice. "With so much at stake, I won't take that chance, will you, general?"

The President leaned back in his chair. "I suppose you have someone in mind?"

"Yes." He wondered if she'd changed, if she still thought of him. "Mei Ling, professor of Asian languages at Harvard."

"*A damn chink!*" The air force general swore like a trooper.

Zebastion struggled to ignore the slur. "I've worked with Mei Ling before, she's a consummate professional, an expert in her field."

The air force general shook his head, his face turning bull-red. "A chink and a woman, now you've gone too far."

Zebastion pinned the general with a daggered glare. "She runs the Boston marathon every year, always placing in the top ten percent. And as to her heritage, it's true her parents were immigrants from China, but Mei Ling was born in *this* country, and last I checked, America is still a melting pot, the home of the free and the brave."

"Enough." The President intervened. "We'll do a level four security check on her, and if she passes, you'll have her on your team." A hint of annoyance leeched into his voice. "Anything else?"

"Yes, we'll need hazmat suits in case the mercury levels are too high. And one last thing, we'll need a portable seismograph to confirm the entrance to the tomb."

"You're not sure of the entrance?"

"According to Sima Qian, there are four entrances at the four cardinal compass points, but I believe only one of them is real. The Chinese government unearthed the south gate, so we know that's not the true entrance."

"So which one is it?" The President sent him a sharp glare. "You won't have time to dig potholes all across the site."

Zebastion smiled. "Archaeology is like a game of chess, with the present trying to outwit the past."

"So?"

"So, to find the entrance, we have to think like the ancient Chinese." Zebastion reached for the projector's remote, thumbing through the slides till he found the aerial photograph of the site. "The emperor's magicians and soothsayers choose this site because it has great Feng Shui, great mystical power. Nestled between the Lishan Mountains in the south and the Wei River in the north, the strip of land chosen for the site is shaped like a dragon." He used his finger to outline the head and body. "And the tomb itself is located here, at the dragon's eye. And how does one enter the dragon? Through the mouth." He stabbed his finger at the photo. "The true entrance is here, in the west."

"Dragons and thieves," the air force general shook his head, his voice filled with disgust, "the defense of the nation depends on dragons and thieves, God help us."

A faint rumble shook the bunker.

Everyone froze, watching as dust drifted down from the ceiling.

A red light flashed overhead and the outer door burst open. Six secret service agents poured into the chamber. "Our location is compromised! We have to get the President out!" Klaxons blared from the outer control room, adding a surreal threat to the inner chamber.

The President blanched ghost-white, held in the grip of the secret service. But then he recovered, pointing to Zebastion. "Get the archeologist out on my chopper! He's got top priority, presidential clearance."

Hands grabbed Zebastion, pulling him toward the only door. And then he was running for his life, caught in the crosshairs of a world at war.

#

One week later, Zebastion found himself strapped in a webbed seat, sitting in the belly of an air force cargo plane, somewhere over central Asia. The airplane shuddered and shook but he told himself it was just turbulence. Sweat beaded his forehead; he was an archeologist not a soldier, yet he wore army fatigues, gray mottled with black, dark camouflage for a high altitude night insertion called a HALO jump. The marine instructor said they'd be jumping from thirty-five thousand feet using stealth parachutes. *Thirty-five thousand feet,* the number echoed in his mind, more than enough to smack a man into a pancake. At least his fate would be in competent hands. They'd jump in tandem, strapped close as lovers, with the SEAL sergeant pulling all the strings from behind. Nervous as a virgin, Zebastion tried not to think about his first jump; his stomach already doing barrel rolls.

Desperate for distraction, he turned his mind to the task ahead, surveying the special equipment strapped in camouflage bundles to the center of the plane. Zebastion chose much of it himself, a state-of-the-art portable seismograph, LED lanterns, hazmat bio suits, and good old-fashioned crowbars. Of course the bundles also contained extra ammo, camouflage netting, plastic explosives, and spare Uzis, a grim reminder that his next archeological dig was deep behind enemy lines.

Overhead, the light changed from white to red, proof they neared the drop site.

His small team of tomb raiders sat on either side of the cargo hold, their faces distorted by the red light. They made an odd group, a thief, a linguist, an archeologist, and six SEAL soldiers looking like something straight out of a Rambo movie. At six-foot-one, Zebastion was tall and lean and kept himself in fairly good shape for a thirty-six year old professor, but sitting next to the SEALs he felt like the runt of the litter. Built like blocks of concrete, the SEALs sat shoulder-to-shoulder, listening to music or dozing in their seats, professionals waiting to do a job. Zebastion admired their sense of calm; to these battle-hardened veterans the adventure of archeology must seem like a slow dance.

He dared a glance at Mei Ling, a petite figure sitting on the far side of the plane, her beauty undisguised by camouflage fatigues. Dark raven hair tied back in a ponytail, he remembered the silky feel beneath his fingertips. He shivered, forcing the thought away. She'd made it plain she was here for America first, and the emperor's tomb second, and those were her *only* reasons. He supposed he couldn't blame her; their rocky breakup was more his fault than hers, but deep inside he hoped she was just playing hard to get.

The red light began to blink, throbbing like a slow heartbeat; another fifteen minutes and they'd need to suit up.

Fidgeting with the Velcro on his thigh pocket, he removed a battered postcard, a souvenir from his last visit to Xi'an, a memory from a more peaceful time. The backside remained blank, still waiting for a message to Ling, but the front held the image of an ancient painting. The first emperor stared back at him, a stern-faced man in golden robes captured by the brushstrokes of another time. The red light throbbing overhead gave the emperor's face an evil cast, but Zebastion knew it was just his imagination.

Beside him, the sergeant leaned close, pulled by curiosity. Catching a glimpse of the postcard, he barked a laugh. "Most soldiers carry a photo of their wives or sweethearts, but you're obsessed with a dead emperor!"

Thankful for the distraction, Zebastion grinned, yelling over the roar of the engines. "Archeology is a battle of wits. And this is our opponent. To be successful we have to out-think the first emperor and all his court."

The sergeant sobered. "Can you do it? Can you defeat him?"

"The discovery of the terra-cotta army is what drove me to archeology. All my life I've studied the first emperor, obsessed with the unopened tomb. Now I have a chance to solve one of archeology's greatest mysteries." His shoulders hunched, feeling the weight of history. "The Chinese have a saying; be careful what you wish for." He studied the inscrutable face staring from the postcard. "We'll soon find out if the present can outwit the past."

The sergeant's voice dropped to a low growl. "Well, I'm wishing for an end to the war."

The answer pushed Zebastion toward a long-held question. "How can the Chinese be winning? America's supposed to be the greatest superpower the world has ever known."

Sergeant O'Malley gave him a grim look. "Arrogance."

"What?"

"We always knew they outnumbered us, and they're willing to spend their soldiers like cannon-fodder, but we thought superior technology would save us." The sergeant shrugged. "Turns out their technology is just as good as ours. We're losing the war in the science labs not the field of valor. We need an advantage, something to even the odds." The sergeant drilled him with a deadly stare. "Will breaking into a tomb make any difference?"

"History casts a long shadow. And in China, no ancestor casts a longer shadow than the first emperor."

"But this is the 21st century, the modern world?"

"The Chinese are very sophisticated and very superstitious. Chinese architects use the ancient art of Feng Shei to design buildings, businessmen consult fortunetellers before signing contracts, and hundreds of thousands of dollars are spent each year to purchase lucky license plate numbers." Zebastion shrugged. "It all depends on the strength of the emperor's shadow.

"Let's hope it's an f-ing eclipse."

Overhead, the red light pulsed to a frantic heartbeat.

The sergeant clapped him on the shoulder. "Time to suit up."

Zebastion struggled to keep his supper down; he never liked heights. The sergeant helped him into the HALO jumpsuit, tightening straps and checking the oxygen gage. All too soon, the cargo bay doors whooshed open, revealing an infinite darkness studded with jewel-bright stars. Zebastion gaped at the view, he'd never seen stars so bright, or so cold, but then it was time to go. With the sergeant strapped tight against his back, he shuffled forward like an overburdened penguin. Teetering on the edge, he hesitated, wondering if he stood on the brink of history or oblivion. And then he took the last step, falling into darkness.

#

Midnight in the heart of China, they ran like wraiths in dark camouflage, melting through the empty fields. The SEALs took the lead, setting a fast pace, running in an arrowhead formation. Hunched with equipment and weapons, they looked like gargoyles sprung to life, come to plunder an emperor's tomb.

Cold and dark, the night seemed surreal, full of promise and threat. Zebastion ran next to Ling, struggling to keep pace with her marathon stride. She ran like silk beside him, but for once he wasn't distracted, his mind obsessed with the task ahead. His heartbeat thundered loud in his ears. Exertion vied with excitement, so much depended on his theories.

Night-vision goggles painted the countryside red, like running through a demon-landscape. And then he saw it, a truncated pyramid thrust up from the plain, a man-made mountain guarding the emperor's tomb.

Approaching from the west, they avoided the other excavations and the night guards at the terra-cotta museum, making their way toward the base of the mound. The SEALs used GPS to find the location of the western gate, and then they knelt, unpacking the seismograph.

Zebastion slumped to the ground, gasping for breath, suddenly riddled with doubt. He'd chosen this site, but his talk of Feng Shui and license plates nagged at his mind.

The seismograph gave a muffled thump, sending green lines snaking across the scope.

"This isn't right."

The others froze, staring at him.

"But the scope shows a gate below."

"It's not the right gate." He tried to explain. "The government claims the tomb has four entrances, but in Chinese numerology, four is the most unlucky number, the number for death."

"But we're looking for a *tomb*."

"You're thinking like a Westerner. To the ancient Chinese, this tomb was meant to be heaven on earth. According to Sima Qian, the emperor always favored the number six. We need to find the sixth gate."

"We only get one chance." The sergeant stared at him. "Time is our enemy."

"I know."

"You're the expert," the sergeant shrugged, but his voice was tense. "Where?"

"To the southwest, halfway between the west and south gates."

They moved the equipment across the manicured grass, using the pyramid to estimate the location of the sixth gate. Five times the seismograph thumped and five times there was nothing but dirt beneath their feet. The SEALs wrestled the machine to a new location while Zebastion paced, a sheen of sweat building on his forehead.

"We found it."

Relief flooded through him. "How far down?"

"Four meters to the top of the gate."

"That's it!" So there really was a sixth gate! Zebastion pumped his fist in victory.

A SEAL knelt, cutting a doorway in the sod and rolling it aside. Three others began to dig. Shoveling dirt onto tarps, they tunneled straight down like moles toward the gate. Two SEALs ferried dirt to other pits to hide the new excavation while the sixth kept watch, an Uzi held at the ready.

Zebastion started unpacking equipment, looking for headlamps and crowbars, hoping he'd have a chance to use them. Ling joined him, a petite figure in dark camouflage. "You were lucky."

Her words pricked his pride. "Or maybe I'm just good."

She ignored his riposte. "How will you know if this is the right gate?"

"Opening would be a good start."

"So the others are blinds, false gates?"

"That's one theory."

She gave him a sloe-eyed glance. "I don't remember you being this taciturn."

"It's business, not pleasure."

Her voice dropped to a hushed whisper. "It used to be both."

His breath caught. He wondered if she meant it or if it was just a silken tease. He decided to be cautious. "You're here because you're the best. And because we can't afford any mistakes."

"So I'm supposed to keep you out of trouble?"

Her smoky voice always got to him, like silk rubbing across the back of his neck. "Something like that." Avoiding her stare, he found a tool belt and buckled it around his waist.

"What will we find inside?"

"Nobody knows. That's the mystery of archeology."

"Treasure," the thief interrupted, a thin wiry man slumped next to the equipment, his Bronx accent jarring in the night. "It's filled with treasure, a fortune in gold and pearls and jade, worth way more than King Tut's tomb."

Jack Tanner was the last to join their little team, a thief on loan from Sloan Penitentiary. Zebastion had taken an instant dislike to the greasy little man. "Is money all you care about?"

Tanner grinned. "Money and a full pardon. And, hey," he spread his arms wide to the night, "an all expense-paid vacation *behind enemy lines*." He leaned close, his voice dropping to a whisper. "You know, I figure we deserve hazard pay, a little gold here, an ancient jade there, nothing the emperor won't miss. What do you say?"

Zebastion's anger boiled over. "For the thousandth time, we're not here for treasure, we're here for a provenance, proof the emperor's tomb has been opened."

"Oh sure," Tanner winked, "I've seen the movies. You archeologists are just thieves with fancy names."

Disgusted, Zebastion turned his back on the little man, but that brought him face to face with Ling. She gave him a Cheshire-cat smile. "You know what I said earlier about being lucky? It's not a bad thing."

"What do you mean?"

"We're in China." Her smile deepened to a taunt. "Confucius says a small fortune depends on diligence, a great fortune depends on luck."

"I guess I left my fortune cookie at home." He settled down to wait, listening to the SEALs dig, wondering if his luck would hold.

#

Hours ticked by and still the SEALs shoveled. Zebastion paced the edge of the pit like an expectant father. His gaze kept returning to the star-studded sky, dreading the first hint of dawn. According to the plan, they had one night to gain entrance to the tomb. Another couple of hours and they'd have to abort.

A pair of SEALs returned for another load of dirt. The moist clay made for hard digging but it also kept the shaft from caving in.

A steel shovel scraped against stone. "Hey Doc, we've cleared the gate."

Zebastion leaped into the pit, never mind the six-meter drop. He landed hard, boots pounding into clay, but he soon forgot the pain. Lantern light revealed a stone doorway, dragons and tigers carved deep in the lintel, the work of a master stonemason, but it was the swords that caught his attention. Seven massive swords barred the gate. "Seven swords for the seven kingdoms united by Zheng." His hands caressed the metal hilts, large enough to be wielded by giants. "The swords alone are an archeological treasure."

Beside him, the sergeant said, "Why aren't they rusted?"

"Because they're made of bronze. See how each blade is embossed with the seal of a different kingdom? The Smithsonian would pay a fortune to get these intact."

"Should we try and open it?"

The question sent a shiver down his back. For more than two thousand years the doors had remained closed, guarding the secrets of the emperor's tomb, and now they were his to open. "Give me some room." The small pit was crowded with three SEALs and one archeologist. Schmidt and Clark climbed the rope ladder, leaving him with just the sergeant. "Make sure your video camera is on, we need to record everything." Lipstick-size cameras were embedded in the collars of their fatigues, designed to capture another form of proof. Zebastion turned his on, and then he stared at the doorway, the threshold to a dream. "Help me ease the swords from the stone fittings. Try not to harm them." Metal scrapped against stone. One at a time, they drew the swords from the stone's embrace.

His heart hammering, Zebastion gripped the doors. "The moment of truth," and then he pulled. Stone ground against stone. The double doors slowly swung open, revealing a portal to another time.

"You've done it, Doc!" The sergeant slapped his back, hard enough to rattle his teeth. "You've found the entrance!"

"It's just the beginning, just the outer doors." But Zebastion's heart thundered with excitement, belying the calm of his words. "Get the others down here."

The sergeant disappeared up the rope ladder, leaving Zebastion to stand alone on the tomb's threshold. A chill swept down his back. The mystery of the past beckoned him forward, the dreams of a lifetime. He picked up a lantern and stepped inside.

Faces glinted back at him, reflected in the lantern light. An honor guard of soldiers lined both sides of the hallway, standing rigid at attention. Life-sized, with all the details of the terra-cotta warriors, but these were made of bronze. Zebastion shivered. Only two steps into the tomb and already he'd discovered wonders.

He breathed deep, testing the air. Stale and musty, to Zebastion it held the tantalizing scent of forever. He raised the lantern, peering into the gloom. The corridor ran straight and true, tunneling toward the pyramid, toward the cold heart of the tomb. He knew he should wait for the others but he couldn't resist.

His footsteps sounded in the corridor, the first in over two thousand years. History echoed back at him, the thrill of discovery. He aimed his lamp left and right, drinking in the details. The stonework proved amazing, granite glistening in the lantern light, blocks of stone flawlessly fitted together. And overhead, the corbelled ceiling was painted to look like a summer sky, creamy white clouds in a sapphire vault, the vibrant colors undimmed by time. Twenty steps, thirty, forty and he reached another doorway, this one solid bronze, sealed shut with molten metal. He ran his hand along the rough seal; proof the tomb was still intact.

Footsteps came from behind. Beams of light played against the walls, against the company of bronze soldiers. The others crowded into the corridor, sounds of amazement echoing through the hallway. To

Zebastion, the sudden chatter seemed like a sacrilege, shattering the peace of the tomb.

Sergeant O'Malley reached him first. "We moved everything down from the surface. Clark, Stangle, and Schmidt will camouflage the mouth of the shaft and stand guard." He checked his watch. "Sunrise is less two hours away. We've got nineteen hours underground and then we need to be out of here."

Zebastion nodded, gesturing toward the doors. "We're going to need the acetylene torch. These doors were locked with molten metal, sealed for all eternity."

The sergeant nodded. "Corporal Vasquez, we need the acetylene torch!"

"Yes, sir!" A SEAL rummaged through one of the large packs and then approached with goggles and a torch. The torch made quick work of the bronze. "All done here."

The others gathered around, headlamps and flashlights illuminating the doors.

Smooth as polished mirrors, the bronze doors had no handles.

Zebastion opened his pocketknife and eased the steel blade between the two doors. The knife met no resistance. The doors whispered open...and a skeleton fell into his arms. Zebastion leaped backwards and Ling stifled a scream. Mummies poured out of the doorway. Jammed together, screams frozen on their faces, they toppled to the floor like cordwood.

Beside him, Ling shivered. "What's this?"

Zebastion knelt to study the dead. He'd seen mummies before but none quite like these. Leathery skin stretched taut over desiccated bones, their eyes sunken to dark pits, their hands clenched into fists, their mouths stretched into a frozen snarl, every gesture imbued with horror. Silk tatters clung to the skeletal limbs, the bright colors incongruous with the leathery horror of their faces. The silk scraps marked them as the elite of an empire, all condemned to death. "So the legend is true."

"What legend?"

"The emperor wanted to protect his tomb from violation, but too many knew its secrets. So he ordered every architect, artisan, and master craftsman to be entombed alive, locked between the middle and inner doors for all eternity." Zebastion rubbed his hands on his fatigues. "You might say, he took his secrets with him to the grave."

"How many of them are there?" The sergeant eased the doors open wide.

Lantern light revealed a hallway straight from hell. Mummies crammed the inner corridor, forced to stand in place for thousands of years.

Ling shuddered, her face ghost-pale. "It's horrible!"

"It's absolute power. One of the many reasons god-emperors went out of style. Life was hard in 210 BC." He looked at the others. "We have to clear the corridor to reach the inner doorway."

The task was repulsive. Some mummies crumbled to dust as soon as they were touched while others proved tough as old shoe leather. Working together, they slowly cleared a passageway through the dead.

Beyond the bodies, they found a third set of double doors. A metal plate bearing six horizontal tumblers inscribed with Chinese characters sealed the third barrier. Zebastion had never seen anything like it from the era.

Beside him, the thief jostled for a view of the doorway. "A cryptosystem!"

"You know this?"

Tanner shrugged. "It's a letter combination lock, with the locking mechanism embedded in the door, but I didn't expect to see one here." He shivered. "Kind of gives me the creeps."

"Why?"

"Because it means the Chinese are too damn clever."

Zebastion hid his surprise; perhaps the wiry little man was smarter than he looked. "So can you open it?"

Tanner shrugged. "I can try. Or we can cut the lock out with the acetylene torch, but the easiest way is to solve the cryptogram." He smirked, a hint of challenge in his dark gaze. "I figure that's your work, *Doctor* Kole."

Zebastion ignored the snide remark and stepped to the doorway. Archeologists rarely found ancient locks intact; he didn't want to ruin this one. Despite the lock's age, the tumblers turned with ease, clicking as they settled on each character. "Six tumblers, each with six characters, more proof of the emperor's lucky number."

Ling stepped to his side. "Let me see." She thumbed through the tumblers, reading the characters out loud. "Emperor, heaven, remember, exalted, conquered, tiger, victory."

Zebastion leaned forward. "Try the emperor's name, Qin Shi Huang Di, the first august god of Qin".

Ling shook her head, "Not enough characters, and besides," she gave him a wry smile, "it's a bit too obvious."

"True." Zebastion felt his face redden, "then it must be a phrase, something about the emperor." He turned the last tumbler, puzzled by one of the characters, "labor exerted?"

Ling studied the character. "*Deeds*, that would best translate into deeds."

"And this one here, grass ceremonial mat?"

Ling laughed. "You're being too literal, you have to find the meaning implied by the combination of characters. This one translates to *by means of*."

"And this one here?"

"Hand of a scribe, translates as *history*."

Zebastion nodded, "Of course," but then he had a thought. "Sima Qian had a favorite phrase when he wrote about the first emperor, *history will know him by his deeds*, but Qian lived a hundred years after the death of the emperor."

Ling shrugged. "Worth a try. Let's see if the characters fit the phrase." One by one she turned the tumblers. "*History, remembers, the emperor, by means of, his, deeds.*" The last tumbler clicked into place...and the door sighed open.

"We did it!" He pulled her into his arms, kissing her hard. A spark jumped between them, something long buried and presumed dead. It startled them both. They pulled apart. Zebastion stared at her, like studying a rare Ming vase. A mixture of surprise and embarrassment rode her face, and something else, something he yearned to decipher.

"Bravo!" Tanner clapped, an irritating sound. "And I thought we came here to raid a tomb."

Flustered, Zebastion got back to business. "This doorway should lead to the inner tomb." Imagining the wonders hidden inside, he took a deep breath and tugged on the doors, but the emperor was not so easily defeated.

The doors opened onto a large square room. Three walls gleamed with gold leaf inscribed with text. Script flowed from floor to ceiling in elaborate Chinese characters, a flourish of brushstrokes, an art form all its own. The fourth wall, opposite the bronze doorway, contained a massive door made of solid granite. Two wrist-thick bronze chains ran from the bottom of the stone door up to the ceiling, disappearing into the stone vault overhead. A pair of huge bronze windlasses, looking like giant turnstiles, dominated the center of the otherwise empty chamber.

"What's this?" The thief was first to enter. "Where's the treasure?"

"Too easy." Zebastion shook his head. "Three doors would have been too easy, especially for the first emperor."

Ling gravitated to the walls of script, while the sergeant studied the windlasses. A pair of bronze Fu Lions, the guardians of Chinese graves, sat atop the center of the windlasses with four handles radiating outward. The sergeant gripped one of the handles. "These look like the windlasses on a ship, used to raise an anchor."

Understanding struck. "Or raise a door." Zebastion gestured to the other two SEALs. "Let's see if they still work."

Two men stepped to each windlass. Zebastion and the sergeant took one, Vasquez and Ritter on the other. Gripping handles carved like dragons, they strained to turn the central shafts. The ancient bronze mechanisms groaned in protest. Step by step, they forced the windlass to turn. Chains clanked around the central shaft, winding tight, but nothing else seemed to happen. And then the massive stone door slowly shuddered upward, the chains pulling taut from the ceiling, like raising an inverted drawbridge. "Keep turning." Zebastion bent over the handles, using the strength of his legs to drive it forward.

The sergeant said, "Seems like we're doing a lot of turning for not much lift in the door."

And then he understood. "Energy."

"What?"

"This tomb has lain dormant for more than two thousand years. The price of entrance is energy. For each turn of the windlass, we raise the door but we also arm all the traps and tricks hidden inside."

The sergeant gave him a piercing glare. "Clever devils."

"That's just what the first Westerners thought." Zebastion was sweating by the time they got the stone door raised. Setting chocks on the windlasses, they clustered around the opening, their flashlights sending beams of light into the gloom.

Beyond the drawbridge-door, a stone corridor burrowed into the depths of the pyramid, intricate carvings of the Chinese zodiac adorning both walls. Zebastion flashed his light ahead. Gold gleamed bright like a temptation at the far end of the corridor.

"Treasure! Now that's what I'm talking about!" Tanner leaped forward, a grin on his face.

"Stop!" Zebastion grabbed for the small man, but the thief was too quick, darting into the hallway.

Something clicked inside the walls. The air in the corridor came alive. Arrows hissed from holes in the carvings. One struck the thief in his arm, another in his butt. Howling in pain, he flopped to the floor. The fall probably saved his life.

"Stay where you are!" Zebastion turned to the sergeant. "Can we get a rope and pull him out?"

Tanner squirmed, leaving a smear of blood across the stone. "Help me!" His movement released more arrows. A hail of steel quarrels hissed between the walls, all of them shooting above the thief's head.

"Stay down and you'll be okay." They threw him a rope and pulled him back. Two SEALs knelt over the thief, attending to his wounds, while Zebastion studied the hallway. Straining forward, he reached for one of the spent arrows. "A crossbow quarrel." Made of bronze, the tip was razor sharp. "Pressure plates in the floor release the crossbows and the quarrels shoot from the mouths of the zodiac. If we stay below the zodiac we should be alright."

Ling grabbed his sleeve. "But how could anyone get through this?"

Zebastion considered her question. "Perhaps they sent peasants through first to clear the way. Life was always cheap in China."

"I don't like this."

"It just means we need to be careful."

"And lucky."

He didn't disagree. The sergeant drew him aside. "Our thief wasn't so lucky. His injuries are deep. We'll have to carry him out of here. That cuts our time underground in half. You have less than five hours to get in and get out."

Less than five hours to defeat the traps of the emperor, Zebastion shook his head. "I need more time."

"If the Chinese catch us here, we're as good as dead, and the story of opening the emperor's tomb gets buried with us. We can't afford to wait."

Zebastion's mouth went dry. "Then we best hurry."

The sergeant nodded. "I'm leaving Vasquez and Ritter with the thief. They'll stabilize his wounds and carry him back to the entrance, so it'll just be the three of us going forward." He shrugged a small pack from his shoulders. "I'll go first. I'm the most expendable."

He grabbed the sergeant's arm. "Be careful."

"I will." The sergeant dropped to the floor and then slithered forward, pushing his pack ahead of him. Nothing happened till he reached the spot marked by the thief's blood. As the sergeant crawled forward, the air above became a deathtrap, spitting crossbow bolts.

Zebastion followed with Ling in the rear. It might have been safe to walk in the sergeant's wake, but Zebastion didn't want to take the chance.

The sergeant's voice echoed back to him. "I've reached the end. Is it safe to stand?"

"What do you see?"

"It opens onto a large square room. The walls are plastered and painted like a mural, like sitting in a Chinese pavilion and looking out onto a sunny countryside. I'll try standing, it seems safe enough."

Zebastion kept crawling, pushing his backpack ahead, careful to keep his head below the zodiacs. He stared forward, the beam on his headlamp illuminating the sergeant.

"I'm okay." The sergeant's voice held a touch of awe. "You have to see this chamber. It's stacked with treasure!"

Zebastion reached the far end and stood, shouldering his pack. He helped Ling to her feet and then he joined the sergeant. Treasure crowded the chamber, stacked floor to ceiling. Lacquered chests embossed with gold, exquisite carvings of jade and alabaster, porcelain plates and urns, a golden tea set, cedar furniture adorned with gold leaf, and along one wall, twelve life-sized terra-cotta servants kneeling with their heads to the ground, waiting to serve the emperor. "The stuff of daily living." Except a single piece of this *stuff* would fetch a small fortune at Sotheby's. "At least we know we're in the tomb proper."

"Yeah, but where to now?"

The far wall held six silver doors, each embossed with a different scene. "More choices." Zebastion trained his light across the doors. The craftsmanship was superb, a rare prize for any museum. The first carried the relief of a life-size warrior etched in silver, waiting to be called to battle. The second showed a map of the seven kingdoms united into one empire. The third showed a heavenly dragon holding the Veil of Stars, the crown of the first emperor. The forth showed a classic measuring scale superimposed over rows of Chinese characters. The fifth showed a detailed map of the Yellow River conquered by massive dams and a series of canals. And the last door carried a single Chinese character, the symbol for eternal life.

Ling joined him, her lamplight playing across the doors. "History remembers the emperor by his deeds."

"Exactly, the deeds of the emperor's life." Zebastion paced the length of the wall from left to right. "First he was a warrior-king, modernizing the army. Then he conquered the seven kingdoms, uniting them into one empire. Then he made himself a god, the first god-emperor of Qin. Then he became a reformer, standardizing the weights and measures and the written language of the empire. Then he became a builder, taming the mighty Yellow River and starting the Great Wall. And last but not least, he wandered the land as a mystic, searching for the secret of eternal life."

The sergeant joined them. "So, Monty Hall, which door do we choose?"

Ling said, "The sixth door, the symbol for eternal life, the ultimate prize."

"I don't think so." Zebastion paced in front of the doors, considering.

The sergeant said, "Maybe we should split up, each one trying a different door?"

"No. It's too dangerous, better if we stick together." Zebastion came to a stop in front of the third door. "We take this one. His greatest achievement was to become the first god-emperor of China." Zebastion grinned, feeling the certainty of his choice. "The Veil of Stars will lead us to the emperor's final resting place."

The sergeant shrugged. "It's your party, Doc."

Zebastion opened the third door, half expecting a trick or a trap, but the door swung open revealing steps leading down.

The sergeant crowded behind. "We have to go down? Is this right?"

"It feels right." Zebastion aimed his headlamp into the gloom. "In the tomb of Li Zhongrun, an emperor of the Tang period, archeologists had to descend a series of steep stairs to reach the tomb chamber hidden beneath the apex of the pyramid."

"Whatever you say, Doc, just let me go first." Sergeant O'Malley led the way, light from his lantern swaying with each step. Zebastion went second, followed by Ling.

The stairs were wide but steep, blocks of granite expertly fitted together. But it was the walls that caught Zebastion's attention. "Look at these paintings!" The plaster was perfectly preserved without any sign of water damage. Colors and details remained bright and exquisite. Legions of armies thundered across the left-hand wall, battle banners flying in the wind, while on the other side, rows of court officials held scrolled documents waiting for the emperor's decision. Zebastion drank in the details, hoping the small camcorder mounted on his collar captured the tomb's stunning beauty.

Ahead of him, the sergeant fell hard, clattering to the floor. "Watch the last step, it's a real bitch."

Stone ground against stone.

Zebastion froze, a shiver running down his neck. "Watch out!"

The corridor at the base of the stairs shimmered with silver. Massive metal axes whooshed out of the walls, slicing back and forth in a gauntlet of death. The sergeant swore, scuttling backwards. "We picked the wrong doorway."

Zebastion studied the axes, each one decorated with the head of a dragon or a tiger. "I don't think so."

"What? Are you crazy?"

"These axes are called *Fu,* they're reserved for the bodyguards of emperors. The presence of the Fu proves we're on the right track."

"But how do we get through?"

"Very carefully." Zebastion jumped down from the last step, carefully approaching the first axe. The massive metal blade sliced back and forth like a deadly pendulum. "Looks like there's just enough room between each axe for a person to stand. It's all about timing, a test of nerves."

Ling shook her head. "I don't like this."

He'd never known her to be afraid. "I'll take you through it." He offered his hand. "Trust me?"

She nodded and then she was in his arms, close enough to feel her heartbeat. He struggled to catch his breath. "It's all in the timing." He met her dark gaze, trying to ignore her enticing scent of jasmine. "Ready?" She gave him a small nod. He turned away and studied the swing of the axe, feeling the deadly cleave of air with each pass. "Now." They leaped forward as one, coming to a sudden stop as the second axe sliced past, narrowly missing their faces, and then they leaped again. Like a pair of dancers, they threaded their way past eight axes. "Stop!" Zebastion held her tight. "Look down." Beyond the ninth axe, the floor vanished into a deep pit lined with sharp stakes. "Another trap."

Ling shivered against him. "We have to go back."

"No," he flashed his light ahead, "the floor continues beyond the tenth axe, we just have to jump the pit."

"And avoid two axes."

He flashed her a grin. "Come on, it's the emperor's tomb!"

"Your idea of a romantic date?"

"Better than that stuffy accountant you've been seeing."

"Charles is not stuffy."

"Yeah, but I bet he's boring."

From behind, the sergeant yelled. "Are we going forward or back?"

They both answered at the same time. "Forward!"

She laughed like the daring grad student who'd first caught his heart, and then she took his hand, lacing her fingers with his. "Together."

He nodded, gripping her hand tight. "Wait for my word," and then he turned his attention to the two axes. Forward and back, he timed the rhythm, waiting for the perfect moment. "Now!" They leaped the pit, stretching to reach the far side. Zebastion found solid footing but Ling fell short. Her weight jerked him backwards, but he held his ground, gripping her hand tight. For a moment, he teetered on the edge, and then the tenth axe began to descend. She stared up at him, her feet scrabbling for purchase. "Hurry!" He pulled upward, frantic with strength, and then she was in his arms just as the tenth blade swung past.

"We made it!"

He kissed her hard.

The sergeant yelled. "Is the way clear?"

"Keep coming. Just be careful of the pit after the eighth axe. It's a long jump but you can make it." And then he took Ling's hand and led her into the depths.

The corridor turned left and then right, branching into many side passageways. Three times they ran into dead ends and had to backtrack. Beside him, Ling said, "At least we haven't run in to any more traps."

"Yeah, but the blind passageways are eating time. We can't afford any more mistakes." Zebastion could feel the pressure mounting, wondering if he'd chosen the wrong door. And then they came to an elaborate doorway, the lintel carved with celestial dragons. Hanging from the dragons were strands of giant black pearls strung on fine gold wires, like a curtain of beads obscuring the way forward.

Ling stopped and stared. "Oh my god, they're beautiful." She ran her hands along a single strand, caressing the pearls.

The sergeant whistled. "Look at the size of those pearls! A bloody fortune used as a curtain!"

"It's not a curtain." Zebastion touched the strands, his voice filled with awe. "It's the Veil of Stars, a representation of the emperor's crown. To the Chinese, the emperor was a god, his face hidden by the stars in the heavens, thus the Veil of Stars became the official crown." A grin leaped to his face. "It means we're close."

They stepped through the veil and into another world.

Zebastion gasped. "So the legends are true!" They stood on the threshold of an immense room, a vaulted ceiling soaring thirty meters overhead, the hollow of the pyramid. "We've reached the heart." He drank in the details, his pulse hammering as he played his flashlight across the ceiling. Painted a deep midnight blue, the ceiling sparkled like jeweled stars. Diamonds and pearls encrusted the vault in a panoply of constellations, a priceless replica of the heavens.

"Look here." Ling's flashlight danced across the floor, revealing a miniature empire, complete with mountains, rivers, cities, and temples.

"It's the empire of China, wrought small." Zebastion's voice dropped to a hush. "Sima Qian had the truth of it, a universe for the emperor to rule in the afterlife."

"But mountains of amethyst and rivers of molten silver? How can that be?"

"It's not silver, but mercury. To the ancient Chinese, mercury was a mystical metal. Liquid at room temperature and capable of dissolving gold, they saw it as a supreme substance, the metal of immortality."

They stood on an elevated stone walkway that ran around the perimeter of the central chamber. Four bridges of bronze, one at each cardinal compass point, arched from the walkway over the miniature empire toward a small island of stone in the center. And on the island stood a petite palace made of gold and silver and bronze. Zebastion trained his headlamp on the palace. "The emperor's final resting place."

The sergeant whistled like a man appreciating a beautiful woman. "That's some tomb, enough to make King Tut jealous. But we're running out of time. We best get what we came for." He started toward the bridge, but Zebastion caught his arm. "It's too easy."

The sergeant stopped. "Then how do we get across?"

"Give me a moment." He played a beam of light across the span of the bridge. Lacquered squares decorated with silver dragons and gold tigers covered the walkway in a checkerboard pattern. "The emperor was known as the Tiger of Qin." Removing his backpack, he crouched by the edge of the bridge. Holding the straps, he let the weight of the pack crash onto one of the dragon squares. The black lacquer fractured like a dropped plate. The pack punched a hole clean through the square, dangling over the miniature empire below. Retrieving his pack, he tried the same thing with a tiger square, but the floor remained solid. "Only step on the tiger squares."

"Thanks, Doc."

"No problem." Zebastion led the way, careful to step on the tigers. Reaching the apex of the bridge, he stopped to stare at the miniature empire spread below. "Amazing. All this beauty hidden away for thousands of years, and we're the first to see it." He laughed. "Now I know how Howard Carter felt in the Valley of Kings."

Ling stood beside him. "A childhood fantasy?"

"Every archeologist's dream."

A muffled boom came from the stone doorway.

Zebastion gripped the bronze railing. "What's that?"

Behind him, the sergeant said, "Either someone's set off another booby trap or the boys have run into trouble."

Zebastion broke into a cold sweat. "Then we better hurry." He ran across the bridge, leaping from one tiger to the next. The bridge took him to the doorway of the petite palace. A pair of imperial guards stood on either side, their Fu-axes held rigid at attention, but instead of terra-cotta, these were cast in gold, a marvel of ancient metalwork. And the door they guarded was another wonder. Jade dragons and golden tigers entwined around the emperor's name, but Zebastion saw no lock, no sign of any tricks or traps. He paused for just a heartbeat and then he pushed.

The door swung silently inward and he stepped into the tomb.

Lamplight glittered off a thousand treasures, gold and silver, diamonds and pearls, alabaster and jade. Like an elaborate jewelry box, the petite palace held a single magnificent room, the mausoleum of an emperor, every wall covered in exquisite works of art. Dragons danced along the walls, embedded crystals reflecting light from the vaulted ceiling, but Zebastion ignored the artistry, drawn to the heart of the mausoleum, to body of the first emperor. Clad in a magnificent suit of jade armor, he lay in state on a block of green marble, arranged as if he slept, a golden pillow-box beneath his head. His armor was breathtaking, scales of green jade interlaced with fine gold wire. And covering his face, a death mask of the palest jade, individual eyelashes painstakingly carved, so life-like it looked as if he might wake from two thousand years of slumber.

The others entered the tomb, beams of light flashing across countless wonders.

Ling gasped, turning from one treasure to another. "Unbelievable!"

The sergeant joined him at the heart of the tomb. "So this is the mastermind, the god-emperor of China?"

"Yes."

"You said we needed a provenance, proof we were here."

The sergeant's words brought him back to the present. "Yes."

"What will you take?"

The choice was easy. "Three things." A bronze stand placed at the head of the marble slab held a black lacquered hat. Zebastion was amazed to see that it was still intact. A flat lacquered board designed to sit across the top of the emperor's head; it dangled strands of black pearls in front and in back, screening the divine countenance. "This is the very first Veil of Stars, the symbol of the emperor's divinity. We take the emperor's crown, the Veil of Stars, and the jade death mask."

"And the third?"

"Perhaps the greatest treasure of all." Zebastion moved to the foot of the marble slab, where a single massive piece of jade was carved into a crouching tiger. The workmanship was superb. "If my guess is right, then this is the twin to He Shi Bi, the first imperial seal of China, known as the Heirloom Seal. The wielder of this seal carried the authority of the gods." Using both hands, he carefully lifted the jade tiger. It was heavy, weighing a good thirty pounds or more. His heart hammering, he turned it over, and found a carving etched deep on the reverse side. "This is it!" Ling and the sergeant crowded close as Zebastion read the inscription. "*The one who has received the Mandate of Heaven shall enjoy longevity and prosperity.*" He clutched the great seal to his chest. "This is the provenance we've been looking for, the mandate of the emperor's power on earth."

The sergeant nodded. "Then let's take it and go."

Zebastion agreed. Dumping the contents of his pack, he settled the great seal inside, wishing he had something to better pad the precious jade. Shouldering the pack, he moved to the bronze stand and removed the Veil of Stars, handing it to Ling. Last of all, he hovered over the emperor, gently removing the jade mask. Beneath the mask the magnificence was lost, just a leathery face with eyes sunken to dark pits. For a heartbeat he stared into the true face of Qin Shi Huang Di, the first god-emperor of China. "Mortal after all. How he'd hate to be seen this way."

"We need to go."

Zebastion tucked the jade mask into the sergeant's pack and then they were running, across the bridge and through the veil of pearls. Something snagged at Zebastion's pack, trying to tug him backwards, but he pulled free and never looked back. They ran through twists and turns of stone corridors, heading for the gauntlet of swinging Fu-axes.

Footsteps rushed towards them.

"*Stop!*" Zebastion and Ling both froze at the whispered command. The sergeant dropped to a crouch, an Uzi suddenly in his hands. "Who goes there?"

Voices echoed back. "Corporals Vasquez, Ritter, and Schmidt."

"Come ahead." The sergeant gave them a baleful glance. "Something's wrong."

They met up with the others in an empty corridor, three SEALs reeking of sweat and explosives. The sergeant's voice dropped to a low growl. "Report."

Vasquez answered, a nasty cut streaming blood from his forehead. "Local guards discovered our excavation and raised an alarm. They ordered us to surrender and when we refused, they opened fire. We held our own until a truckload of regular army arrived. They started lobbing grenades into our little bunker. Clark and Stangle bought it, along with the thief, not enough left to fill a single body bag. The rest of us retreated into the tomb. We rigged a booby trap inside the second doorway, enough plastic explosives to bring down the hallway. We heard it go off a while ago, so the chinks are trapped outside and we're inside." The corporal looked from the sergeant to Zebastion, weariness lining his face. "We need to find another way out."

"*Another way out!*" Zebastion exploded in anger. "There *is* no other way out!"

The corporal stared at him in disbelief. "But what about the other gates? I thought you said there were six?"

"Six gates, yes, but only one is a true opening. The others are just blinds, dead ends lined with tricks and traps."

"So you mean we're trapped in the tomb?"

Zebastion could only nod, the taste of acid rising to his mouth.

Ling took his arm. "There has to be another way out." Short and petite, she remained cool as a summer breeze. Zebastion wished he had a different answer. He shook his head in grim denial, but Ling overruled him. "Let's go back to the main chamber and think about it."

They trooped back through the stone corridors, sullen and silent, returning to the inner tomb. Vasquez and the others took a moment to gape at the wonders, but then they quickly turned professional, prowling the walkways, searching for hidden doorways. Zebastion knew the search was futile. He slumped to the floor, his back to the wall, and pulled a chocolate bar from his pack, wondering if it was his last meal. The irony hit him hard. "Chocolate in the emperor's tomb. In another time it would have been a marvel of the age."

Ling sat beside him. "Tell me what the ancients believed. Why such an elaborate tomb?"

With nothing else to do, he obliged. "The tomb is a statement of power." He gestured toward the soaring ceiling. "That's why so many dynastic tombs are found under earthen pyramids, a man-made mountain, a blatant symbol of power on earth."

"But what did they believe?"

He took another bite of chocolate, savoring the taste. "The ancient Chinese believed each person has two souls, shen, the spirit, that flies up to heaven to become divine, and gui, the ghost of the body that remains underground. All this," he gestured to the opulence around them, "was meant for the enjoyment of the emperor's gui."

"And the emperor's shen, his spirit?"

"Ascends to the heavens." He sat up straight, staring at the celestial ceiling. "That's it!" He leaped to his feet. "We need light!"

The others gathered around, pulled by the urgency of his shout. "What is it?"

"We need light. Ignite every flare. If this doesn't work then it won't matter." The SEALs rummaged through their packs, lighting flares and scattering them across the floor. A bright glow filled the tomb, like a final sunset.

Ling stayed close to him. "What are we looking for?"

Zebastion pointed overhead. "Sometimes the ancients left secret shafts in the top of the tomb, shafts to allow the spirit to ascend straight to heaven."

"So we're looking for a shaft directly over the emperor's mausoleum?"

"No, that would make it too easy for tomb raiders. We're looking for something else, something subtle." He studied the constellations overhead while the others trained their flashlights across the soaring ceiling. "The dragon, the rat, the monkey, the rooster...and there, the tiger, it has to be the tiger."

One of the SEALs produced a pair of binoculars and Zebastion studied the ceiling, praying his eyes did not betray him. "There's a faint indentation around the tiger." He handed the binoculars to the sergeant.

"I see it."

Zebastion's heartbeat quickened. "But how do we get up there?"

The sergeant flashed him a broad grin. "We're SEALs."

An answering smile spread across Zebastion's face. "The cavalry to the rescue!" But the SEALs were already hard at work. Vasquez removed a small modern crossbow from his pack and a reel of fine wire. He bent over the crossbow and then raised it to the ceiling. A steel bolt whooshed upward, thunking into the ceiling. A small shower of plaster drifted down like snow but the bolt remained fixed overhead, a thin steel wire trailing back to the corporal. Using the wire as a thread, Vasquez rigged a nylon rope through the bolt. The sergeant secured one end, serving as the belay, as Vasquez shimmied up the rope. He reached the top and hammered a series of climbing rings into the ceiling. More rope was strung through the rings, and then the corporal leaned out toward the tiger, using the hilt of his K-bar to tap the celestial ceiling.

Zebastion held his breath. Ling clutched his arm.

A few taps of the K-bar and the ceiling shattered to dust, revealing a rectangular shaft in the side of the pyramid.

"*Yes!*" Zebastion pumped his fist while Ling cheered.

The corporal trained his headlamp into the shaft. "It slants away from the pyramid and then turns upward. I'm going to investigate." Vasquez hammered more climbing rings inside the shaft and then he disappeared.

"Hey, Doc." The sergeant gave him a piercing stare. "Will it reach the surface?"

"No, but it might come close. Do you have any explosives left?"

The sergeant looked at Ritter.

The big blond-haired SEAL replied, "We've got half left."

"Good." The sergeant nodded. "Sounds like we're going to need it."

The SEALs set to work, cool and professional, while Zebastion paced the walkway, nervous with energy. Vasquez returned to the opening and the others hoisted the makeshift bomb to the ceiling, and then there was nothing to do but wait and worry.

Zebastion found himself drawn to edge of the walkway, staring down at an empire wrought small. The details were amazing, a stunning snapshot of ancient China. Mountains of amethyst, tiny temples crafted of silver and gold, crushed malachite serving as grass, rivers and lakes of molten mercury, and even a host of miniature terra-cotta peasants working the fields. A peerless archeological treasure hidden away for more than two thousand years, he wondered if any of them would live to tell the tale. His gaze moved toward Ling, cool and calm despite the danger. An odd laugh bubbled out of him. Surrounded by splendors, by his life's dream, yet he'd trade it all for a way out and another chance with Ling. He crossed the walkway; close enough to catch a hint of jasmine. "Ling, if we…"

"*Stand clear!*" Vasquez reappeared, zipping down the rope like a greased fireman's pole. "Fire in the hole."

Zebastion hugged Ling close, shielding her with his back.

A small roar came from the shaft, followed by a shower of dirt and stone.

When the dust cleared, Vasquez climbed back up the rope, disappearing into the shaft. More earth rained down, filling the tomb with the smell of a fresh-dug grave.

Everyone stared at the open shaft. The waiting proved hard. Another shower of dirt startled them all. Scrapping sounds echoed from the opening, like rats trying to dig their way out. A desperate sound, the scrapping grated against nerves already frayed. Zebastion balled his fists, frustrated by the wait. Time seemed to slow. The flares began to sputter and die. Darkness threatened to reclaim the tomb, but then Vasquez reappeared, a broad grin on his dirt-smeared face. "We're through! And the sun has set. Now's our chance."

The SEALs sprang to action. First Ritter and then Schmidt shimmied up the rope like monkeys. Ling went next. Graceful and lithe, her athleticism served her well. Zebastion sighed in relief when she reached the top.

"Your turn, Doc."

He grinned at the sergeant. "No. The first one in should be last out, my way of paying respect to the emperor."

"If you say so." The sergeant gripped the rope, climbing hand over fist. He reached the top and then Zebastion was alone in the tomb, standing amidst the dying flares.

"Time to leave, Doc." The sergeant's words drifted down from the ceiling like a ghostly summons.

Zebastion knelt, tying his pack with the great seal to the end of the rope, and then he began to climb. It was harder than it looked. Twice he slipped, the nylon rope burning the palms of his hands. Sweat soaked his fatigues by the time he reached the top. The sergeant gave him a hand, pulling him into the well of the shaft. Zebastion pressed his back against the cool granite wall, glad to take the strain from his arms.

"No time to rest, Doc, we need to get out of here before the chinks investigate the blast."

Zebastion struggled to catch his breath. "Help me pull this up." Working together, they hoisted the pack up toward the shaft. "Almost." Zebastion reached down, but the knots unraveled, and the pack began to fall. He lunged, but it slipped from his fingertips. *"No!"*

He watched it fall, a sick feeling in the pit of his stomach.

It hit hard, like a clap of thunder.

Zebastion grabbed the rope, staring down into the darkening tomb.

"What are you doing?"

"We need the seal!"

The sergeant gripped his arm. "We don't have time!"

"You don't understand. It's the proof we need." And then he was sliding back down the rope. His hands burned but he refused to let go. He landed hard enough to jar his knees, but nothing mattered except the seal. Zebastion raced to the pack, his fingers fumbling with the straps and then it open. *"NO!"* The seal was ruined, broken by the fall, sundered into seven pieces.

A groan echoed through the tomb as if the very stones were in pain.

And then the floor began to pitch and buck, like an angry dragon trying to wake. A second tremor knocked Zebastion to the ground. He landed hard, like the slap of a giant hand. Stunned, he grabbed the pack, wondering if the broken seal carried a curse, incurring the wrath of the dead emperor. The tomb shuddered and shook. Chunks of plaster fell from the ceiling, threatening to entomb the living with the dead.

The sergeant shouted from above. *"It's an earthquake! Get out of there!"*

Zebastion closed the pack and slung it on his back. He grabbed the rope and began to climb. His arms ached and his hands burned but he fought his way upward despite the added weight.

"Hurry!"

Desperation lent him strength. He reached the top and the sergeant pulled him into the shaft. Swinging the heavy pack around to his chest, he put his back against one wall and his feet against the other. Step by step he spider-walked up the shaft. Dark soil rained down, pelting him in the face, like a persistent gravedigger determined to fill the tomb. Struggling to keep the dirt from his eyes, Zebastion rushed to keep pace with the sergeant, desperate to reach the top before the opening caved in. The granite shaft ended in a jagged hole of raw earth. A rope waited for them, hanging down one side. Hand over hand, muscles aching, Zebastion clawed his way up out of the earth till he emerged beneath a starry sky. Clutching the grass, he stared at the stars, amazed to be alive.

Chaos ruled the night. Sirens blared and somewhere to the east a fire raged. The earth continued to buck and heave with waves of aftershocks. Zebastion figured it had to be an eight on the Richter scale. The others crouched around the opening, night-vision goggles on their heads, Uzis in their hands, looking like modern-day gargoyles. They gave him a moment to catch his breath and then they started to run. Cloaked by chaos, a handful of tomb raiders ran for their lives in the dark heart of China.

#

Fleeing China proved harder than getting in. For three long months they leapfrogged south, from bolt-hole, to safe-house, to hideout, always lurking in the shadows, always heading for the coast. To Zebastion it seemed they traveled at a snail's pace, stealing rides on slow-moving freight trains or hiding in truckloads of onions, desperate to stay one step ahead of capture. But while their own progress was slow, the video recordings from inside the emperor's tomb took another route. Edited and spliced and given voice-overs in a dozen languages, portions of the tapes were seeded into the world-wide-web. In chat rooms and blogs, on mainstream sites and underground webs, the news traveled at the speed of thought. And as it always did, in China's past and present, superstition played a part.

China was ripe for change, in ways the West never understood. Hiding in the shadows, Zebastion experienced first-hand the devastating effects of the rice shortage and the swine epidemic. Food riots were common, people scrambling to feed their families. Exorbitant oil prices and the burden of a pre-emptive war against America only made the situation worse. The common people were reeling, barely able to make ends meet.

And then the rumors started, adding fuel to the fire. The tomb of the first emperor was violated and China was cursed, doomed to dissolve into seven parts. Superstition lit a firestorm to the people's discontent. Rumors ran rampant, claiming the ancestors were angry. Footage from the video appeared everywhere, replayed countless times. The dead emperor's face stared from televisions and computer screen, but all the mystery and majesty was gone. Stripped of the Veil of Stars and despoiled by death, his sunken eyes stared from a leathery mask, the past come to haunt the present. Video clips showed a mortal's face, dead and decayed, yet the very land seeemed linked to the emperor's tomb. Devastating earthquakes rocked the country, proving the potency of the emperor's curse.

As the tomb raiders made their way south, scurrying from one hiding place to the next, Zebastion watched it all unfold, amazed by the power of superstition. Images of the dead emperor's face became a haunting symbol of the central government's decay. Starving and desperate, the people rose up, sparking demonstrations and riots across the land. The police and the army proved no match for the angry multitudes. In just a few short months, the dragon of many parts crumbled from within.

#

Zebastion fumbled with the knot, too nervous to get the bowtie right. The tuxedo felt like a straightjacket and the hotel suite felt stiflingly hot, but it was the small box in his pocket that really put him on-edge. "Do we have to go?"

"And turn down an invitation to the White House?" Ling emerged from the other room, stunning in a strapless gown of red silk. As always, she took his breath away. "You are a vision."

"My handsome archeologist, I like you in a tux."

"It's a straightjacket, I'm more of a chinos kind of guy."

She crossed the room and reached for his tie, smiling up at him. "You should wear a tux more often."

"Only when we save the Western world."

Her smile sobered. "We did, didn't we?" She finished his tie, her hands resting on the lapels of his jacket. "What will happen to the three treasures we took?"

"The Veil of Stars and the jade death mask will go on exhibit at the Smithsonian."

"And the great seal?"

"The seal's the most important of the three. It'll be kept in a secure place where it can never be re-assembled."

"But why?"

"In the West, the scepter and crown are the highest symbols of royal power, but for the Chinese, the emperor's chop, his seal, is the symbol of supreme authority. A gift from the gods, the imperial seal is the mandate of heaven."

"So when the seal broke, the Chinese lost heaven's mandate?"

"Something like that." He couldn't wait any longer. Reaching into his pocket, he removed the small black box. "This is for you."

She gave him a questioning look and then slowly opened the box. A ring nestled inside, two diamonds flanking a flawless black pearl. Ling gasped, "From the emperor's tomb?"

He nodded. "Somehow a single strand of pearls from the final doorway snagged on my backpack. I put it in my pocket and forgot about it till later."

"A whole strand?" Her eyes flew wide. "It must be worth a small fortune!"

"But it's not mine." Puzzlement filled her eyes but not disappointment. "I gave two pearls to each of the families of the slain SEALs and one to each of the SEALs who survived. But I saved the best for you." He reached inside the box and removed the ring. "It seemed fitting since it was the emperor who brought us back together." His voice dropped to a dry husk. "Will you marry me?"

She answered him with a deep kiss.

A sharp knock on the door brought them back to reality. They looked at each other and laughed. "It's probably the secret service."

Zebastion smiled. "I hate it when they interrupt."

Ling left his arms, rushing to repair her make-up, but her gaze met his in the mirror. "You know, Zebastion, we really were lucky."

"Lucky?"

"The earthquake happening just when the seal broke. It seems like a miracle."

"It wouldn't be the first time America was saved by a miracle." He offered her his arm.

"So it was luck?"

"And history. Never underestimate the power of the past. Despite all of China's advancements they were still living in the emperor's shadow."

"A potent shadow." She took his arm, her face thoughtful. "And whose shadow is America living in?"

Zebastion smiled. "That's another story." Arm in arm, they went to receive the gratitude of the nation.

A Man's World

Coal dust under his fingernails, just like his father, proof he worked hard for a living. Danny grinned, his first day underground and already he felt like a miner. Lamplight from his helmet glowed against the exposed seam, four feet of prime black coal, shiny and bright, destined for the Illawarra steel mills. He tucked his thumbs into his utility belt, his re-breather bulging at his left hip, a constant reminder of the risks. A thousand feet of rock hung overhead but it didn't bother him a bit. Mining was a man's calling, high risk and high pay, the only job he'd ever wanted.

Cold and damp, he slogged through the puddles. Rough rock walls lined the corridor, tall enough for a man to walk, wide enough for a coal crawler. Bundled cables formed an electrical spine along the ceiling, the occasional light bulb reflected in puddles. Everything else was pitch dark and black as coal. He turned his head, directing a beam of light into a side passage, but they all looked the same. Attila mine was a confusing labyrinth of tunneled roadways and collapsed goafs. Without Bart as a guide, he'd be well and truly lost. Danny kept close to the thirty-year veteran, trying to mimic the older man's swagger.

A low growl shook the tunnel, the sound of metal chewing rock. He turned a corner and a roar of noise avalanched against him, a throbbing vibration punching clear to the bone. Danny hunched forward, as if walking into a storm. They'd reached the longwall, the heart of the mine. Men with coal-blackened faces worked among mighty machines, everything on a massive scale. A ninety-ton shearer chewed coal from the ore-face, spitting black lumps onto a conveyor belt. Hydraulic jacks held the ceiling in place, massive metal pillars bearing the burden of Atlas. The scale thrilled him. A thousand feet underground, men triumphed over nature, wresting a wealth of coal from the depths, truly a man's job.

Bart leaned toward him, tapping his watch. "Shift's nearly ended. We'll watch the change-out and then head for the surface."

Danny nodded, staying close to Bart.

The longwall never slowed, a voracious metal beast gnawing on coal and rock. Lost in the roar of the mighty machines, Danny almost missed the anxious glances darting between the miners. Beside him, Bart shifted from one foot to another, staring at his watch, a scowl on his face. Danny leaned close, shouting over the noise. "What's wrong?"

"The blokes are late." He hawked and spat. "Somethin's not right." Throwing hand signals to the other miners, Bart growled, "Come on," and set off at a blistering pace.

Danny kept close to the older man, a shadow at his back, hurrying to keep up. Anxiety gnawed at him; no one ever hurried underground. The roar of the longwall receded, replaced by a brooding silence. They reached the crib, grabbed their lunch pails and then headed for the lift, the only way up.

A blare of lights surrounded the lift, like a star chained in the dark, but the corridor stood empty, not a single man in sight. Bart shook his head, "Somethin's not right."

They entered the lift, a rectangular metal box, big enough to hold a coal crawler. Bart closed the safety grate and then pushed a green button on the controls. A klaxon sounded and the massive doors whooshed shut like an airlock. The lift shuddered, the only proof of movement. Danny sidled close to the veteran miner, the emptiness of the massive lift closing around him like a threat.

Bart shook his head, his voice a low growl. "The lift should be crowded for shift change. Somethin's not right."

Danny wished he'd quit saying that; it made a thousand feet feel like a million. He stared at the metal doors, yearning for a breath of fresh air.

The lift shuddered to a stop. A klaxon sounded and the doors whooshed open. Bart fumbled with the grate and then they both stopped and stared. At first, Danny thought it was some kind of joke, a gag to test the nerves of the newbie, but then he heard the strain in Bart's voice. *"Bloody hell!"* Bart bolted from the lift. *"Tom, Ed, Harold, what's wrong?"*

Three men lay sprawled across the concrete floor, still as death, their hardhats tumbled aside. A styrofoam cup sat upright near the lift, half full of coffee. A splash of brown surrounded the cup like an impact crater, as if it'd been dropped in mid-sip.

"*Help them!*" Bart's voice cut through the shock. Danny leaped to the first man, the one who'd dropped the coffee. He rolled him over, a big man with gray hair, mutton-chop sideburns, and a gut from too much beer. His face was slack and his skin clammy, no pulse at his neck. Danny had never seen a corpse, let alone touched one. "I think he's dead." He backed away, wiping his hands on his coveralls as if death was something you could catch.

"Get help!" Bart crouched over a red-haired man, furiously pumping on his chest, giving him CPR, as if he could raise the dead. "Go!"

Danny ran from the ready-room, screaming for help. Down the corridor and around a corner, he almost tripped on a fourth body. Another miner dropped dead, sprawled across the floor, something was seriously wrong. He sidestepped the corpse and ran for the mine manager's office. More bodies slumped at their desks, even Margaret the secretary, and Brett, the mine manger. He yelled but no one answered. Fear seized his stomach. He staggered outside, spewing his lunch across the grass. Drenched in sweat, a sour taste in his mouth, he leaned against the brick building, soaking up the sun-baked warmth. The world looked normal, the afternoon sun still hung in a pale blue sky, the brick buildings all looked the same, rows of cars parked in the lot, but there was no sound, no movement, as if he was the last man on earth.

Panic struck like lightning. Danny bolted for the nearest door, sprinting through the corridors, desperate to know that Bart still lived. He burst into the ready-room, gasping for breath, relieved to see the older man working the phone.

Bart slammed the receiver down, worry lining his face. "There's a dial tone but no one answers. Ambulance, fire department, they're all just answering machines." His voice dropped a notch. "And my wife's not home."

"They're all dead!" The words burst out of him.

"What?"

"I ran to the manager's office, everyone's dead! It must be mine gas or something."

"A gas leak," Bart snorted, "if it came from the mine we'd be the first ones killed." His tone changed from cynical to serious. "The men underground, we have to get them out."

"I don't know the way."

Irritation flashed across the older man's face. "You stay here. If something happens, we'll need a man on the surface." He strode to the shelves, grabbing three extra re-breathers and a survival kit. The grate clanged open and Bart stepped into the lift. The klaxon sounded and the massive doors began to close. Danny shifted so he could stare through the narrowing gap, watching Bart's face, clinging to his humanity. The doors closed, the lift shuddered, and he was alone.

Alone with the dead.

His stare crawled to the nearest corpse, the gray haired man with the beer belly. The dead man's coveralls had long ago turned gray, khaki impregnated with coal dust, the sign of a veteran miner, but there were no bloodstains, no bullet holes, no sign of a struggle. As if he'd just dropped dead, felled by an invisible force. Danny shuddered and turned away. So much safer to stare at the styrofoam cup, half full of coffee, surrounded by a brown splash pattern, like a Rorschach inkblot staining the cement floor. He wondered how many times he'd have to drop a cup to get the same pattern. A thousand? A million? Or maybe some patterns never repeated, like coming up from a thousand feet under ground to find a mine full of dead men. Maybe Bart wasn't coming back and he'd be left alone, locked in some kind of Twilight Zone.

The klaxon blared.

Danny jumped, kicking over the coffee cup, changing the pattern on the floor. He turned toward the lift, half afraid to look. Metal doors whooshed open and coal-blackened miners spilled out. Twenty-two grim-faced men, veterans of the underground, strode from the lift like a squad of heroes. Danny sighed in relief.

Bart nodded toward him. "This way, kid."

Danny fell in behind the veterans. They made another search of the mine but nothing changed. Men sat slumped at their workstations, phone calls answered only by machines, no sign of any life. Even the cat was dead; an orange tabby sprawled by her food bowl.

Rocco, the shift foreman, a big man of Italian descent with a gold cross gleaming from his black chest hairs, made the decision. "There's nothing we can do here. Best if we head into town."

By grim agreement, they strode to the parking lot, not bothering to change into their street clothes. Danny stuck close to Bart. "Can I ride with you?"

Annoyance flashed across the older man's face. "Don't you have a ride?"

Danny could only stare, knowing his eyes brimmed with pleading, like a hound dog desperate for a reassuring touch.

Bart's face softened. "Sure kid, this way."

Danny followed Bart to a red pick-up truck, dented with spots of rust, a Ford with too many kilometers on it. Candy wrappers and newspapers littered the passenger seat, but Danny didn't mind. "Try the radio, kid." Bart started the engine and backed out of the parking spot. Danny twirled the dial, searching for a news station.

Nothing but static.

Bart shrugged. "Reception's bad out here." It was a lie but Danny didn't disagree.

The red truck was first out of the lot, turning down the side road and heading for the main highway. The countryside looked the same, stands of eucalyptus trees baked by the summer sun. The road curved east, merging onto the highway, heat rising from the asphalt.

Bart slammed on the breaks. Tires squealed and the truck slid to a stop.

Cars littered the highway, some crashed together, some run off the road, others just stopped, their drivers slumped at the wheel.

"God!"

Bart shook his head, "Somethin's not right."

Danny's hands started to shake. "I wish you'd quit saying that."

"It'll be better in the city." Bart got the truck moving, swinging around the wrecks, gunning the engine on the rare stretches of open road. It was a white-knuckle ride. The closer they got to the city; the more wrecks blocked their way. Both men pretended not to notice.

Twenty minutes and they reached the lip of the escarpment. Danny gripped the dash, half afraid to look. The highway took them over a low hill and started down the steep switchbacks. Sheer sandstone cliffs gave them an eagle-eye view of Wollongong, the city by the sea. A pillar of dark soot billowed into the sky. The steel mills were burning. Fires dotted the city but nothing else moved.

"Oh God!"

"Marie!" Bart's voice sounded strangled. He mashed on the accelerator and the old truck rocketed down the switchbacks. Rounding a curve, a flutter of white feathers hit the windscreen. Danny flinched, but Bart never slowed the truck, his knuckles white on the steering wheel. Cockatoos littered the road, as if a whole flock had fallen dead from the nearest gum tree. Danny stared, fear knotting his stomach. "Something's not right."

Dodging dead cars and cockatoos, they reached the bottom of the escarpment. Bart drove straight through the traffic lights, heedless of their color. Nothing else moved, no sirens, no alarms, no cars, no pedestrians.

Bart turned off the main street, onto the side roads, driving like a madman. Careening around a corner, he turned onto Keira Street and stopped dead in front of a redbrick bungalow. Leaving the keys in the ignition, he burst from the truck and ran for the front door. Danny waited, rocking back and forth in the passenger's seat. The house was pretty, pink roses trained to a trellis over the front walk; Bart's wife must be a gardener. The front door banged open and Bart went inside. Danny studied the stand of eucalypts across the road, hoping to spy a cockatoo or a kookaburra. Nothing stirred, not even a breath of wind. The kookaburras usually sang at sunset, a chorus of raucous laughter, somehow he doubted there'd be any laughter tonight.

"Noooo!" A man's voice shattered the silence, a raging howl against fate.

Danny shut his eyes and stayed in the truck. His parents were long dead, his mother when he was five, his dad a few years ago to emphysema. He didn't have anyone else to lose, anyone new to mourn. A bitter laugh bubbled out of him, finally an advantage to being orphaned.

The sun set on the escarpment, a brilliant blaze of orange and red, too glorious for such an evil day. Shadows crept across the city, twilight slipping into night. Streetlights began to glow but the houses remained dark, no one home to turn on the lights. The front door banged opened and Bart appeared, haloed by a porch light. His shoulders were stooped and the swagger was gone from his walk. An old man climbed into the truck. "All dead. My wife, my mother-in-law, even the damn dog." He shook his head, his voice hollow. "How could this happen?"

Danny could have cried, but instead he took a deep breath, realizing it was his turn to be strong. "Maybe it'll be better in Sydney."

Bart nodded, "Maybe," but his voice held little hope.

"We'll go to my place."

Panic flared in Bart's brown eyes.

"I live alone."

"Okay, no more dead tonight." Bart's hands shook but he got the truck in gear and followed Danny's directions. It wasn't far, four blocks over on York Street, a cheap one-bedroom apartment on the second level. Danny climbed the steps and unlocked the door, flicking on the lights. Cool air blew out, proving the air-conditioner still worked. "Make yourself at home." Familiar smells of stale beer, day-old pizza, and plastic leather filled the apartment.

Bart slumped into an overstuffed black pleather chair. "Try the TV."

Danny grabbed the remote, thumbing through the channels. Mostly static but then the screen cleared showing a set of faces and an all too familiar tune. *"A poor mountaineer barely kept his family fed."* Danny barked a laugh. "The world ends and we're stuck watching re-runs of the yanks' sit-coms," but he left the TV on, preferring hillbilly banter to the gaping silence.

He went to the fridge and grabbed a six-pack of cold four-X beer. Twisting the cap, he downed one in a single long swill. He took another for himself and handed one to Bart. The old man didn't move; he just sagged into the armchair like a permanent fixture at an old folk's home.

The phone rang.

Danny jumped, his heart racing. Lunging for the phone, he spilled half his beer. Swearing, he pressed the receiver to his ear. "Hello?"

His heart thundered as a man's voice answered. Hope sank with every word. A final "yeah" and he gently set the receiver in the cradle. "That was Rocco." He couldn't take Bart's dead-man stare, so he looked at the TV instead, focusing on Jed Clampitt's smile. "He's calling all the miners. It's the same all over the city. The other men are coming here, looking for a place away from the dead." There was nothing else to say. Danny sank into the worn leather couch, making steady progress on his six-pack, listening to Granny get the better of Jed.

A soft knock on the door.

They arrived in ones and twos. Underground miners, still in their coal-stained coveralls, shattered expressions on their faces. They brought cases of beer and bags of groceries, too much for his little fridge. Jake had stopped by a sporting goods store, handing out sleeping bags, enough for everyone. No one had any appetite, but they did major damage to the beer.

Jed Clampitt's hour ran out and the TV turned to static. Danny turned it off; no one else seemed to mind.

There wasn't any talk, just a bunch of lonely men huddled together, swilling beer, trying to forget. When they had enough, they crawled into their sleeping bags, layered like sardines across the floor.

Danny stayed on one end of the couch, preferring cramped quarters to the loneliness of his bedroom.

A few men snored like foghorns in the dark, but Danny didn't mind. Unable to sleep, he watched the glowing hands of the kitchen clock. Midnight was supposed to be the witching hour; maybe the nightmare would end when the clock struck twelve.

He startled awake.

Somewhere in the dark, a man cried, bawling like a baby, a flood of grief.

Other men stirred, a rustle of nylon sleeping bags across the floor, but no one turned on a light. Darkness was a haven. Unseen and unnamed, a man could cry in the dark, weeping for a world that was lost.

Day Two

His head felt like a jackhammer and his mouth tasted like sawdust. Danny opened one eye, squinting against the sunlight, hoping the world had changed.

Sleeping bags crowded the floor. Men stretched and scratched, bleary-eyed, fresh beards shadowing their faces.

It was all true. Groaning, Danny closed his eyes, sinking back into the couch, groping for the oblivion of sleep.

The smell of fresh-ground coffee teased him back to life. He stretched, trying to ease the knot in his back. Rocco and Jake worked behind the kitchen counter serving up plates brimming with scrambled eggs, toast, and rashers of bacon. The smell proved hard to resist. Danny staggered to the counter and claimed a plate.

A few of the men had showered and shaved, but most looked unkempt, bed-head hair matching their hollow stares. Danny perched on the edge of the couch; shoveling down breakfast, coal dust still lining his fingernails. The other men crowded into the living room, everyone balancing a plate and a steaming mug of coffee. Harry flicked on the TV but it was nothing but static.

Simon barked a laugh, "You'd think we'd at least get that annoying broadcast, you know, the one that says this is nothing but a test."

A few men forced a laugh but it fell flat.

Bart shook his head, his face etched with loss. "Some test."

Silence descended like an iron fist.

Danny choked, the food suddenly tasting like ashes.

James, a pot-bellied miner with gray hair broke first. "How in hell could this happen?"

Stares ricocheted around the room, avoiding the question, but James persisted, a hint of panic in his voice. "What is this, the bloody end of the world?"

His question broke the logjam. Opinions flooded out. "It had to be the steel mill, we all saw that pillar of smoke. One of the furnaces must have blown, releasing a toxic gas."

Simon sneered, "A toxic gas that spread all the way to the mine? I don't think so."

"It was those damn tea-towel heads in the Middle East, setting off one their secret bombs. They blew themselves up in mushroom cloud and the rest of the world fried."

"It couldn't happen that fast." Bart shook his head, his voice thoughtful. "And besides, they died without a mark on them. No radiation burns, no nothing."

The men turned silent, their eyes plagued with memories.

Rocco stood, his fist clutching the gold cross at his neck like it was the key to heaven. "It was the hand of God. Armageddon is upon us."

Bart raised his stare. "No way. My Marie was a devout Catholic, a firm believer, mass on every Sunday. No way God would take her and spare a sinner like me."

James chimed in. "Besides, God would never be so cruel."

"Oh yeah, remember Sodom and Gomorrah? Or how about Noah's flood?"

Tempers flared. Jake intervened. "This isn't getting us anywhere. We need to figure out what to do." Twenty-two pairs of eyes turned in his direction. "First thing we need to know is how far this thing's spread. Is it just here or all along the coast?"

"It can't be just here, otherwise help would've come already."

"Yeah, that fire at the steel mill is sending up a hell of a distress signal. If they don't come for that, then they aren't coming."

Jake nodded. "Okay, then the disaster is spread along the coast."

Bart shook his head. "More than that. There's no TV and no radio, that means Sydney and Melbourne are both gone."

Danny swallowed hard, staring at a stain in the carpet; he'd never even been to Melbourne.

"Aren't there stations in Perth? Maybe it's all of Australia."

Bart's voice sank to a hoarse whisper, "Maybe it's the whole world."

Dread crawled through the room. Like hearing words read from your own tombstone, too grim to believe.

Danny looked away, fixing his gaze on the kitchen clock, watching the second hand tick off time. Could time keep ticking if the world stopped? "It can't be the end." He pointed to the clock. "Things still work."

A few men turned his way, a glimmer of hope on their faces. "Yeah, that's right kid. We still have electricity, and the phones."

A whisper of relief rippled around the room. Men nodded and grinned, pulling away from the edge of a fatal cliff. But then James dropped another bomb. "Why did we survive?" His gaze circled the room. "Why are we the only ones left alive?"

Most of the men looked away, a few made the sign of the cross, but Jake had an answer. "Because we were underground. A thousand feet of rock protected us from sure death."

James began to shake. "Then only miners survived?"

"Only *underground* miners."

Danny stared at his hands, coal dust beneath his fingernails, the only reason he still lived. "But if we're still alive then there must be others."

A spark of hope leaped around the room. The men began to talk of friends in other mines, about mounting search parties and bringing them all together. Maybe they'd find pockets of other survivors. Maybe they'd even find some women.

And then the power went out.

Day Seven

Danny grabbed the feet and Bart took the shoulders. Together, they manhandled the corpse onto the wheelbarrow. "*Phew!* This one really stinks." He wiped the sweat from this forehead, pulling the bandana back up to cover his nose. It didn't help. "We should've kept our re-breathers. Never knew the dead could stink so bad."

Bart nodded, a green tinge to his face.

"One more and we'll head back outside." Danny took the handles, pushing the wheelbarrow down the corridor. They found another corpse in the next classroom, a woman this time. She might have been pretty, before the bloat.

They stuck to their routine, feet and shoulders, lift and swing, heaving the corpse onto the barrow. Three was their limit. Danny strained against the weight, struggling to keep the grizzly load from tipping. Bart went ahead, holding the doors. They used the wheelchair ramp to get down the steps, through a set of double doors, and then out into the summer sunshine. Danny tugged his bandana down, gulping fresh air, never mind the heat.

They kept to the sidewalks, maneuvering through the campus, heading for the rubbish tip. It was Rocco's idea to take over the university. A quick scavenge of the city turned up thirty-three petrol generators, more than enough to power the core buildings. Jake set up work rosters and the men paired up, drawing straws for duty. Danny stuck with Bart, his work partner and his roommate. Today they had corpse cleanup; tomorrow lookout duty, and then they'd work the library. Nobody really thought the library held any answers, but nobody complained about looking. It was the lightest duty on the roster. Some of the men were already talking about the treasure trove of old magazines. Danny was looking forward to it.

A pillar of black smoke marked the rubbish tip, almost there. Once they got the corpses burnt, the campus would be a lot more livable.

A siren blared.

Danny dropped the wheelbarrow, his heart pounding.

Simon and James burst from a nearby building, sprinting across the grass. "What's up?"

Danny shrugged, "Must be the lookout siren." Hope warred with fear. "Maybe help's finally come." They ran for the Science Building, the tallest on campus, following the blare of the siren. The others came running, some of them looking like they were going to have a heart attack, but nobody let up.

Jake waited on the steps of the Science Building, a grin bursting from his ruddy face. "We're being rescued!"

For half a heartbeat they couldn't believe it, but then the cheering started.

Bart had the good sense to ask for more. "What do you mean?"

Jake danced a jig on the steps, pointing toward the escarpment. "A convoy of cars is threading its way down the highway. We need to make noise so they know where to find us." He pumped his fists like a victorious prizefighter. "We're being rescued!"

Danny leaped into the air, shouting and yelling, dancing around like a madman. The street became a festival of noise. Horns blared and men pounded on the hoods of cars. Others shouted at the top of their lungs. James and Harold linked arms, bellowing an off-key version of "Advance Australia Fair". Simon found an Australian flag, waving it high and low, racing up and down the street. Someone yelled, "They're coming!" Danny joined the others, racing to the far end of the street, whooping and yelling, kids once more.

Rocco gave Danny a boost and he shimmied up a lamppost. The added height let him spy over the row of shrubs. A blue Volvo barreled down the road, the first in a line of twelve cars. *"They're coming!"* He slid down the pole and joined the other men, laughing and shouting. Beside him, Bart murmured, "Where's the army? There should be army trucks," but no one listened. The survivors stood together, twenty-three miners, laughing and cheering, watching the cars come closer.

The Volvo pulled to a stop, the other cars braking in a line behind it.

Sunlight glinted on the windshield, making it hard to see.

The doors flew open and two men got out. Two big men, rough and unshaven, coal-stains on their denim coveralls. "Creswell Mine" was stenciled on the flap of their left pockets, the company logo stitched right over their hearts.

The cheering fell silent.

Hope sank like a rock in Danny's stomach.

The bigger of the two men stepped forward. "Name's Nate Tasker, from Creswell mine." A flicker of anger passed across his face. "We gathered up the survivors from the other mines, hoping to find life in the city." His gaze turned bleak. "Are you all that's left?"

Jake nodded.

Nate scowled. "More god-damn miners." He spat. "And not a sheila among you."

Day Fourteen

"Calling the world, is anybody out there? Over." Danny flicked a switch and waited, staring at the knobs and dials.

Nothing but static.

Bart sat beside him, doodling stick figures on the logbook. "Are you really supposed to say "over"? It sounds stupid."

Danny shrugged. "How should I know? They do it all the time in the old movies, so why not." He turned the dial, trying another frequency. *"Calling the world, is anybody out there? Over."* It was Jake's idea to try ham radios and Danny thought it was a good one. He'd had a friend in high school who'd claimed to talk to people on the far side of the world, bragging about a girlfriend in Paris. Jake figured that's what they needed most right now, to find other people. So they scoured the city, scavenging the biggest radio set and setting it up in the Science Building. They took turns manning the radio twenty-four seven.

More static.

Danny turned the frequency dial up another notch. "Didn't Rocco say he'd picked up some Chinese chatter the other day?"

Bart shrugged. "Yeah, but who can speak Chinese?"

"Still, it means someone's out there, that others survived."

"Lots of coal mines in China. Doesn't mean there's any Chinese women left." Bart hawked and spat. A wad of brown goop landed in the wastebasket.

Danny shook his head. The old man had taken up chewing tobacco, a disgusting habit, but Danny couldn't talk him out of it. After a week of badgering, he'd given up trying. *"Calling the world, is anybody out there? Over."*

More static. He worked his way to the end of the dial, trying all the frequencies, and then he started over. *"Calling the world, is anybody out there? Over."* It was a lot like playing the lottery, the odds were long, but you never knew when you'd get lucky.

Another turn of the dial, *"entify yourself."*

"Was that English?" Danny lunged for the volume control. More static. Maybe he needed to answer. He flipped the switch and gripped the microphone. *"We're here! Who are you?"*

Bart gave him a scathing look.

"This is NORAD Command, identify yourself!"

They both leaped out of their chairs, jumping and shouting like they'd won a million dollars. "It's them! It's the yanks!"

Bart gripped Danny's arm. "Answer them! Say something!"

"Oh, yeah." He flipped the switch, grinning like his face would split. *"We're in Wollongong Australia, at the university, over!"*

"Ho ny ar yo?"

"They're breaking up! Get them back!"Danny nudged the dial, his hand sweaty on the microphone. *"Say again! You're breaking up."*

"This is NORAD Command. We're taking a census. How many are you?"

Danny swallowed, a sinking feeling in his stomach. *"There's forty-eight of us here."* His mouth felt suddenly dry but he forced the question out. *"Have you found anyone else in Australia?"*

It seemed to take forever to get a reply. *"You're the first onshore."* Danny's mouth dropped open, his shock echoed on Bart's face. *"But we've been in touch with the Royal Australian Navy."* The navy! *"Five of your submarines have survived. They're monitoring frequency 148.80 megahertz looking for survivors."*

"The navy's coming!" He nudged Bart into action. "Write the number down!"

Bart grabbed a pencil, scrawling spidery numbers across the logbook. "Ask them if it's the same there." His voice shook as bad as his hand.

Danny nodded, flicking the switch. *"Did it happen to you too? Is it the same over there?"* He sat on the edge of his chair, rocking back and forth, praying it wasn't true.

The speakers crackled. *"It happened worldwide."*

No! He gripped the microphone, refusing to believe. *"But how? Who did this? Was it a bomb? Or a plague? Or what?"*

Another long pause. Sweat drenched the back of Danny's shirt, like waiting to hear a murder verdict. *"We're still collecting data, but all evidence points toward a burst of radiation from a star called Cassandra. The star went hypernova, emitting lethal pulses of a new type of radiation. Earth took a direct hit. We're still analyzing the data from the Chandra, Swift, and Hubble telescopes but our scientists are calling the event Cassandra's Curse, a worldwide catastrophe."*

Danny closed his eyes. It sounded so simple. A single star gone nuts and the whole earth died.

More static from the speakers. *"We're taking a census of survivors. Do you have any women among you?"*

And that was it. The only question that still mattered.

Day Sixteen

Danny's head ached from yesterday's hangover so he stuck to soda, avoiding the beer. Most of the men sat in folding lawn chairs, but

Danny chose to lie in the grass, oblivious to the green stains on his chinos. *Fresh cut grass,* Danny breathed deep, one of the smells of civilization. The campus was going back to nature, growing wild, but they kept the central commons cut, using it for their meetings.

Rocco and James worked the barbie, flipping fish and stirring hash browns. Aside from canned food, fish and potatoes had become their main meals. Turns out there were still fish in the ocean and potatoes took forever to rot. He supposed they'd have to start a garden, a bunch of miners turned farmers, another twist in a brave new world.

Jake took center stage, a sheaf of papers in his hands. The murmur of conversation died without prompting. "Thanks for coming. We've got some important decisions to make. But first a report from the library; seems the science papers held some answers after all."

Simon stood; his reading glasses perched on the end of his nose, looking like a professor in his rumpled street clothes. "Before we talked to the yanks, we didn't know what to look for. When we searched under "extinction" we found it."

Extinction! Danny shivered despite the heat.

Simon raised a glossy magazine with a Hubble space photo on the cover. "It's happened before, a mass extinction during the Ordovician period caused by a gamma ray burst from an exploding star over five hundred million years ago."

"Five hundred million years!" James snorted, spraying a mouthful of beer. "What the bloody hell! We won the damn celestial lottery!"

Simon shrugged, looking over the top of his glasses. "That's what it says. So maybe the yanks are right. I've got the magazine if anyone wants to read it."

A chorus of jeers served as an answer. Simon retreated to a lawn chair and Jake took over.

"You've all heard the news from NORAD. The whole world's in the same mess. The yanks are taking a census. Seems there's small pockets of survivors dotted all around the world. So far they've made contact with groups in China, Russia, the UK, Germany, South Africa, the emerald mines of Brazil, anywhere with underground mining. So the situation's not as bleak as it first seemed." He glanced around the circle of men but there was no response. "The good new is the navy's on its way. The HMAS Robert Menzies is steaming for the port of Sydney and should arrive in another eight days. So we have to decide if we stay here, or meet the navy in Sydney."

Nate sneered, "What's the use? No sheilas on subs. The navy's no better off than we are."

"Yeah, miners, submariners, and a bunch of missile jockeys, what the hell was God thinking?"

"Don't take the Lord's name in vain." Rocco had started carrying a rosary, going all religious on them.

"Well why the hell not?" James was turning red, like a boiler about to blow. "God's in charge of the universe. It was his star that blew up. He's the one that put us in this mess."

"Not really."

Calm words cut through the tension. They all turned to Martin, one of miners who'd come with Nate's convoy, a quiet bookish man with a long narrow face and close-cropped gray hair. "The star exploded but we decided who survived."

Danny sat up straight. "What do you mean?"

"We never let women work in the mines." Martin shrugged. "We had one start at Creswell once, a young woman of Indian descent. She wanted to be an underground miner, wanted the great pay and a good career, but we made sure she didn't stay." A few of the other men nodded. "And it's not just the mining industry. The navy doesn't allow women on subs. And I bet there aren't many women working at NORAD." He shrugged, a sad smile on his face. "So you see. God shattered the star, but we shaped the world that survived. I guess we got what we always wanted, or maybe what we deserved. Now it truly is a man's world."

A man's world. Danny shuddered. The phrase had never sounded so cold, or so lonely.

The others looked away, struggling with their own memories, but Nate began to laugh, a hard cruel sound, full of scorn. "I told ya, it's all about the sheilas." He reached for a beer, flipping the lid from the bottle. "And the yanks didn't call to help. They're looking for sheilas too, same as the navy." He hefted the bottle in salute. "You mark my words, whoever finds the sheilas, wins."

"Maybe it's not about winning anymore." Danny didn't know where the words came from, but they felt right.

Nate smiled like a crocodile. "So the kid speaks." He took a swill of beer, his eyes as black as coal. "You're right, kid," he showed a flash of teeth in a deadly grin, "it's all about getting laid." Laughing, he turned and sauntered away. Seven men followed.

The other fell silent, watching them go.

Harold muttered, "What if he's right? What if there are no women left?"

A sense of doom fell across them. Men reached for beers, slouched in their lawn chairs.

Jake rallied. "We have decisions to make." He waved his papers, trying to enliven the others. "We need to send a delegation to Sydney to meet the submarine. I'm calling for volunteers."

A burnt smell billowed from the barbie. "Somebody flip the damn fish, our supper's burning!"

Danny stared at the grill, *fish on the barbie*. An idea bubbled in the back of his mind. "There must be some women left." Everyone turned to stare at him. "I mean, there are fish in the ocean." He seized the thought, desperate to reel it in. "The men on submarines survived, the fish survived...so why couldn't a diver survive?"

"You mean a scuba diver?"

Danny nodded. "Yeah, lots of women dive, don't they?"

"Not lots, but some."

Danny grinned. "Some would do."

"Yeah, but the timing would have to be right. They'd have to be diving when it happened."

"And they'd have to be deep enough to matter."

"And the boat would have to be anchored, or they'd be lost at sea."

"A lot of ifs, but it might work." Bart gave him a slow smile, a glint of pride in his eyes. "And Australia just happens to have the diving capital of the world, the Great Barrier Reef. If any divers survived, that's where we'll find them."

Danny grinned. "I'm going to Cairns. Who's with me?"

Day Twenty-one

Danny kept his foot on the pedal, racing the Land Cruiser into the north. He'd wanted a sports car, a jag or a convertible, but Bart insisted on a "practical" vehicle. Turned out the old man was right. More than once they'd had to go off road to avoid a snarl of wrecked cars. And the added petrol tank meant they didn't have to stop and siphon so often. The Land Cruiser proved a good choice, a dependable car for a world turned hard.

He flicked a glance in the rearview mirror. A big black Hummer rode his tail, and behind it another Land Cruiser. Nate and six of his cronies, Danny wished they hadn't come. "They're crowding me again."

Bart nodded, maps and guidebooks spread across his lap. "Of course they are. They're racing you to the prize."

"It's not a prize."

"You're right," Bart's voice held a tinge of sadness, "but to men like Nate, women are nothing more than a prize waiting to be claimed."

They lapsed into silence, kilometers ticking by. The number of wrecks began to increase, a sure sign of an approaching city. Danny slowed the cruiser, weaving around the dead. "Why didn't any of the others come?"

"What, the men from Attila?"

"Yeah, Rocco and Jake and the others." Danny swerved off the road, avoiding a tangle of five cars and a jack-knifed semi. The cruiser rumbled back onto the asphalt and he hit the accelerator. "So why didn't they come?"

Bart sighed. "The truth is, men are creatures of habit. All of us grew up in the Illawarra. We got married, got a mortgage, raised our kids, and watched our hair turn gray." He shrugged. "You're the only young buck among us." He reached for a soda and popped the lid. "If there are any women left, they'll be looking for young men willing to change, willing to build a different world."

Danny gripped the steering wheel; grateful the older man had stuck with him. "Do you think we'll find women in Cairns?"

"We can always hope." The smile faded from his face. "But when we get there, you'd best watch your back."

"Why?"

Bart flicked a glance in the rearview mirror. "Nate's not the kind of man to welcome competition." He sighed. "The world's gone hard. I saw the same thing in the army when Vietnam fell. There's no law left but the rule of might."

Day Twenty-four

Night was the worst. Nothing but darkness, not a speck of light in all the land, a vast primordial blackness, proof that civilization had died. Danny rubbed his eyes; afraid he'd fall asleep at the wheel. "Enough for today." He pulled the Land Cruiser off the side of the highway and killed the engine. By unspoken agreement, they avoided hotels. It was far better to camp in an open field than deal with the horror of rotting corpses.

He slid from the driver's seat, assaulted by the hot muggy air of a tropical night. The other cars pulled up behind, a sudden blare of headlights. Danny squinted, temporarily blinded.

A car door opened and Nate stood in the lights, throwing a massive shadow. "We're almost to Cairns. Take a deep breath boys, I can smell the sheilas waiting for me!"

Bart and Danny moved away from the others, setting up a domed tent more for privacy than protection. The inflatable mattress looked inviting; the best the camping store had to offer. Danny pulled off his boots, and sprawled on his back, exhausted from the long day's drive.

He bolted awake, startled by the sound of men fighting.

Danny nudged Bart awake and then peered from the tent flap. A camp lantern provided the only light. A scrum of men fought, a tangled knot of flying fists and savage kicks. One man fell, rolling on the ground in agony. Another cursed and limped away. Nate's voice bellowed above the rest, "You'll bloody well do as I say." A shotgun boomed. A man spun and fell.

Danny gaped, a spurt of fear rushing through him.

Another man moaned in pain. Another shotgun blast and the moaning fell silent.

Murder!

Bart gripped Danny's arm, his voice a harsh whisper. "We have to get out of here!" Danny started through the tent, but Bart pulled him back. "No, this way." Pulling a knife from his belt, Bart slashed the back of the tent. They crawled through, scuttling towards the scrub. Danny reached the bush when he heard a muffled fall behind him. Bart lay on the ground, clutching his ankle.

Flashlight beams played across the bush, coming near, too near. Nate's voice boomed in the dark. "Where the hell are they? Check the tent."

Danny scrabbled through the dirt, searching for a rock. Finding one, he hurled it to the far side of the field.

"What's that? Look over there." Flashlight beams gave chase, following the sound.

Danny ran back to Bart. Desperation lent him strength. Hoisting the older man to his feet, they hobbled toward the brush.

Shotguns boomed in the night.

Danny flinched, expecting a shot in the back. Drenched in sweat, he got Bart to the scrub. They crawled in deep, ignoring the thorns. Hugging the ground, they listened for footfalls. Bart handed Danny his knife, his voice a whisper. "You take this. My ankle's cactus, I'll be no good in a fight."

Danny gripped the knife, *a knife against a shotgun*; he tried not to think of the odds.

More shotgun blasts ripped the dark, the sound of heavy slugs hitting metal.

Nate bellowed, "Cairns is mine. If I see your ugly faces again, you're dead."

Car doors opened and slammed shut. Headlights flared sending twin beams into the dark. An engine rumbled to life, the low growl of the Hummer. A single car pulled away, roaring down the highway.

Danny waited, hugging the ground, listening for an ambush. The night was still as death, not a sound in the bush. The world teetered on the brink of extinction yet murder still ruled the dark. Maybe man didn't deserve to survive. Anger pulsed through him; something had to change. There had to be a better way.

Day Twenty-five

Dawn revealed the grim details, four men dead and two cars shot to hell. Danny studied the carnage, still shocked by the violence. "Murderers. I've led murderers into the north."

Bart leaned on a shovel, using it as a make-shift crutch. "Nate and his blokes are hard men. They take what they want and damn the consequences. But I thought he'd wait till we hit Cairns."

"We have to stop them."

"We're outnumbered." Bart gave him a long measuring look. "And it takes guns to fight guns."

Danny straightened his shoulders. "Then I guess we have some scavenging to do."

Day Twenty-six

They waited till the first light of dawn before heading into the heart of Cairns. Danny drove and Bart rode shotgun. The red convertible issued a low throaty growl, the first car they'd found with a full petrol tank. It wasn't practical but it would do.

The Esplanade was deserted. Palm trees lined the long straight street, tourist shops on the right, the sea on the left. A salty breeze blew in from the north, providing relief from the charnel-house stink. Corpses lay bloated on the sidewalks, the height of tourist season. If anyone survived, the stink alone would drive them from the city.

Danny drove straight to the pier and parked in the open, easy for anyone to see. Bart chose his hiding place while Danny searched the parking lot. Near the back, he found just what he wanted, a big white Ford truck with chrome roo bars on the front. The keys were missing, so he hotwired the car. Strange the things you learned when the world came to an end. The engine revved to life and he moved the truck into position, leaving it idling in park. Satisfied, he returned to the convertible. He took a last look around the peaceful harbor before issuing his challenge. "Come get me, Nate!" He leaned on the horn, a loud blare splitting the morning. A few rounds of duct tape kept the horn blaring.

Danny ran to the truck and slumped into the driver's seat, his hand on the gearshift, his foot hovering on the accelerator. Playing dead, he peered over the steering wheel, hoping Nate would take the bait.

The waiting seemed to take forever, a trickle of sweat running down his back, but then a black Hummer cruised into the parking lot. Crouched like a mechanical monster, it blocked the only exit, the tinted windows hiding the men inside. The doors opened. Nate and two others got out. All three carried shotguns, looking like they knew how to use them. They circled the convertible, one of them reaching for the duct tape.

Danny mashed his foot on the accelerator, keeping his head low. The truck leaped forward, charging like a bull.

Shotguns boomed. The windscreen exploded in a shower of glass. More slugs hit the back of the cab, shattering the rear window.

Danny never let up, gunning for Nate, driving into a storm of bullets. The engine choked and sputtered but momentum prevailed. Something soft struck the front of the truck. Heavy chrome bars rammed the convertible with a sickening crunch. Flames erupted from the engine. Danny bailed from the truck.

A shotgun swung toward his face. *He'd missed Nate!* Danny leaped for the gun, twisting the barrel away. *Boom!* The shotgun fired, deafening Danny. Nate yanked on the gun, but Danny clutched the barrel with a death-grip, desperate to keep it pointed away. They grappled for the gun. Slamming to the pavement, they rolled back and forth, kicking and gouging. Nate had all the advantages; stronger and heavier he rolled on top. He pressed the barrel across Danny's throat, cold steel crushing down on his windpipe. "Time to die, kid."

Danny gasped, his vision darkening. He tried to knee Nate in the groin, but the big man only pressed down harder.

Nate sneered, "You're not man enough for this world."

A shotgun boomed.

Nate's head exploded like a ripe watermelon.

Spattered with gore, Danny pushed the corpse away, gasping for air. Bart stood over him, a shotgun held in his right hand, his left hand extended in friendship. "The killing's done." The two men hugged like father and son.

Day Thirty

All the shotguns were gone, flung into the ocean, consigned to a watery grave. Danny hoped he'd never have to kill again. Barefoot, wearing a tourist shirt and khaki shorts, he sat on the edge of the pier, watching the sun rise on another beautiful morning. For four days, he and Bart had scoured the docks looking for clues. All the big diving boats were gone, lost to sea or moored elsewhere. Danny took their absence as a sign that some groups had survived. He couldn't blame them for deserting Cairns. The tropical heat and the hordes of dead tourists made for a fearsome combination.

Footsteps from behind, "I brought breakfast." Bart handed him a can of peaches and a spoon.

Danny had to laugh. His friend had gone tourist, a straw hat, chino pants, and a shirt brighter than the plumage of a macaw. "I think I need sunglasses."

"The sun's barely up."

They sat on the end of the pier, eating peaches from tin cans, slurping the sugary juice. Danny surveyed the harbor. "There has to be a clue here, something we've missed."

"We've checked all the larger boats." Bart waved a spoon toward the harbor. "There's got to be two hundred docked here. They're all starting to look the same."

"Yeah, but we're missing something." He swallowed the last peach, savoring the taste. "You said the world would be different if women ran it."

Bart nodded. "Bound to be different."

Danny sat straighter, reaching for the binoculars. "Then maybe the message is different."

"So we're looking for a message in a bottle?"

"More like something hidden in plain sight. Something a man like Nate would never see." He scanned the harbor, always returning to a small sailboat stranded in the mangroves. "Something about that sailboat." Danny tightened the focus of the binoculars. Bold blue letters named it the *Sea Goddess*. A small white boat with furled sails, it looked abandoned yet something fluttered from the mast. "It's flying a small Australian flag, but the flag is upside down. It's a distress signal!" He leaped to his feet. "I've got a hunch about this one. Come on."

They found a small flatbed fishing boat and got the outboard engine puttering. Maneuvering out into the channel, they crossed to the stand of mangroves. Danny grabbed the side of the sailboat and leaped aboard, lashing the two boats together. "Hello the boat!" But there was no answer. The deck was deserted, not even a corpse onboard. Bart walked to the prow. "That's odd, the anchor's down. Why would they moor in a mangrove swamp?"

Danny shrugged, "Let's try the cabin." A set of steps led to a small cramped cabin. Sunlight poured through the porthole-windows, illuminating a nautical chart tacked to the wall. Danny gasped, his heart pounding. "I found it!"

Bart clattered down the stairs. "What?"

A message was scrawled across the chart; red letters in a bold hand. "Is that lipstick?"

Bart gently touched the edge of one letter, his finger leaving a red smudge. A grin burst across his face. "It is!"

His heart thundering, Danny read the message again. "If you want to help, start here." A simple street address was scrawled below. "Find a pen!" Danny found it first. Red ink, he laughed, writing the address on his left forearm like a tattoo, a message he never wanted to lose. They took a last look around the cabin, leaving everything the way they found it. Climbing back onto the flatbed boat, they castoff, laughing like a couple of beered-up fishermen.

It took a couple of hours before they were ready to leave town. Danny insisted on finding another convertible, something fun and sporty to celebrate a new world. He finally spied a Miata, the color of bubble gum blue. They stocked the trunk with presents, canned peaches, Cadbury chocolates, a tinned ham, a Christmas pudding, and a couple of bottles of fine red wine. Bart found the address on the map and they zoomed out of town.

An hour's drive north of Cairns, they pulled off onto a dirt road, red dust raising a cloud behind them. Banana trees lined the road, lush leaves forming a canopy overhead. The road ended at a classic Queensland cottage, a red corrugated tin-roof, a wrap-around porch, wooden shutters, all raised on stilts. Painted a bright tangerine, the house looked well cared-for, a welcoming haven in the midst of the rainforest.

They parked the convertible and got out. Danny spied the carport and nudged Bart. Scuba tanks sat in a neat row next to a yellow Land Cruiser. A lycra diving suit hung from the rafters, swaying in the breeze. The suit was bright pink, petite, and shaped for an hourglass figure. Danny couldn't stop grinning.

"Go ring the doorbell."

Danny took a deep breath and sprinted up the steps. He pressed the doorbell and then sheepishly realized the electricity was off. He knocked, but there was no reply.

"Try the back. She must be home."

Walking around the porch seemed like a rude intrusion, so he went back down the steps and followed the dirt path. Red banana trees lined the side. He opened the gate and entered the back garden. So many flowers, an explosion of color, like stepping into a tropical Eden. He found her working at the back, facing away from him, raking a fresh patch of garden. Petite yet athletic, she wore a man's long-sleeved work-shirt over khaki shorts, a braid of pale blond hair hanging below her waist. She was a vision. Danny watched her work, struggling for the right thing to say. He finally settled on the message from the boat. "We came to help."

She raised her head, but she didn't startle, as if she'd known all along that he was there.

Danny held his breath, eager to see her face.

She turned slowly. He struggled not to gape. Tanned to crinkled leather, her face was a map of wrinkles. She was sixty if she was a day, too many years spent under a tropical sun. But her eyes were bright and keen, a hint of humor in her voice. "Not what you expected?"

Flummoxed, he didn't know what to say.

"You must be a miner. You certainly don't look like a navy submariner."

Danny swallowed; she seemed to know everything. "My name's Danny Jenks, a coal miner, come all the way from the Illawarra."

She flicked a glance toward the front of the garden. "Just the two of you then?"

He turned to find Bart hovering near the garden gate. "Just the two of us, ma'am."

She gave them a slow appraising look, as if weighing their very souls. Danny sweated under the scrutiny, hoping he wasn't found wanting.

"You answered the distress call of the *Sea Goddess*, choosing to help rather than take." She flashed a radiant smile, like a burst of sunshine after a thunderstorm. "You'll both do."

Her smile was like a balm to his soul. He breathed a sigh of relief. "So there's others then?"

"Three boat-loads of divers from Cairns and two from Port Douglas, more women than men, enough for a fresh start." Her eyes darkened and her face turned stern. "But part of the price is that you can never tell another soul. The other survivors, the miners, the submariners, and the missile men, they must all make their own journeys and pass their own tests to earn a place in the new Eden."

The two men gave their solemn promises.

"Now come, I'll make you some tea and scones and then we'll get out a map and I'll show you where the others have gone."

They started to walk toward the house, but Danny stopped in mid-stride, the question bursting out of him. "Who are you, ma'am? And how do you know so much?"

She laughed and the sound held all the wisdom of the ages. "My name doesn't matter. But I'll tell you a secret." She leaned close, her voice dropping to a whisper. "God is a woman, and She finally put Her foot down. You best not disappoint Her again."

They left clutching a map, looking for an Eden in the north. Earth was no longer a man's world.

Pieces of the Truth

Electricity thrummed through the chamber, raising the hairs on the back of his neck. Linus smiled, knowing his reaction was more than just static electricity, part fear, part eager anticipation. Ozone swirled around him, the sickly sweet smell reminiscent of mad scientists. Dressed in vintage clothing, everything as close to authentic as possible, even down to the smallest coin in his pocket, he waited for the signal. In front of him, the quark-door shimmered silver turning to gold. As a physicist, he understood the equations of time travel but the experience remained a mystery. Linus took a last breath of the twenty-fifth century and leaped into history.

Such a long leap.

Light flashed from every direction, a confusing jumble of images. He tumbled in the currents of time, dizzy with centuries, and then he was through, staggering into the fresh, crisp air.

Cobblestones beneath his feet, horse dung on the street, he struggled to find his balance. Heart hammering, Linus looked up and gasped.

Color! He never expected so much color. Green leaves budding on trees, red geraniums bursting from window boxes, and golden sunlight shimmering on stone buildings four stories tall. He stared in wonder. All those years of studying sepia photographs, he'd come to expect a black and white world. He laughed out loud. History held only pieces of the truth.

And then it hit him; he'd done it, he'd gone back through time! But was this the right when and where? Sounds of the city tugged him forward. Hoisting his book bag over his shoulder, he made his way toward the mouth of the alley, anxious to learn the truth.

The alley opened onto a bustling square. So many people, women in long skirts and fancy hats, men in dark suits with starched white collars, a vision from another era sprung to life. A boy hawked newspapers, a dog barked at the trolley, everything in motion, defying the photographs of old. Bicycles zoomed through the square. Ridden by men in suits, they swerved to avoid horse drawn carriages and a central trolley, but Linus saw no motorcars, not yet. And overhead, electrical cables crisscrossed the sky, yet the air carried the dingy stench of burning coal. So many paradoxes, he'd journeyed to a time of change, of startling innovation, the cusp of the 20th century.

A passing stranger doffed his hat. "Guten Tag!"

The quaint gesture made Linus smile, more proof he was really here, a voyeur from another time. Eager to confirm the date, he crossed the square and tried his German, handing the lad a timeworn penny for a newspaper. The headlines made no difference, but the banner leaped out at him, *Anzeiger der Stadt Bern, Mai 24, 1905*. Just as they'd planned, he'd arrived in Bern Switzerland at the start of the miracle year. He clutched the newspaper aloft in victory, but his victory dance drew stares, and stares were the last thing he wanted; he'd come to observe not to influence.

He gave himself a day to get acquainted with the city and the era. Strolling the promenade, he practiced his Deutsch with passing strangers. His wanderings eventually took him to the arcades, markets crowed with tempting smells, all competing for his attention. The food was otherworldly, whole spit-roasted chickens and sizzling bratwursts, so different from the organic nutrients of his era. Succumbing to the temptation, he bought a sizzling bratwurst drenched in onions and wrapped in a thick slice of rye bread. Closing his eyes, he dared to take a bite. Flavors flooded his mouth, rich with spices, so this was what meat tasted like! He licked his lips, more proof the past was full of surprises. Linus ate as he walked, hot grease running down his fingers. He grinned in delight, knowing his friends would be appalled. Licking grease from his fingers, he staggered left, narrowly avoiding a pile of horse dung, enthralled by the pleasures and pitfalls of a by-gone age.

His footsteps took him to the edge of the river, a beautiful blue-green ribbon meandering around the walls of the old town. Bern was a cozy medieval city tucked in the curve of the Aar River, the Swiss Alps forming a stunning backdrop to the church spires and the red-tiled roofs. Vibrant and alive, the city was nothing like the dusty pages of history. But he hadn't come for history; he'd crossed time for science, for a deeper understanding of the genius behind the famous equations, for a chance to learn what might have been lost.

Sunset drew him to the corner of Speicherstrasse, anxiously watching the entrance to the Patent Office.

And then Linus saw him. The Great Man exited the building with another man. There was no mistaking his face. Even at the relatively young age of twenty-six, Einstein's dark hair grew wild, foreshadowing a famous future. Deep in conversation, he walked with a sprightly step, a book tucked under his left arm, his right hand waving as if to pluck an equation from the very air.

Lost in their own conversation, they passed him unawares. Linus followed, gathering the courage to hail them. *"Herr Einstein!"*

The Great Man turned, a quizzical look on his face. *"Ja,* do I know you?"

Linus offered his hand, forcing an introduction. "Linus Singer, a graduate student of Heidelberg University, I was hoping to find you."

Einstein's bushy eyebrows rose in surprise. "Looking for me?"

"Yes, I've studied your paper on capillarity."

"Capillarity? But no one is interested in capillarity these days, electricity and x-rays and magnetism, these are the topics that burn with excitement."

"But your work on capillarity is also important. Truths to the universe can sometimes be found in the smallest paradox." Linus held his breath, hoping to snare the Great Man with a paraphrase of his own words echoed from a distant future.

Einstein cocked his head, a gleam in his dark eyes. "I like you, Herr Singer, you give evidence of a mind worthy of further investigation. Come and walk with us, and let us discuss the paradoxes of the universe."

Introductions were made and Linus fell into step with the two men. Keen to gain the acceptance of the Great Man, Linus asked, "So how did you come to study capillarity?"

Einstein chuckled like a man amused by the world. "A simple observation! Why does water rise in a straw all by itself when gravity should pull it down? What force in nature allows this to happen? For it must be one force acting against another. And by understanding these forces, we better understand the whole." Einstein grinned like a boy stealing an apple. "In such paradoxes God reveals his best kept secrets."

They walked through the cobbled streets, bouncing ideas back and forth in a wide-ranging discussion. Linus hung on every word, careful not to betray the future. All too soon, they turned onto Kramgasse

Strasse. In Linus's time, the four-story row house was preserved as a museum, a shrine to relativity.

Einstein paused before the door. "And so we have reached my humble flat, but there is no need for our discussion to end, for tonight is a meeting of the Olympia Academy." He gestured to Michelle at his side. "A small group of us meet to discuss physics and philosophy and music. The dinner is plain but not the company. You are welcome to join us."

It was the invitation he longed for. "The honor is mine!"

"Then come and meet my little family."

They trooped up the narrow staircase to the second floor flat. A battered door opened onto a small apartment, chintz curtains on the windows, a throw rug on the floor, an upright piano along one wall. Faded pink wallpaper added a dash of color to the room, but it was the clutter that dominated. Books tumbled from overstocked shelves, papers lay strewn across the table, a violin propped on a chair, abundant proof of an intellectual life.

"Liebchen, I'm home!"

A young child squealed in happiness, crawling across the floor. Einstein hoisted the diapered baby into the air. "This is my son, Hans Albert."

A dark-haired woman limped into the room. Prim and proper, she wore an ankle-length dress of blue muslin, rows of tiny white buttons running all the way from her narrow waist to the stiff collar beneath her chin. Her hair was pulled back in a severe bun but her dark eyes glittered with mystery. Linus bowed, so this must be Einstein's first wife, the mother of his three children, the woman history nearly forgot.

"My wife, Mileva." Einstein made the introductions and the men found seats at the small round table. A pipe appeared in Einstein's hand and he fished in his pocket for a match, adding a plume of blue smoke to the small room. Mileva circled the table, setting plates and silverware while gathering up papers.

Linus strained to catch a glimpse of the papers, rows of equations written in a neat hand, a tantalizing hint of genius, just the type of papers he'd hope to find. When Einstein immigrated to America, he brought few papers from his early days, leaving modern scientists to wonder what might be lost.

A knock on the door and two men entered. Linus recognized them from old photographs, more members of the Olympia Academy. Maurice Solovine hefted a bratwurst wrapped in newspaper and Paul

Habicht carried a sack of freshly ground coffee. "We've brought sustenance for the mind!" More introductions were made and the two men settled around the table.

Linus watched the dynamics of the dinner meeting, so different from the culture of his own time. While the men talked, Mileva served the meal, a tureen of potato soup with sliced bratwurst, and cups of thick Turkish coffee, and then she retreated to a chair in the corner.

Curls of smoke drifted to the ceiling and coffee was replenished countless times. The men waged a spirited discussion, meandering from philosophy and human nature to a reading of *Don Quixote*. Linus did his best to contribute without betraying the future.

Outside, night crept across the city but electric streetlamps held the darkness at bay. Inside, Mileva lit a pair of oil lamps bringing a warm yellow glow to the room. Linus stifled a smile, wondering if Einstein's theory of relativity would be written by the light of an oil lamp, another paradox of the era.

"There are so many marvels of our age, so many things to study." Einstein leaned back in his chair, blowing smoke rings toward the ceiling. "A wire telegraph is kind of a very, very long cat. You pull his tail in New York and his head is meowing in Los Angeles. Do you understand this? And a radio operates exactly the same way. You send signals here; they receive them there. The only difference is that there is no cat."

In the corner, Mileva stirred, a suggestive smile on her face. "Yes, but darling can you say the same thing with an equation and leave out the cat?"

"Mine Liebchen has the truth of it." Einstein slapped the table, rattling the china cups. "But first we must start with physical inspiration." He gestured to the open windows, to the violin on the chair, and the books on the shelf. "Observe the marvels around us and then describe it in the form of an equation, for mathematics is the true language of God." He pointed a finger at Linus, as if to emphasize his words. "Find the solution in the purity of mathematics and then you will understand the workings of nature. When the equation is elegant then you know it is right, for elegance is the true hallmark of God's handiwork."

Linus wanted to ask more, but Einstein grabbed his violin, launching into a lively Bavarian folk-melody. After a rush of music, the discussion careened away from physics, plunging back into philosophy. Night deepened outside the windows and still they talked. Einstein showed amazing stamina, jumping from one topic to another. The party lasted till the wee hours of the morning. When the old clock tower chimed three, Linus found himself walking back to his hostel, staggering under the breadth of the discussion but no closer to any answers.

#

Linus became a nocturnal creature, sleeping by day and attending the Olympia Academy by night. His mind thrummed with intellectual discussion but there was never enough physics. So many nights he sat next to Einstein, tempted to steer the conversation toward string theory, or the inconsistency of black holes, but Linus always bit back his questions, afraid of changing the future. And always he stared at the papers littering the small apartment, wondering what secrets they held. So tempting just to slip a few pages in his pocket but he never did.

The nights passed in an intellectual blur. Linus marked the days on a calendar, surprised to find he'd frittered away most his allotted time. Only two days remained yet he'd gained none of the answers he sought. Linus decided to change tactics. It was a bold move but the Einsteins were bohemians, so perhaps he'd not give offense.

Rising earlier than usual, Linus made the rounds of the arcades, purchasing a basket of goodies with the last of his francs. Weisswurst and loaves of fresh-baked bread, bars of Swiss chocolate, and a small sack of fresh ground coffee, the fuel of inspiration. By noon he was ready. Armed with a basket of bribes, he dared to knock on the door of the small apartment.

The door cracked open and Mileva peered out. "Yes?"

Linus proffered the basket. "I return to Heidelberg in two days and I wish to repay your hospitality."

"Oh!" A smile lit her face and the door swung wide. "So kind of you, come in!"

Linus had never been inside the apartment without Einstein. Without the Great Man's incandescent presence, a host of details annoyed him. For the first time he noticed dust on the bookshelves, and dirty dishes stacked on the sideboard, and a stinky diaper abandoned on the floor. Mileva was not much of a housekeeper. But it also meant that Einstein's papers were scattered about the room like a temptation.

"Please take a seat." Mileva accepted the basket. "I'll make coffee."

A book lay open on the table. While she fussed with the kettle, Linus snuck a peak at the title. *The Economical Nature of Physical Inquiry* by Ernst Mach, the father of the Mach number. "Doing a bit of light reading?" He spoke in jest but she took him seriously.

Mileva set a steaming cup of coffee in front of him and joined him at the table. "Yes." Her hands captured the book, pulling it toward her in a protective way.

Linus struggled to make conversation. "And do you find Mach interesting?"

"Mach is rigorous in verifying all of his theories, especially his work on the speed of sound." She caressed the spine of a book, an enigmatic smile on her face, like a bohemian Mona Lisa. "I find it interesting that he too rejects the concept of absolute space and time. Absolutes are so rare in this world. As if everything in nature is a matter of perspective. It makes one think."

It was the most he'd ever heard her say, and the closest he'd come to discussing Einstein's famed theory of relativity. His surprise must have shown on his face, for she laughed, a light sound, full of mischief. She gave him a sloe-eyed glance. "You know I almost got my doctorate in theoretical physics."

It was something he didn't know, for this intriguing woman was nearly lost to history. "Why didn't you?"

Melancholy washed across her face. "Children take time. And some things aren't proper." She stared down into her half-empty cup, a faint blush rising on her cheeks.

He was losing her to embarrassment, but he did not want the conversation to end. Desperate for something to say, he blurted one of his burning questions. "How does Albert find time for physics?"

She gave him a startled look and he wondered if he'd made a mistake, but then she answered with a laugh. "Ach, mein Albert can find inspiration in anything, so he is always working, scribbling on every scrap of paper." She shrugged. "There is always time for physics, for physics is everywhere."

"But working in the Patent Office all day and holding court in the Olympia Academy all night, when does he find time?"

Leaning toward him, she gave him a mischievous smile, as if she were about to share a great secret. "Everything is tangential, everything is related. Physics is a connected argument. One idea leads to another. Like the apple falling from the tree and the water rising in the straw, an observation so simple can spark a great idea." Her fingers caressed the edge of the book. "My Albert is always saying that imagination is more important than knowledge," she gave him a hooded stare, "but do you know what I think?"

He stared at her, surprised to realize how much he wanted to know *her* thoughts.

"I think it takes both. Imagination provides the leap in logic, but it takes knowledge to explain the stepping-stones. Without knowledge others will never make the leap."

So simple yet so profound.

The baby cried from the other room. "I must see to my son."

She disappeared into the back room and he shook himself awake, like a man coming out of a trance. Now was his chance. He pulled a sheaf of papers from beneath the book. Equations and diagrams spilled across each page, all written in a neat hand. His mind drank up the notes, feasting on the details of electromagnetism, and the photoelectric effect, and the thermodynamics of light. Brilliance shown from every page, this was the treasure trove he'd crossed time to find, the details behind the famous papers. He lingered over the notes in the margins, memorizing every word. But then he noticed something odd; the notes were written in two distinctly different hands, two different styles of penmanship. Perhaps Michelle Besso or one of the other Olympians helped Einstein with his work. Even a genius like Einstein sometimes needed a sounding board.

The crying stilled to a hush. A soft lullaby came from the other room; Linus was running out of time. He hurried to tidy the papers but one fell to the floor. A simple grocery list, apples and milk and cloth for the baby's diapers, and scrawled on the corner in neat script, a description of Brownian motion. And then it hit him. Molecules and milk written in the same flowing script; *the handwriting was the same!*

Mileva came from the other room, holding the baby in her arms. "What's wrong?"

For the first time he noticed the ink stains on her fingertips. "Did you write this?"

"What?"

He held the paper to her face. "Did you write this?"

"It's just a grocery list."

"Did you write the equations? The explanation for Brownian motion?"

"Oh." She slumped into the kitchen chair, a wane smile on her face. "I'm a physicist too."

"No, it can't be." In a single sentence, she'd shattered his life-long image of Einstein, the hero he'd crossed time to meet. *"No!"* Refusing to believe, he ran from the room, down the narrow stairs and out into the clean sunshine. "It cannot be!" Raving like a lunatic, he wandered the cobblestone streets, a crumpled grocery list in his fist. This was not what he'd come back in time to discover.

All day and into the evening he walked, mulling his discovery. Two sets of handwriting proved nothing. Einstein was a genius; the world had ample proof of his brilliance...yet Mileva *had* helped. The conviction grew in his mind, clawing at his conscious. But how much work was hers? Einstein always said that inspiration was more important than knowledge. Perhaps he was the inspiration, the lightning leap in logic, and she provided the stepping stones of knowledge, showing others how to follow the leap. Inspiration and knowledge perfectly married, and together they were sheer genius, forever changing our perception of the universe. Linus shuddered, realizing his hypothesis fit the data. Einstein never duplicated his brilliant achievements of 1905, his miracle year. Did his brilliance fade when he divorced Mileva, confining her to the dust motes of history? How many women were lost in time, erased from history books?

Linus could not face the Olympia Academy, not with doubt riddling his mind, so he spent his last evening wandering the cobblestone streets. Morning came and he was still awash in uncertainty. With his last day ticking away, he found himself walking back to the apartment on Kramgasse Strasse.

Up the narrow stairs to the second floor apartment, he stared at the door, daring a soft knock, but there was no answer. He knocked harder. "Mileva I need to know!" Still no answer. Frustration lent him strength and he pounded on the door. The flimsy lock burst and the door banged open. A trespasser from another time, he stood on the threshold, embarrassed by his anger. "Mileva?"

But there was no reply, not even the cry of a child.

Papers lay scattered across the room, dirty coffee cups on the sideboard, a stack of books on the chair, much the same as yesterday, but she was gone. The emptiness ate at him like acid. He stood in the small room, staring at the papers, a wealth of knowledge strewn about the small apartment, but physics no longer drove him. He'd come for the truth, the truth lost to history.

Outside, the tower clock tolled two, almost out of time.

He remembered the grocery list. *Perhaps she's gone shopping!* Hope rushed through him, lending speed to his steps. He clattered down the stairs, emerging into the bright sunshine. So many arcades, each with its own specialty, he started with the fruit market, then the flower stalls, and finally the meat market. Women crowded the stalls, but none with her mischievous smile, and none with the ink stains of genius on their fingertips.

Frustrated and nearly out of time, he emerged from the arcade, blinking at the sunshine. The crowd parted and he saw her on the far side of the square, a small woman in a blue muslin dress, holding a baby on her hip, limping away from him. *"Mileva!"*

A trolley thundered through the square. The crowd parted and reformed across the tracks, a solid sea of humanity. Linus rushed forward, but Mileva was gone, as if the crowd had swallowed her whole, erasing her from the notice of history.

The clock tower chimed three.

He was out of time. He took a last look and then he ran. Back through the cobblestone streets, back to the alley where he'd first appeared. The golden door shimmered in the alleyway...and then it began to shrink.

"No!" Linus sprinted for the doorway, refusing to be trapped in the past. The door shrank to half its size. Linus leaped, lunging for the portal.

The world tilted and blurred. Linus tumbled in an endless fall. Light sizzled around him and then he landed on his shoulder, slamming hard against a concrete floor. Bruised and battered, he took stock of his surroundings. Technicians in white coats flocked to his aid, the distinctive smell of ozone filling the chamber.

He was back in the twenty-fifth century, a grocery list clutched in his fist.

"Are you alright?"

"Ich bin gut," he forced his mind back to English. "I'm okay." He rushed to the nearest computer, obsessed with the need to know. His fingers flashed across the keyboard, but all he found were pieces of the truth. The archives held millions of references to Einstein but only a few pertained to Mileva. After bearing his three children, Einstein divorced her in 1919 and she died penniless and alone in 1948. Her name never appeared on any technical publications, but Einstein's early love letters to Mileva repeatedly mentioned "our theory" and "our

work." Released to the public after Einstein's death, the world was stunned to learn of Mileva. Physicists and historians of the late 20th century debated the love letters, discounting their scant evidence, condemning Mileva to the margins of history as nothing more than a wife.

Linus gently laid the grocery list on the table, smoothing away the wrinkles, wondering if he held the only proof. But who would believe him? And how many other women were erased by history? Perhaps time travel could serve a greater purpose. History was supposed to be the signpost to the future, but what if mankind only knew half the truth? He looked up at the others gathered around, a legion of questions on their faces, and he made a promise to himself and Mileva. "History is broken. Someone needs to find the missing pieces. Send me back."

Snakes and Ladders

L ynn Gallant expected profits to matter more than prejudice, but so far the upper rungs of the corporate ladder eluded her, always dangled just out of reach. Whispers said she'd hit the glass ceiling, but Lynn refused to give up, putting her trust in hard work and merit. Lynn figured she just needed one *fair* chance to show the "good old boys" that a woman could compete in the corporate world.

The multi-million dollar Whiskey project was her chance to smash the glass ceiling.

Armed with facts and figures, Lynn led her five-man team from Quest Oil into McGiven's wood paneled boardroom. A petite but ambitious Yankee-blond, she straightened her blue suit jacket, set her briefcase on the boardroom table, and gave the oilmen her most professional smile. A dozen men stood to exchange business cards. Southern drawls from Texas and Louisiana dominated as the men sorted out the pecking order. They did their best to ignore the only woman in the room, but Lynn waded into the group, offering a firm handshake, always the odd suit in the stacked deck of business cards.

The boardroom doors burst open and John Falco, the senior Vice-President of McGiven Oil, strode into the room. An older gentleman with a square jaw and salt-and-pepper hair, he wore a perfectly-tailored blue pinstriped Armani. Exuding corporate power, Falco drew the other men like money drawn to a bank. The lesser managers circled around, paying homage. Falco acknowledged them with a nod or a smile while claiming the seat at the head of the table. Tapping his gold watch, he said, "Let's get this meeting started. Who's presenting?"

The other men shuffled for seats near Falco, a corporate power-game of musical chairs, but Lynn remained standing. "Lynn Gallant, presenting for Quest Oil."

Falco's eyebrows jerked upward. He raked her with his stare, an appraisal that was more fitting for a bar than the boardroom. Smiling, he hissed, "This should be interesting."

Smirks circulated the room.

Lynn stood her ground, throwing down the gauntlet. Charts and numbers flashed across the overhead screen, an arcane dance of facts and assumptions. Lynn mixed science and economics with the crystal ball gazing of business strategy, weaving an explanation for her radical plan to develop Whiskey, the latest offshore oil discovery in the Gulf of Mexico. As the profit numbers blazed from the screen, Lynn leaned on the table and looked Falco in the eyes. "The plan is radical but the rewards more than justify the risk." Surveying the table of poker-faced men, she issued her challenge. "The price-tag is $1.2 billion, but Whiskey will forever change the way oil is developed in the Gulf of Mexico, unlocking millions of barrels for the US market." Lowering her voice, she said, "Are you in?"

The lesser managers squirmed, uncomfortable with such a big decision, but John Falco remained statue-still, a shrewd look on his chiseled face. Falco was the key to closing the deal. Lynn waited, refusing to be intimidated by his scrutiny.

He gave her a shark's smile, drilling her with his stare. "You're sure about these numbers?"

"The cost estimates come from three different contractors. We used the highest costs and applied a risk factor to be safe."

"What about the oil price?"

Lynn played her ace in the hole. "Light sweet crude is currently trading at $89 dollars per barrel...for these economics we've assumed a flat $50 dollars." She gave him a knowing smile. "So you see, the upside is tremendous."

The other men studied Falco, sycophants waiting for a sign. An engineer tapped a nervous pencil against the table, ticking off the seconds. Lynn stood firm in a sea of tension; hoping their greed would overcome their prejudice.

Falco stared at the profit numbers.

Lynn's heart beat loud in her ears.

"You're asking us to take a mighty big risk, little Lady."

Lynn kept her voice steady, ignoring the slur. "A risk with a lot of upside."

"Will you stake your career on this development?"

"The numbers are sound, I stand behind them."

"I'll remember that." Falco nodded. "We have a deal. Good work."

Lynn heard the first crack in the glass ceiling. She stepped forward to shake Falco's hand, struggling to contain her smile. This deal would put her name on the Vice-President's office back at Quest's headquarters. She'd be the first female VP in the sixty-year history of a company dominated by rednecks, educated or otherwise.

Snapping the clasps on her briefcase, she ushered her team out of the conference room, eager to claim her latest victory in the corporate game of snakes and ladders.

#

Charlene, the boss's secretary, saw Lynn coming and waved her through into the Vice-President's office. Lynn knocked in passing on the open door and took a seat in front of her boss's desk, a triumphant smile on her face. "The Whiskey project is going to change the company's bottom line."

Rast raised his head from the glow of the computer screen and flicked a daggered glance in Lynn's direction. Thin and wiry with dark unruly hair, Rast sat hunched behind the screen, peering into the computer like a corporate gargoyle. "Wait till I finish this spreadsheet."

Lynn did her best to keep a straight face. It always amazed her that the dumb prick didn't realize that the reflective coating on the high-tech office windows provided a perfect mirror of his computer screen. Rast was playing solitaire, *again*, and he wasn't even winning. The words *"red jack on the black queen"* quivered on the tip of Lynn's tongue but she resisted the temptation. The smart move was to let Rast play in ignorance. The more people who caught the dumb bastard playing solitaire the better. Like they said in Star Trek, *revenge is a dish best served cold.*

Blanking the screen, Rast leered at her from across the vast expanse of his empty desk. "What do you want?"

Ignoring his curt tone, Lynn flashed a triumphant smile. "I closed the deal on Whiskey and even managed to get a promote on the next three wells. Our partners liked the plan so much they gave us everything we wanted. The promote alone will bring the company an extra thirty million in profits."

Rast gave her a blank stare, almost as if he didn't understand a word she'd said. On reflection, Lynn decided it was a distinct possibility. Trying again, she said, "This new development plan makes deepwater fields profitable. Whiskey will yield a profit of four hundred and twenty million dollars and that's just Quest's share." Leaning forward, Lynn tapped her index finger on Rast's desk, driving home her point. "Sealing this deal is my ticket for the promotion you promised." She gave Rast a steely-eyed stare. "Doubling the value of the group is surely worth a Vice-President's chair."

A look of panic scurried across Rast's face.

Before Lynn could press home the advantage, Jay Bexcell walked in.

Fawning and disgustingly differential, Bexcell greeted Rast in his usual smarmy voice, "Excuse me boss, I hope I'm not interrupting anything, but you said you wanted to talk to me about my performance appraisal?"

Annoyed at the ill-timed interruption, Lynn nevertheless had to stifle a smirk. Bexcell was almost as incompetent as he was spineless. About the only thing he never bungled was organizing the yearly Christmas party.

Relief washed across Rast's face. He waved Bexcell into his office while casting an annoyed glance at Lynn. "We'll talk later." As she stepped towards the door, he added, "And write me up a memo on the deal to develop Whiskey. I'll need it to brief the CEO on our latest success."

Lynn left Rast's office with anger in her stride. She'd write the memo, but instead of sending it to her solitaire-playing fool-of-a-boss, Lynn would send the memo straight to the CEO. Ignoring corporate protocol, she'd by-pass Rast and go straight to the top. The profit margin on Whiskey field was sure to grab the CEO's attention...and this time, Lynn intended to get full credit for *her* work.

#

Three cups of coffee later, chance and a full bladder found Lynn innocently ensconced behind the door of the last stall in the lady's room while Rast's secretary, Charlene, and the CEO's secretary, Thelma, met for a gossip break in front of the make-up mirror. Lynn didn't normally listen to office gossip, but this was too good to resist.

Thelma's smoky voice said, "So you're finally moving up to the thirty-third floor. Who would have thought that Rast would pull it off?"

Charlene replied, "Rast obviously had no doubts. The weasel had me order his business cards with the *Vice* deleted from his title more than three weeks ago. He probably has "President" sewn on his jockey shorts."

Both women shared a laugh but Lynn didn't think it was funny.

Over the sound of running water, Charlene said, "So who's taking Rast's place?"

Lynn leaned forward to catch the name, wishing her stall was closer to the sink.

"I shouldn't tell you ahead of time, but what the heck, the announcement will be posted by the end of the day. You didn't hear it from me, but Rast picked Bexcell to fill the VP's chair."

Lynn's heart stopped.

"Mmm, Lynn Gallant won't be happy with that decision; she worked hard to bring that new field forward."

"Charlene, there's only *one* executive washroom in this building and it doesn't have a woman on the door. It's about time Lynn Gallant figured that out."

Filled with rage, Lynn's mind went into overdrive, thinking of ways to salvage her career.

#

Lynn's practical low-slung leather heels beat an angry drumbeat into the marble floor as she strode toward the stairs. The "golden staircase" led to the offices of the powerful men who ruled Quest Oil from the thirty-third floor. She'd had the "balls" to ask for and get an impromptu meeting with the CEO. Hoping that greed would overcome prejudice, Lynn dared to take her case straight to the top. If anyone deserved the VP's office, she did.

Walking through the hushed corridors of power, Lynn passed beneath the stern-faced portraits of past CEOs, a shrine to capitalism – but all of the patron saints were white, Anglo-Saxon males. The portrait gallery served as an elaborate Keep-Out sign, warning that women could be martyrs but never patron saints. Glaring at the portraits, Lynn dared to walk in uncharted territory – someone had to be the first to break into the club.

At the CEO's office, Thelma escorted Lynn to the inner-sanctum, the palatial office of Dion Law, the venerable chief executive of Quest Oil.

Ever the polished gentleman, the silver-haired CEO rose from behind his massive desk and gestured toward a pair of leather armchairs near the wall of windows.

Following the CEO's lead, Lynn settled into the plush leather. She crossed her legs and smoothed her dark blue skirt, wearing her own version of a poker face. "Thank you for seeing me on such short notice."

"My door is always open. What can I do for you?"

"I suppose you've seen the profit projections for the new Whiskey field?"

Beaming his famous paternal smile, the CEO said, "Yes, I talked to Bruce Rast about the field over lunch. Rast has done an outstanding job. We need more people of his caliper in the company."

Gritting her teeth, Lynn said, "Did he explain about the promote that I negotiated from our partners? My idea is worth at least thirty million to the company."

"Yes, you and your team did an excellent job of negotiating the agreement. I am sure you will continue to perform at the same level of excellence under Jay Bexcell's leadership. Bexcell's idea to try for the promote was nothing short of brilliant."

For a moment Lynn wasn't sure she'd heard him correctly. Then the message behind his words hit home, punching her in the gut. She struggled to breathe. Rast had beaten her memo to the top floor, and of course, the CEO was eager to believe that Rast and Bexcell deserved all the credit. Short, petite blonds weren't capable of doubling the profit margin of an entire business group.

Trying to hide her anger, Lynn lowered her gaze to the coffee table. Glaring from the tabletop was her memo about Whiskey field. The bastard knew the truth. He knew it and he didn't care. Lynn raised her gaze from the telltale memo and stared Law full in the face.

He met her challenge, a Cheshire cat grin stealing across his face. In an oily Texas drawl, Law said, "Some day you'll make a really significant contribution to the company...and then we'll talk promotion.

Rage smoldered within her, a volcano threatening to erupt.

Oblivious to the danger, Law prattled on, dangling a string of corporate carrots that would never be awarded, but Lynn wouldn't bite. All her hard work and innovative ideas were wasted, the credit always given to someone else. In a haze of anger, she mouthed polite words and nodded appropriately, waiting for the first chance to escape. It was time to appeal to a higher power.

#

Lynn stopped in her office long enough to grab her purse and her briefcase and then headed straight for the elevator. This time she was going down. Relieved to be alone, Lynn rode the sleek glass-encased elevator to the ground floor, silently watching the million-dollar view of New Orleans, the city of Creole cooking, black oil, and voodoo magic. Some might think it ironic to find the corporate towers of Big Oil in heart of the Big Easy, but Lynn knew the business of hunting for black oil had a lot in common with voodoo magic. They were both a sort of dark art.

The elevator opened and Lynn's footsteps echoed in the marble foyer of the cathedral-like entrance way. Spinning the revolving door, she escaped from the carefully conditioned corporate air into the fierce heat and swamp cocktail of smells that could only be New Orleans.

Air, thick as southern molasses, wrapped her in a malaise of late afternoon heat. Knowing better than to fight the elements, Lynn surrendered to a slower pace and a different, seductive way of thinking. Easing her blue silk jacket off her shoulders, she unbuttoned the top of her crisp white blouse. Turning her back on the corporate towers, she headed for the depths of the French Quarter. Four city blocks later, she left the wide modern streets behind for the narrow lanes of mystery. Wrought-iron balconies, gas lanterns, and shuttered windows spoke of a bygone era, a time of riverboat gambling and voodoo queens, when superstition triumphed over science. Bespelled by the possibilities, Lynn drank in the details. Tantalizing aromas of Cajun spices permeated the air but they couldn't mask the underlying stench of spilled beer and urine that marked the dark side of the Quarter. Normally the city's shadier side repulsed her, but not this time. Lynn was done playing fair.

Avoiding Bourbon Street and the rush of tourists, Lynn sought out the small narrow alleyways where the mistresses of tarot plied their trade. She'd heard rumors at parties and conferences, always whispered by professional women always with frozen careers. She'd listened but she'd never believed, trusting to merit and hard work to get her to the boardroom. Lynn still didn't believe, but she was angry enough to take a walk on the dark side and see where it led.

Gas lanterns lit the narrow alleyway, the flickering light adding a sense of mystery to the lane. Lynn studied the worn wooden signs, searching for a scrap of rumor that might hold a desperate remedy. *Gypsy Lady*, *Crystal Ball*, *Emperor Tarot* and then, over the green door, the face of the *Man in the Moon* stared back at her, proving at least some of the rumor was true.

Lynn reached for the door handle shaped like a coiled serpent, and then jumped backwards as the door swung open. A dark-haired woman in a sleek business suit burst from the shop, panic written across her face.

Startled, Lynn said, "Is something wrong?"

The woman shrieked and rushed past Lynn, running down the alleyway despite her stiletto heels.

Such an odd encounter, but Lynn refused to be deterred. Gathering her courage, she passed through the door, walking from the light into dark. Strands of beads brushed across her face like cobwebs. The heavy musk of incense enfolded her like a shroud. A disembodied voice said, "Welcome to the House of the Moon, may you see the future clearly."

Lynn's eyes adjusted to the gloom. The small room was decorated like an old-fashioned parlor. Heavy green drapes cloaked the widows, faded gold wallpaper covering the walls. Candles provided the only light, illuminating the central table. An old crone sat at the lace-draped table, peering at a spread of colorful tarot cards. Wrinkled hands bejeweled with rings gathered the cards into a single stack. The crone began to shuffle with a practiced, patient motion. Lynn found the sound of shuffling cards somehow soothing, somehow seductive, ripe with possibilities.

"Have you come for a reading, dear...or have you come for something else?"

"I've come...for something else."

The old woman laughed and gestured to the seat on the opposite side of the table. "Have a seat, dear, the cards told me to expect you."

Lynn sat perched on the edge of the chair, not really sure what to expect. Pushing doubt from her mind, she focused on her anger instead.

The old woman nodded. "That's it, dear, let the anger come to the surface...that's why you're here isn't it, the anger."

Tongue-tied, Lynn could only nod.

The sound of shuffling stopped and the crone spread the tarot deck in a fan across the lace tablecloth. "Now the Questioner picks a card, and we see what has brought her to the House of the Moon."

As an engineer and a business strategist, Lynn didn't believe in this type of mumbo-jumbo, but she'd play along for now. She reached for the antique deck, selecting a card from the middle. Turning the card, Lynn's breath caught in her throat. A winged woman filled the card, blindfolded and holding the scales of justice. Lynn stared, shocked by the truth revealed in the tarot.

The crone laughed. "*Justice*, something always sought by honest folk but rarely ever found...at least within the confines of *this* world."

Candles on the edge of the table flickered, as if a ghost walked past. The crone husked, "Choose a second card, and we'll learn about the nature of the Questioner."

A shiver ran down Lynn's back, she wasn't sure if she wanted to learn more about herself in this kind of place, but she was too far into it now. Choosing a second card, she turned it over to reveal a prancing man dressed in motley. The second card was the *Fool*. Puzzled and mildly insulted, Lynn stared at the old woman demanding an explanation.

"It is not what you think, dear." Smiling, the crone tapped the up-turned card. "The *Fool* is always chasing a dream that seems just out of reach. To achieve the dream the Questioner will have to pay a great price. It is up to the Questioner to decide if the dream is worth the price."

The old woman's words rocked Lynn's soul.

"The cards know, dear, the cards always know. The Tarots are the messengers of the higher powers. The powers see you and they understand. Now choose a final card for the price."

Swallowing hard, Lynn obeyed. Her hand trembled as she turned the card. A winged-grotesque grinned up at her.

The pounding of Lynn's heart seemed to fill the room.

"Yes, dear, it is the card of the *Devil*." Chuckling under her breath the old woman said, "You shouldn't really be surprised, dear. The Other Fellow will give you justice in the next life, but if you want justice here on earth, in this lifetime, then the Devil is the one you seek."

The old woman's words made a strange kind of sense. "But what does it mean? What do I have to do?"

"Relax, dear, the Devil is more fair than he ever gets credit for."

Lynn had read enough fiction to know this was the part where she got tricked, suckered into doing something she didn't really want to do. In a cautious voice she said, "So what do I have to do?"

"Merely help another woman achieve the same justice that you seek."

Cringing inside, Lynn waited to hear the rest.

"I'll tell you a secret, dear, the face looking out from the moon is *female* not *male*. Under the sign of the Moon, the scales of Justice always, eventually, balance out. Help another woman, and in turn, you shall be helped."

The idea appealed to Lynn. Taking a deep breath, she made her decision. "Tell me what to do."

The old woman crossed Lynn's palm with a photo and a business card. Whispered instructions followed. Lynn listened, hearing words that would change her life.

#

Lynn needed a drink. Maybe a tall frosty Hurricane to settle her nerves as well as her mind. She found O'Donal's bar and claimed a corner table. It was still early for alcohol, even pink alcohol, but Lynn didn't care.

Catching the waiter's attention, she ordered a pink Hurricane and then scanned the room for her prey. She found him at the bar, six-foot tall, blond hair and blue eyes, just as the crone had said. Sipping her drink, Lynn took her time to check him out. He must have been eye-candy in his college years, but age and the sedentary lifestyle of the office had taken their toll. His chin was trying to double itself and while he still had the shoulders of a linebacker, he was also working on a beer gut. His fading looks would work in her favor, but this wasn't going to be easy, especially since she knew him.

Tim Jefferries was a rising star at Tempco Oil. Lynn had worked with Jefferries on more than one joint venture project. Tim had an enormous ego and a reputation for getting ahead on the backs of others, especially women. Bastards were everywhere in the oil business, you just never knew what package they'd come in.

Taking a long pull of courage from the too-sweet but very strong Hurricane, Lynn left a generous tip on the table and then made a bee-line for Jefferries before she lost her nerve.

Putting a casual hand on his shoulder, Lynn said, "I'm surprised to see you here. Mind if I join you?"

His face reflected surprise and a touch of interest. He gestured toward an empty barstool. "Lynn! Please join me. What brings you to the Quarter at this time of day?"

"My team sealed the deal on the Whiskey development, so I thought I deserved a treat. How about you?"

"Performance review time. The office is really tense since our last four wells were dusters." He raised a glass filled with an amber-colored liquor. "I needed to take the edge off before facing the traffic to the burbs and the wife and kids."

They talked shop for a while, only about the wells that were already in the trade rags, no company secrets. This kind of conversation was easy for Lynn. She understood his problems at work and praised him at all the right moments, giving him what he couldn't get at home, and all the while Lynn wondered if she had the nerve to go through with it.

Tim seemed to enjoy her attention. While he bragged about an office triumph, she studied him through hooded eyes. Tall and blond, Tim had all the right rings on his fingers: the class ring from Texas A&M, the ring from his college football championship, and a gold wedding band, all pre-requisites for the boardroom. As a good old boy, Tim had all the advantages that Lynn would never have. Doors would open effortlessly for him, while Lynn would be locked out regardless of how much she achieved. It was enough to tip her decision.

Several drinks later, Tim took matters into his own hands. Leaning close, the smell of bourbon on his breath, he stared at her with bedroom eyes. There was no mistaking his intentions. Tim's advances should have made the task easier, but they only repulsed her. Dropping her stare, Lynn hid behind a shallow smile, burying her revulsion beneath a mountain of anger.

Tim hovered close, waiting for a response. "I always liked you." He brushed a finger across the top of her hand, slow and suggestive.

Lynn couldn't stall any longer. Remembering the crone's promise, she slowly slid her hand over Tim's, lowering her voice to a husky whisper. "I know someplace special, someplace more...intimate."

He gave her slow smile. "What are we waiting for?"

Hinting at a romantic suite tucked away in the Quarter, she led him through the twilight streets, her arm eventually going around his waist.

The wrought iron gate was open. Slipping the liveried doorman the crone's business card hidden inside of a ten-dollar note, Lynn got the key to a suite of rooms tucked away on the far end of the second floor balcony.

Fumbling with the key in the lock, Lynn had second thoughts. Married men were always strictly off-limits, and one-night stands weren't her style, but she supposed it was too late for that now.

The door opened and Lynn stepped into an antebellum boudoir complete with an antique four-poster bed piled high with pillows, scads of Chantilly lace, and an open bottle of red wine breathing on the nightstand. Lilac and the scent of jasmine completed the illusion of southern intimacy...perhaps this wouldn't be so hard after all.

"So you *have* done this before." Tim grinned.

She fought the urge to slap him. Instead, she drew him into the room, closing the door and steering him toward the bed. He came willingly, leaving a trail of business attire strewn across the carpet. His hands groped and squeezed, but she eased them away, taking control. Pushing him down on the bed, Lynn crawled on top and closed her eyes, pretending it was Brad Pitt instead of an aging oilman, trying to delay the point of no return.

Tim moaned in pleasure. "That's it, little lady, now ride your cowboy."

That made Lynn open her eyes, and then she saw the mirrored wall.

The mirror reflected the whole bed...the whole truth.

It was ugly.

It was everything Lynn despised.

Disgust crawled across her face as she realized what she'd almost done. Leaping from the bed, Lynn grabbed her clothes and rushed to the bathroom, locking the door behind her. Frantic to escape, she dressed with no care for her appearance.

"Sugar, come back here!"

Lynn fumbled with her nylons.

Tim banged on the door. "Come back here! I'm just getting started!

Hot and sweaty, it was hard to get the nylons up her legs, but she persisted, ignoring the urgency of Tim's voice and the fresh runners in her stockings. Pulling on her suit jacket, she opened the bathroom door.

Startled, Tim took a step backward. "What's going on?"

"I can't do this." She rushed past him, ignoring his outrage as well as his limp nakedness. Gathering up her purse and briefcase, she ran for the door, desperate to escape the nightmare.

#

The muggy air of the Louisiana night offered no relief, but at least it was dark. Lynn plunged into the sleepless streets of the French Quarter, walking without thinking, trying to escape from the deeds of the night. Her footsteps eventually took her to the narrow lane that served as the home to the voodoo queens and the fortunetellers. It was well past midnight but a flickering gas lantern still illuminated the sign painted with the face of the moon. Drawn like a moth to the flame, she approached the green door. Her hand rested on the serpent-shaped handle. The shop couldn't be open but she pulled anyway. The door swung wide, releasing the cloying smell of incense.

A voice from the dark said, "Come in, dear, I've been waiting for you."

The old woman sat at the table studying a spread of tarot cards. Nodding at Lynn, the crone smiled. "You've done well, dear."

"But I didn't..."

"You've done enough." She turned a card, revealing winged justice. "You've played the game the only way you could, the only way *they'd* let you."

Reaching beneath the table, the crone produced a manila envelope.

Just an ordinary manila envelope, the type she'd used in the office a million times. But sitting here, on the same table as the tarot cards, there was something sinister about it. Like a coiled snake summoned by black magic.

"Come on, dear, this is for you. The Devil always keeps his bargains."

She'd come this far; she might as well go all the way. Lynn snatched the envelope from the table. Her hands shook as she broke the seal, letting the contents tumble onto the antique lace. Like a modern set of tarot cards, the photos stared back at her. Photos that clearly showed the face of Dion Law, the CEO of Quest Oil, but the nude woman snuggled next to him was *not* Law's high society wife. A smile of triumph slowly spread across Lynn's face.

"Yes dear, you've learned to play the game, the same way the men do, with threats and favors. Use the knowledge well, dear."

Lynn left the shop clutching the envelope. The photos were her key to the executive washroom...only this time Quest Oil would have to change the symbol on the door. Lynn smiled. Once in power, she'd change the rules in favor of merit and judge the men accordingly. Bexcell would be looking for a new job and Rast's solitaire-playing days were numbered. Lynn smiled as she walked, a sense of justice thrumming through her. She'd teach the good old boys a new way to play the corporate game of snakes and ladders. She wondered how many would survive.

The God Planet

The lid of the sarcophagus rolled back and light poured in. *Light,* so bright it hurt my eyes, eyes that had seen nothing but dreams for the last nine hundred years.

"Let me help you, sir." A medbot leaned over me, metallic hands removing needles and probes. So cold the robot's touch, I shivered as the probes snaked out of me, some from the most unmentionable places. It left me feeling empty and unplugged, drifting in a surreal haze.

"Just lay there, sir. You'll feel better once the stimtabs take effect." The medbot's voice was warm and soothing; a congenial male without a hint of dialect or dominance, but the face was pure machine. According to the Galactic Concord, robots had to look like robots. No one wanted a repeat of the android rebellion of 7830.

I blinked, realizing my thoughts were my own, no longer floating in a daze of dreams. Flexing my hands and stretching my legs, I took deep breaths of stale metallic air, reconnecting with my body. Strength from the stimtab flowed through me, and I almost felt humanoid again.

"Let me help you, sir." Cold metallic hands lent support as I sat up. I stared down at my naked body, two arms, two legs, a flutter of gills on my chest, six fingers on each hand. Everything seemed to work, but my natural tan was gone, bleached to an ugly dead-fish white. So pale and mottled, my skin was dotted with red pinpricks and circular sucker marks, as if I'd been held for centuries in the embrace of a Vernian-squid at the bottom of the Deneabian Sea. I shook my head, repulsed by my own body. Chalk it up to another side effect of cryostasis.

The medbot's metallic voice intruded. "Your vital signs are strong, brain activity normal for a class-M humanoid, only a six percent weight loss, and a slight impairment of the liver."

I couldn't help the sarcasm in my voice. "Nine hundred years without a drink and you're telling me I have liver problems?"

"Only a minor impairment."

"So much for abstinence."

My humor was clearly lost on the medbot. "Get me out of this coffin." It helped me climb from the sarcophagus. I stood pale and naked as a newborn, my knees wobbling, but the medbot never let go. "Here, drink this sir," it pressed a squeeze tube into my hand. My mouth tasted like a chemical dump, I eagerly sucked the tube. The rush of taste thrilled me. *Ah, chocolate!* In all of humanoid-kinds galactic wanderings, we'd never discovered anything as ambrosial as chocolate. The rush of rich sweetness hid a cocktail of nutrients and stimulants, but after three hundred years, taste was the only thing that mattered.

The medbot took the empty tube. "You should be comfortable now, sir. Ship controls are set at Standard temperature and eighty percent of Standard gravity." It handed me a white silk robe, a *Seeker's* robe.

I hesitated, proof I was really here. Faced with my fate, I tried to diminish it with a joke. "White was never my color," but the medbot just waited, a stoic look on its mechanical face. Robots weren't programmed for humor. I took the robe. Cool spyder-silk glided across my skin as I pulled it over my shoulders and tied the sash around my waist, the hem falling just short of my knees. I stared down at my hairy legs. "Real men wear pants."

The medbot swiveled, returning with a flimsy pair of white silk pants. Not something I'd choose on my own, but better than nothing. The white silks made it official, I was a Seeker, or a Pilgrim, or an Anointed, or a Thaglid, or any of the other thousand names depending on your star system. But for me, Josh Brennerman, deep-sea fisherman from the Vernian system, the pristine white silks labeled me a sucker.

"Will there be anything else, sir?"

The milky smooth voice began to grate on my nerves. "Just a home-bound ticket."

Vid-cam eyes stared back at me, my image reflected on the beveled lenses, and then the medbot turned away, rolling to the next sarcophagus.

Abandoned, I stood barefoot in the belly of the cargo hold, trying to get my bearings. The *Psalm Singer* was a long-haul cargo ship, basically a tin can with a Langer drive, nothing like the big luxury cruisers that plied the inner systems. Stripped down to its bare essentials, the ship's cargo bay gaped large and empty. Eight sarcophagi sat huddled in the center, bright lights blinking a steady stream of bio-readouts on their metal lids. Medbots hovered about like ants tending their eggs, everything dwarfed by the cavernous size of the cargo hold. Such a large ship for so few passengers, but all the sects agreed; eight was the holiest number. Turn an eight on its side and you have the symbol for infinity, the measure of the gods. And of all the tetra-trillions of humanoids in the known universe, it was my rotten luck to be one of the eight Seekers. I shook my head in disgust.

The other sarcophagi remained sealed, locked in their slumber. So I was the first one resurrected, the luck of the draw, but at least I was alive. Long haul cryostasis tended to be a risky venture and I was never one to roll the dice unless I had to.

With no one to talk to but the medbots, I decided to head for the ship's living quarters. Might as well claim my bunk before the others woke. I padded to the far end of the bay, the metal deck warm beneath my bare feet like a sun-soaked sea. At least the temperature suited me.

The lift took me to the more habitable parts of the ship. I'd only gotten a brief glimpse before they put me into cryrostasis, now was my chance to explore. The next three levels held sleeping cells, more than a hundred identical pod units laid out in concentric circles, proof the cargo ship was a refit. Each pod was gray, and boring, and compact, nothing but the bare essentials. You'd think for Seekers they might have included a few frills, like senso-beds and stimtab-bars and holographic headsets, but no such luck. Everything looked sterile and efficient and boring as the nine hells. No point in even picking a pod, since they were all identical. Besides, without personal belongings I had no way to stake a claim, another grim reminder of my fate.

Depressed, I followed the markings to the central galley. Another sterile room filled with metal tables and gray chairs, the only decoration a faded star chart on the far wall. At least the food dispensers worked, bright lights illuminating the central screen, but the choices were all too predictable. I punched in butterscotch and tore the top from the squeeze tube. A burst of warm buttery flavor filled my mouth. Taste suddenly seemed like my most exotic sense.

Sipping on warm butterscotch, I followed the markers to the central lift, determined to explore the rest of the ship. The lift doors whooshed open on the last deck, the bulbous nose of the ship. Finally some luxury. Eight sumptuous black leather high-gravity armchairs filled the center of the small circular chamber. Lights winked and blinked on control panels set in the lower walls, all run by the central computer. But the chamber's main feature was the conical ceiling inset with real plazglass windows. I gaped at the unfettered view of space. A real trillion-credit view, not just some computer generated holo-projection. Drawn to the stars, I reached out to the glass, as if I could touch the very fabric of space.

"Dim lights."

The computer complied. And then I was staring at the universe, in all its celestial glory. So many stars, like bright jewels they filled the universe with a glittering glow. Little wonder humanoid-kind was so obsessed with the night sky. But then cold logic smothered wonder. The truth was, the bright glow was all in the past, the place we'd come from, countless light-years away. Few ever saw the Milky Way from such an extreme distance, like having a gods-eye view of the cosmos. Swallowing my fears, I let myself indulge in the sight, mesmerized by the beauty. I don't know how long I stood there but it was long enough for the rotational spin of the ship to slowly change the view. Instead of staring at the past, I stared at the future, at the gaping darkness on the edge of space. So dark and forbidding, legends said even light cannot survive the Big Dark. I shivered, staring at all that emptiness, like a vacuum waiting to suck my soul dry. Yet I could not turn away. There was something fascinating about the dark, something compelling on a primordial level. And I wasn't alone in my fascination. The vast stretch of midnight confounded scientist, taunted explorers, and inspired the religious to a frenzy of worship. And among all that darkness sat a single lone star, set like a beacon to the rest of the universe. I stared at the star, a blue dwarf with a thousand names. The devout called it God's Eye, while the cynical named it Hell's Portal, but my people favored the Pinprick, the one speck of light in a vast sea of night. And around that star orbited a single planet, the reason we'd crossed so many light-years.

The doors to the lift whooshed open.

I turned to greet my fellow Seeker, a short swarthy man with a barrel chest and bulging muscles, telltale signs of a high gravity planet, but it was the metal collar at his throat that grabbed my attention. A wrist-thick gunmetal ring with a winking red light circled his throat, a high-security prison collar. I took a step backward, hoping the ship's computer kept tight control of the convict.

"Collar kills 'em every time." His voice was a low growl.

I raised my stare to his face, a square lump sitting atop a tree-trunk neck, topped by a wild mane of spiky dark hair and set with even darker eyes.

"Name's Brag Turner from Athrid-5. Know it?"

I shook my head no.

He flashed a twisted grin. "A high security penal planet in the Chillod system." He jerked his thumb toward the collar. "And yeh, I've earned it, many times over."

"Does it work in deep space?"

"Take a swing and find out." Brag flexed his muscles, cracking his knuckles. "I could use a good brawl, get the blood flowing after the deep freeze." He flashed a gap-toothed grin. "Go ahead, take the first swing."

Knowing I was no match for the high-gravity brute, con or otherwise, I stepped back, trying to keep a safe distance.

"No takers?" Something dark and predatory lurked in Brag's gaze. "Who in the Intellect are you?"

"Josh Brennerman, deep-sea fisherman from the Vernian system."

"A squib," he laughed and I did not like the sound of it, "awfully far from the sea. Why'd the Intellect pick you, fish-er-man?"

The lift opened, disgorging another white-robed Seeker. I sagged against the plazglass, saved from being alone with a homicidal maniac. My gaze shifted to the newcomer, a tall willowy figure with a baldhead and large luminous eyes the color of deep violet. A blue tattoo rode his forehead, a triangle filled with the all-seeing Eye of BuddhaChrist, the mark of a shamlin monk.

"Greetings of the Light to you. My name is Kayden, a monk of the shamlin order."

The voice belonged to a woman, a female monk.

Brag growled, "A friggin' nun."

She gave him a serene smile. "A monk not a nun, women can be among the devout," but then she caught sight of the view and crossed to the plazglass windows, staring at the single star set amongst the darkness. "Heaven's Gate." Her hands sketched a series of runes in the air, like a prayer in motion, too quick to make any sense of the symbols.

A low chuckle rumbled through the chamber. "A sinner, a saint, and a fish-er-man." Brag sprawled on the nearest armchair, his shovel-sized hands laced behind his head. "Makes you wonder what else they've got in the deep freeze."

The lift doors opened and two more Seekers trickled in.

The first took my breath away, a stunning blond of ballistic proportions. Built like a starlet from a porn-holovid, she walked with a seductive sway, the thin silk robe enhancing every luscious curve. I felt myself stir, proof the best parts of me had survived cryostasis.

"Hello everyone," her voice was just as breathy as her long mane of blond hair.

Brag sat up in his chair, "*Shirah Highlem!*"

I recognized the name and gaped in disbelief. She really was a porn star, famous across the inner systems. Not that I bought much porn myself, but fishermen talked on the deep hauls, and besides, I was only humanoid.

"A condemned man's last wish." Brag's hooded gaze tracked her like a wolf eel in spawn.

"Honey, I'm every man's wish, first, last, and always." She circled the armchairs, slow and sensuous. Sauntering past Brag, she came straight towards me, laying a dainty hand on my chest. "And you are?"

I thought my heart would pound out of my chest. "Josh," I stared down at her, suddenly caught in a stammer, "J-josh Brennerman."

"He's just a soggy squib," Brag growled. "If you want a real man, come to me."

She turned her sea-blue gaze away to consider Brag, and I staggered back a step, as if released from a spell. And then I looked at her, I mean really looked. Tiny wrinkles rode the corners of her eyes and mouth, like the crazed cracks in tempered glass, and her golden hair held a hint of silver. Her figure still dazzled, but the truth was in the details. I struggled to remember how young I'd been when I first heard her name and then I realized this woman wasn't just a starlet, she was an icon. Gene-therapy could do wonders but sooner or later the light-years started to show.

"I...bring...hellos."

The computer-generated voice jerked my gaze toward the lift, to the other Seeker. He stepped forward, only one-meter tall, clad head to toe in a pressurized spacesuit. I assumed it was a he, but who knew? Two arms, two legs, the stunted body of a dwarf, but behind the helmet's faceplate swirled a dense orange-brown fog, a methane breather, or some other cocktail of deadly gases.

He stepped forward, his boots making a faint metallic click against the deck. "I...am...Sil-88."

So the little fellow didn't speak Standard, and his suit's translator seemed to be struggling. As the first to awaken, it felt like my duty to respond. "Welcome to our little group." I spoke slow and clear, giving his translator a chance to work as I introduced the others.

Brag growled. "Welcome to the Intellect's friggin' freak show."

"No need to swear." Shirah flounced onto one of the leather armchairs, her Seeker's robe hiking up to reveal a distracting length of shapely thigh. "Now what do we do?"

Her voice oozed seduction. I found myself getting hot despite the truth of her age. "I suppose we should wait for the others."

A klaxon blared, interrupting my words. The rude sound was followed by the smooth male tones of the ship's voice. "Attention all passengers. Please secure for the next acceleration thrust. Final thrust will commence in ten Standard tarmins." The voice began a slow, steady countdown.

Shirah turned pale. "What about the others? Aren't there supposed to be eight Seekers?"

Brag flashed an ugly grin. "Eight frozen for the long haul but only five survived the thaw."

My stomach churned with a sick inside-out feeling. "I didn't know the odds were so bad."

Brag grinned. "Don't you know, fish-er-man, we're fodder for the gods."

I swallowed, wondering what else I didn't know.

Sil-88 climbed onto a leather chair. "We...best...pick...chairs."

The gas-breathing dwarf had a point. I climbed into the nearest armchair. Leather-gel flowed around me, conforming to a snug g-force embrace. The chair tilted back, giving me a great view of the windows. I stared up at the plazglass, at the infinite darkness broken by a single pinprick of light, like looking into a bottomless well. The *Psalm Singer* was about to enter the darkest place in all the cosmos. I stared at the vast sea of night, wondering what lurked on the other side.

#

I must have dozed, because when I woke, a single planet loomed large in the plazglass windows. Fate stared me in the face and I stared back. It wasn't much to look at, a big dirty snowball of clouds, white streaked with orange and scuffs of dingy brown. If the clouds hid any continents or seas, I could not tell. A feeling of betrayal crept across me. After all the rumors and religious hoopla, I expected something beautiful, like the jewel blue of old Earth, or the stunning blue-green of Verne-4, or the brilliant desert reds of Haldorn-8, not this cold snowball of dirty clouds. Disappointment laced my voice, "It's ugly as sin."

Brag growled. "Can't even see any land. What is it, a friggin' gas giant?"

"It's perfect." The female monk rose graceful from her armchair and approached the window, her hands tracing symbols in the air like a benediction.

"What do you mean?" I could not help asking.

"God's ways are mysterious, and so is His planet." She gestured toward the cloud-shrouded orb. "Heaven's Gate is just as it should be, cloaked in righteous mystery."

A loud braying sound echoed through the chamber. "You friggin' believe that crap? The Almighty Intellect runs the known universe, and if you think anything else, you're friggin' brain dead."

The monk turned her violet eyes on the convict, a tinge of sadness in her voice. "So you don't believe. It is written that the Seekers will find what they most expect. I pity your emptiness."

Brag's voice turned nasty. "Save your pity, sister, cause I'll tell you what *I* believe. Every last one of you is goin' to die." He thumps his chest. "Takes a con to know a con. I'll be the only one walkin' away from this gig."

The saint and the sinner stared at each other, an angry tension flooding the chamber.

"What are those?" The starlet's breathy voice interrupted the argument. She pointed toward the plazglass windows and I took another look. And then I saw what I'd missed before. Derelict ships, cold and dark as tombstones, orbited the planet like swarms of minnows. All different vintages and designs, proof of the Seekers who came before but never returned to tell the tale.

Brag said, "Dead ships, thousands of them."

"All the Seekers who never returned."

Brag scowled. "We're dead meat." But then his bravado returned. "You're all gonna die!"

A cold dread settled in my stomach, wondering if I taken a one-way trip to hell.

#

The ship's hallways all looked the same. I felt like a rat scuttling around a tin-can maze. But then I turned a corner and met a lovely surprise. Shirah Highlem never failed to take my breath away, every fisherman's wet dream. She flashed a suggestive smile and leaned against the wall to block the passage, her silk robe showing her curves to best advantage. "Hello, sugar. What's on your mind?"

I wanted to believe her offer, but survival seemed more important. "Do you think Brag's right? Do you think we're all going to die?"

Surprise flickered across her face. "Sooner or later time claims us all." She smiled and leaned toward me. "What do you think, sugar?"

"I'd rather bet on life."

Her smile dazzled. "An optimist and a gentleman...I like that in my men."

"*Your* men?"

Shirah leaned close, seduction in her gaze. "Since you believe in life, why waste a tarmin?"

I started to answer, but she smothered my mouth with a kiss. A jolt ran through me, like jump-starting an engine. The woman was pure ballistic rocket fuel. And the way she grabbed me, I could tell she needed it as much as I did. Her mouth was hungry on mine, her smell intoxicating. My hands touched curves I'd only dreamt of in my wildest fantasies. I pressed her up against the metal bulkhead. A deep hunger claimed us both. We went at it like two people who hadn't been laid in nine hundred years.

#

An old Earth tradition says that condemned prisoners get a last meal, so I guess it was only fitting that we all met in the galley for supper. Brag arrived before me, sitting at the center table, a handful of food tubes in front of him. I ignored his glare and punched my choices into the synthesizer. Despite my magnetic collision with Shirah, I still couldn't purge the derelict ships from my mind. Sex and the threat of death both made me ravenous. Maybe that's why I ordered so many tubes, indulging in a feast of flavors.

Brag sneered, "A condemned man's last meal?"

"I'm hungry."

"So am I, but not for food."

I ignored his leer and began sampling the tubes, alternating between chocolate and butterscotch.

"I'd rather be doing the blonde. That woman is a star gone supernova. In the joint, cons *killed* just for a hologram of her." Lacing his shovel-sized hands behind his head, he leaned back in the chair. "If the warden had mentioned Shirah Highlem with the Seeker Ship the whole damn prison planet would have volunteered! Hell, there would have been a friggin' riot!"

I glared at the big con but kept my thoughts to myself.

"What's a matter fish-er-man, don't you like porn stars?"

"Shirah's a stunner, in more ways than one."

Brag squinted. "Yeah, well I claimed her first, fish-er-man. A porn star in deep space, every con's wildest dream."

"She's more than that."

"What?"

"I remember holograms of her when I was just a kid getting my first shine. She's an icon, a sexual goddess."

"I could do an icon."

"Maybe you should ask her first."

Brag glared. "You're just sour 'cause you can't compete." He flexed his muscles, a ripple of bulges beneath his Seeker's robe. "Face it fish-er-man, with me on board you don't stand a chance."

The women chose that moment to enter. Shirah and Kayden walked together, a whisper of conversation between them. Shirah must have felt our stares because she made an entrance, swaying as she walked, flashing a sultry smile. "We decided to join you."

Brag nudged the chair next to him. "Sit by me, jailbait."

Shirah gave him a simmering smile. I look away, suddenly interested in my food tubes. The women made their choices and then joined us at the table. Shirah made a show of flouncing her long blond hair behind her back. I stared at her, remembering its silky feel beneath my fingers. Shirah must have felt my gaze. "Well, now that we're here, we might as well get to know each other." Her sea-blue gaze settled on me. "What's your story, sugar?"

Heat rushed through me, as if we were back in the hallway. I struggled to frame a reply, but then her gaze moved on and I sagged back in my chair. Understanding finally dawned. The starlet had to be psionic or perhaps empathic, it would explain her magnetic allure. Humanoids came in all shapes and sizes, some of them with hidden talents. I sat back, watching as her gaze snared another male, the lucky convict.

Hooked on her sea-blue gaze, Brag answered like a fish on a line. "So you want to know about the con?" His voice flushed with bravado. "High grav planets make for tough men. We Chilliods follow the

Intellect, not some fake god. So when our system's number came up, the ruling council looked to the penitentiary on Arthid-5 for a candidate." Brag grinned like a hungry eel. "Since I was already condemned for life, I volunteered for the gig." He leaned back in the chair. "And now look at me, sittin' here with Shirah friggin' Highlem, while the ruling council and everyone I left behind is long since dead, food for friggin' slime-worms."

"So you came as a sacrifice instead of a penitent?"

Brag turned his gaze to the monk, an ugly sneer on his face. "Don't shove your religious crap on me, sister."

The monk bristled but I intervened, trying to smooth the waters. "Why do the shamlin monks make the pilgrimage? What do you hope to find?"

Kayden nodded. "Ours is a poor order, yet we hoard our credits, always purchasing a berth on each Seeker-ship."

"You *purchased* a berth?" I struggled to keep the shock from my face, wishing her order had bought the Vernian berth. "But what do you hope to find?"

She studied me with large luminous eyes, like twin pools of deep violet absorbing the light, drinking in the sight of me as if she measured my very soul.

"No, I really want to know." And I really did. I was desperate to understand this planet, desperate to find a way to survive.

An odd look crossed her face, "Survival is such a small goal. The gods expect far more of you." Shock must have shown from my face, perhaps the monk was a mind reader, but she answered my question anyway. "Each shamlin Seeker carries a single question for the order. I've come to look upon the face of the BuddhaChrist and learn the why of life."

"The *why* of life!" Brag snorted, spraying syntha-food across the table. "What a load of crap!"

I glared at the con. "Let her talk."

Brag sneered, "So the fish-er-man's grown a pair."

Shirah interrupted, her voice breathy, "We'll I can tell you why *I'm* here." She crossed her legs, revealing a flash of shapely white thigh. "Immortality."

"*What?*"

Shirah met my wide-eyed gaze. "That's right, sugar, immortality."

"But why?"

Shirah tossed her long blonde hair, striking a classic porn star pose. "I made all the galactic newscasts when I volunteered. The headlines were priceless, *The Siren Sent to Seduce God!*" She preened. "Those newscasts will replay every time a Seeker Ship launches for the Big Dark." She gave a seductive laugh. "So you see, sugar, I've already got my immortality."

Brag barked a rude laugh. I could only stare. Her logic set a new galactic standard for dumb blondes.

Metallic footsteps approached the galley. We all tensed, our stare riveted on the doorway, but it was only Sil-88.

Brag growled. "Just the friggin' dwarf."

Sil-88 waddled to the table and climbed onto the chair. I'd half forgotten about the dwarf. Darting a stare through his visor, I hoped for a glimpse of his face, but saw nothing but orange gas.

Brag sneered. "Find any demons in the dark?" He made a rude gesture toward the dwarf. "The midget is space-touched. I found him chasing monsters in the lower levels."

Sil-88's mechanical voice replied with the stilted speech of a translator. "Not...space...fever. Prescience. Something...hides. Something...watches."

Brag snorted, "Prescience my ass. Or maybe that's why you packed your own spacesuit. If this tub blows, you'll be the only one to survive."

Brag's banter snared my attention. "Only one spacesuit? What are you talking about?"

"When they converted this tub to a Seeker Ship, they stripped out all the friggin' spacesuits. The shipyard probably sold them for salvage. Nice to know the Intellect spared no expense. A friggin' luxury cruise."

"Or a one-way trip to hell."

Brag nodded, "Now you're gettin' the holograph."

An image of the planet filled my mind. "All those derelict ships should have spacesuits."

"And weapons. All we need is a shuttle."

For once, Brag and I were on the same datascreen. "And a pilot."

Brag grinned. "I jacked more ships than you can count, fish-er-man. How do you think I earned the collar?"

I didn't want to know, but I liked the idea of searching the derelicts. We needed answers, even if it meant working with a convicted killer.

#

Flashlight beams pierced the gloom. Equipment and exposed ducting covered the metal walls, casting eerie shadows. Brag led the way, a flashlight held in one hand, a wrench in the other.

Shirah flinched from a grimy wall. "I don't like this place. It's filthy. And why is it so dark down here?"

I took her arm, guiding her past a greasy puddle. "The ship is designed to conserve power on the unused decks."

"Well just tell the computer to on turn the lights."

"Can't," Brag growled from the front, "this level is designated as non-essential and we can't override the friggin' designation."

Non-essential, I didn't like the sound of that. "Since when is access to spacesuits non-essential?"

Brag flashed me a knowing look.

A metallic clatter came from a side passage.

Shirah stifled a scream.

Sil-88 said, "Not...alone."

Brag hefted his wrench, easing toward the doorway. I dropped to a crouch, standing in front of the women, wishing I had a weapon. Brag peered inside and then stepped back.

A small robot scuttled from the doorway. It started towards us, and then reversed course, racing down the far passage.

"A friggin' mechbot." Brag lowered his wrench. "This ship is lousy with friggin' bots."

Sil-88 said, "Not...alone."

Brag growled, "You're friggin' space-touched."

We continued down the corridor, emerging into a larger shuttle bay. Lights winked on the walls near the airlocks. Brag checked the command panels while the rest of us searched the room. Lockers lined the walls, designed to hold spacesuits, but all the lockers were empty. Sil-88 picked up a discarded helmet and stared at it, the rest of us reflected in the cracked visor.

Brag roved from one panel to another, muttering a curse. "By the Almighty Intellect, we're friggin' marooned here."

My heartbeat quickened. "What do you mean?"

"They left us one shuttle and it's got a burnt engine."

"Are you sure?"

"Can you fish, fish-er-man?"

Shirah said, "What are we supposed to do?"

Brag scowled. "Maybe we're supposed to die."

Kaylen said, "No, there must be a way down to the planet. God will provide."

"Then get your god to fix the friggin' shuttle."

A klaxon blared. The ship's voice echoed through the bay. "Docking complete. Prepare for arrival at docking bay four."

An electric shock ran through me. I looked at the others and saw my reaction mirrored on their faces. "Visitors? But there's not supposed to be anyone here?"

Brag answered. "All those derelict ships! Maybe they're not abandoned after all."

I grinned, liking the idea of survivors. "Someone's come knocking! We better answer the door."

Propelled by the blaring klaxon, we raced down the corridor to the lift. Even Brag remained silent, a clouded look on his gruff face. The lift doors opened and we stumbled into the bright lights of the cavernous bay. The ship's voice blared overhead. "Three tarmins till boarding." Red lights flashed around a small docking port. We gathered in front like a reception committee, or a rogue's gallery of gawkers. I couldn't help wondering what the others expected. For myself, I hoped for a survivor, proof a Seeker could outlive a trip to the Pinprick.

Kaylen said, "I wonder how many survived."

"Or what," my imagination ran wild, "they say Dark Space changes a man."

Brag gripped his wrench, prepared for the worst.

The ship's voice said, "Atmospheric equalization complete."

The klaxon fell silent. Flashing lights around the airlock changed from red to green. The doors slowly slid open. Compressed air whooshed out bearing the faint scent of metal and grease. A silhouette appeared in the doorway, tall and dressed in a long dark robe, two arms, two legs, one head; the shape suggested a humanoid. He walked toward us and the details became clear.

"*An android!*" It was the last thing I expected. Syntheskin covered its hands and neck and a luxurious mane of brown hair sprouted from its head, but its faceplate had been removed, revealing the metal structure beneath. Tiny lights winked within the depths of the braincase, a pair of realistic glass eyes staring out of the metal face. The effect was eerie, like meeting a creature half-humanoid and half-machine.

"Clothes, it's wearing clothes."

Brag was right. Robots never wore clothes, yet this one dressed in a long black robe embroidered with strange white runes running down the front and along the hem. And it wore the robe well, conveying a sense of dignity, as if it had always been clothed.

The android approached. Its voice proved rich and melodic, so unlike the milky monotones programmed into robots. "I bring you greetings. My name is Varjis and I welcome you to the God Planet."

The planet's name chilled me to the core, not a destination meant for humanoids, but Brag just scoffed. "The *God* Planet, more like the butt end of the universe."

Vivid green eyes fastened on Brag, eyes that seemed too real for an android. "Ah, another convict."

"*Another* convict?" Brag leaned forward, his big fists opening and closing, as if he meant to strangle the android.

"Yes, the last convict arrived one-hundred-and-eighty-three Standard years ago. But I suspect you are more interested with the future than the past."

The question bubbled out of me "*Who* are you? And what are you doing here?"

The android's piercing green gaze turned my way. "You must be Josh Brennerman, the fisherman from Verne-4."

My mouth gaped open like a fish out of water. "How do you know?"

"Computers talk." For a millisecond, I thought I saw the glint of humor in its artificial eyes, but that could not be.

"And as to who I am," it spread his arms wide in a very humanoid gesture of openness, "my name is Varjis and you might say I am the concierge for the planet below."

"The con what?" The word made no sense, perhaps something from a dead language.

"A type of doorkeeper."

"So God has a doorkeeper?" Everything about this trip seemed to get weirder by the nanosecond.

"I bid you welcome." Kayden stepped forward, her hands flashing through a series of symbols and signs.

The android responded in kind, its syntheskin hands sketching symbols in the air. I watched the two of them, realizing I didn't like being left out of the conversation. "There's five of us here."

The words came out ruder than I intended, but the hand conversation crashed to a stop and the android nodded toward me.

"Yes, I have much to say to all of you. Perhaps we could adjourn to the altar chamber?"

Brag gaped, "The what?"

I had a bad feeling about this.

"So you haven't found it yet. Come, let me show you." The android led us to the far side of the cargo bay, to a small lift hidden by shadows. The lift doors opened and the android gestured us inside.

Brag said, "How do you know this ship?"

The android replied, "Ship's talk."

I couldn't help staring at our visitor. Its skin and hair looked so real, yet its face was pure machine. And the robes made it worse, as if it dared to imitate a humanoid. Such a freakish combination, little wonder the Intellect had outlawed androids centuries ago.

The lift doors opened and I had something else to stare it. We stood on the threshold of a circular chamber, a strange mixture of mechanical and primitive. Metal pipes and wrist-thick cables crisscrossed the walls, while the center was dominated by a massive block of rough-cut granite. So this was the altar stone. The others left the lift, but I stood frozen, staring at the rough-cut stone. So cold and primitive, it chilled my blood to ice. The lift doors began to close and I slithered between them, not wanting to be left behind. My gaze snapped back to the stone, like prey watching a predator. A shiver raced down my back, the stone was something ancient and primal, something that did not belong on a starship. I stayed close to the others. Kaylen made a flutter of hand signs, a silent prayer in motion.

Brag prowled toward the stone, stopping to read aloud the names etched on the dais. "Yahweh, Adonai, Shiva..." He looked at Varjis in disgust, "What is this, a god-fest?"

"The altar is the gateway to the planet."

Brag growled, "Well, *doorman*, what's waiting for us down there?"

"Whatever you bring."

"I'm done with riddles, tell us something useful or I'll rip your friggin' eyes out of their metal sockets."

I stared at Brag; half expecting the prison collar to blow his head off, but then I realized the collar's programming against violence might not cover androids.

Varjis seemed oblivious to the threat. "You will each go alone to the planet below but you will have a chance to prepare. A storage room has been outfitted to meet your needs."

"Clothes?" The question blurted out of me, I was sick of the flimsy Seeker's robe.

"Yes."

"Weapons?" Leave it to the convict to ask about weapons.

"Yes, weapons from every era, from swords and battleaxes to lazguns and blasters. And there are also amulets and sacred writings from every major religious sect, should you feel the need."

"I'd like to see those writings." Kaylen had an eager look on her face. "So much was lost when the Intellect assumed power."

The android bowed toward the monk. "You are welcome to read them when the turn is yours."

"So...we...take...turns?"

The android nodded to the dwarf. "Yes, each alone, in his own time."

Brag grinned. "One by one? I thought scriptures were always two by two?" He threw a leer at Shirah. "Send me with the blond."

The android said, "Each alone."

Sil-88 said, "Safer...on...the...planet."

The android gave the dwarf a piercing look. "Time to decide the order." Varjis reached within the pocket of its robes and removed a small cloth bag. "Perhaps you would like to choose first?" The android extended the bag, holding it open. Sil-88 reached inside, but whatever he removed remained clenched in his gloved fist.

Varjis turned toward me. "Sir?"

I stared at the small black bag, half expecting it to bite my hand, but I reached inside anyway. Four smooth pebbles waited at the bottom. Four instead of seven, so the android knew only the five of us survived cryostasis. It seemed to know an awful lot. I made my choice and removed my hand. A small black pebble nestled in my palm, a single number inscribed on it, the number five. So I was last. I didn't know whether to feel relief or dread. Sometimes waiting is the hardest part.

The others made their choice and we learned the order. Brag would go first, then Shirah, then Kayden, then Sil-88, and lastly, myself.

"So I'm first?" Brag scowled, an odd squinty look on his face. "And I get my choice of weapons?"

"As many as you can carry."

"They told me this collar would come off." Brag made a rude gesture toward the metal collar.

Varjis nodded. "Yes, the collar will be removed before you descend to the planet."

I tensed, not liking the sound of that.

Brag grinned like a slip-shark about to eat a mer-tuna. "What are we waiting for?"

"You wish to go now?"

"Just show me the weapons, metal-face."

The android bowed. "As you wish." Varjis crossed the chamber to a metal door. The android inserted something into the wall and the door slid open. "Only the first Seeker." The rest of us craned our necks for a peep inside. Brag strode through the doorway, an eager look on his face. Varjis followed, the metal door closing behind.

A hush settled over the chamber.

The other three stood huddled near the door like lost ducklings, but I walked to the far side of the chamber. "I'd move away from the door if I were you."

Shirah said, "Why?"

"When the collar comes off, we'll have a murdering maniac on our hands...and he'll be armed."

The women took my advice and joined me on the far side of the chamber. Nothing to do but wait, my stare was drawn to the altar, a remnant from old Earth carted clear across the universe to the darkest corner of the cosmos, as if the stone held some kind of magic, or divine power. Perhaps the stone's true worth lay in its image, a primitive symbol lodged deep in the psyche of the earliest humanoids, a symbol of sacrifice and divine intervention. I shivered; reminding myself it was just a stone, an inert lump of granite, nothing but a chunk of rock from an ancient planet.

The far door opened and Brag emerged looking like a one-man army. Dressed in gray camouflage fatigues, he carried massive blaster bazookas in each hand, a pair of holstered lazguns strapped to his hips, belts of ammo crisscrossing his chest, the hilt of a samurai sword looming over his right shoulder. Grinning like a starving stun-shark, he prowled into the chamber, a threat in his dark gaze, *but he still wore the collar.*

"By the Intellect, this is what I'm talkin' about." He hefted the guns aloft. "Enough firepower to take out a whole penal planet." His voice turned nasty. "So while you *Seeker-sheep* are up here cowerin' on the ship, I'll be down below, wreckin' some major havoc." His gaze turned to Varjis. "Time to take the collar off."

I sidled backwards, trying to blend into the shadows.

"First you must mount the altar stone."

Brag's gaze narrowed, but then he grinned, an ugly predatory smile. "Have it your way, metal-face." He leaped onto the altar stone. Standing with his feet spread wide, his enormous hands gripping the blast bazookas, he gazed down at us like a laz-shark straining against the bars of a cage. "It's time, android."

The android pointed a black metal rod at Brag. At first, nothing happened, but then the red light winking on the collar turned from red to green. Something clicked, and the collar fell off. *It fell off!*

Brag tilted his head back and laughed. He raised the blast bazookas, a lethal threat. "Change of command, people! I say we turn this ship around and head for the nearest colony, the Intellect be damned. Any objections? Tell it to the blasters, 'cause these babies put me in charge."

Truth be told, I liked the idea of turning the ship around, but not with a mass murderer at the helm.

Varjis stepped forward, his voice smooth and unruffled. "Sir, I need to point out that if you use those blasters inside the ship, you'll not have a ship to turn around."

"True." Brag's face twisted into a sneer. "Then I'll just have to use the lazguns." He let the blasters dangle from their shoulder straps and reached for the lazgun holstered at his hip. Before he could draw the gun, the altar stone began to glow like a star going supernova.

Brag yelled, "What the...?"

I turned away, shielding my eyes.

A rushing sound enveloped the chamber, like the blow of a full-force hurricane, yet there was no wind.

Confused, I hugged the wall, but then the silence returned, as startling as a thunderclap.

I opened my eyes and the blinding light was gone. I dared to look at the altar. Brag had disappeared. *He was gone!* "By the Intellect, what happened? Where'd he go?"

"To the surface below." Varjis stared at me, startling green eyes set in a metal face.

Sil-88 stepped forward. "Teleportation? Or...power...of...God?"

The android nodded. "Yours to decide."

"But teleportation's not possible, a myth of science fiction." I wasn't a tech-brain but I knew that much.

For a millisecond, I thought I saw a ghost of a smile on the android's face. "The universe is full of possibilities undreamt. You fish the seas. Are the deepest places not full of the strangest mysteries?"

I stared at the android, trying to make sense of the answer.

"Can...the...stone...be...studied?"

"As you wish." The android gestured toward the altar and Sil-88 stepped onto the dais. I half expected to see another flash of blinding light, but nothing happened.

Shirah sidled toward the android. "What happens now, sugar?"

"Now we wait."

My gaze snapped to the android. "For how long?"

"As long as it takes."

"Well, I'm not waiting here." I didn't like being so close to the altar. "Call me if anything happens." I backed away from the granite block and entered the lift. The doors shut and I made my escape, stabbing the button for the observation deck. The lift began to move and I sagged against the cool metal wall, struggling to make sense of what I'd just seen. Was it teleportation or the power of God? Both seemed impossible.

The lift doors opened and I found myself alone in the observation deck. I took a chair and stared up through the plazglass windows, searching the cloud-shrouded planet for any sign of life. I'm not sure what I expected to see, maybe the bright glare of blasters exploding beneath the clouds like a mini-armageddon, but I saw nothing different, no proof that Brag was really there. Questions pounded against my mind but I had no answers. The dark side of the universe kept its secrets safe.

The sound of a gong shimmered through the chamber followed by the ship's voice. "A Seeker returns."

I sat bolt upright, *so soon*, and ran for the lift.

The doors opened onto the altar chamber. I burst from the lift but then staggered to a stop. Blood spattered the chamber, sprayed across the walls and floor. A severed foot lay just in front of me, blood pouring from the boot. Nearby a hand still clutched a mangled blaster. Bits of Brag were everywhere, as if he'd been torn limb from limb. Acid filled my mouth and I struggled not to gag. "In the name of the Intellect, what happened?"

The others stood huddled on the far side of the chamber, their faces pale-white. Shirah fainted and the android caught her, but it was

Sil-88 who answered my question. "Altar...blazed...bright." He gestured to the gore. "Brag...returned...broken."

"*Broken!*" The dwarf's calm explanation pushed me close to insanity. "He's bloody well pulled to pieces!" I pointed at the carnage, at the melted blaster. "He went to the planet armed to the teeth, yet someone did this to him! And you want us to go down there!"

Kayden stepped forward. "It is fitting." Her face was dead-fish white but her voice held a calm resolve, pulling me back to sanity. "Those who live by war, die by war."

I was desperate enough to grasp any float in a raging ocean. "So you're saying if we don't take guns to the planet, we'll survive?"

"It is the lesson. And it fits with scripture."

Too much religion, too many things I did not know. "I think Brag had the right idea. Turn the ship around and head for home."

Kayden shook her head, a wistful smile on her face. "I will not return without first visiting the planet."

Sil-88 echoed the monk. "Take...turns."

"Insane. You're both insane." I fled to the lift, relieved when the doors closed on the carnage. Gulping deep breaths of stale ship air, I sought to purge Brag's stench from my lungs, while trying to block his bloody death from my mind. I hadn't signed up for this. I didn't care about religion or solving the mystery of the Big Dark. The others could risk their lives on the planet, but when it was my turn, I knew what choice I'd make.

#

Shirah's turn was next and she actually seemed eager to go. The rest of us waited in the altar chamber, a kind of morbid send-off committee. At least the blood and guts were gone, wiped clean from the altar stone as if it had never happened. An antiseptic smell hung in the air. I wondered if one of the medbots had been reprogrammed to clean the gore. I couldn't imagine Varjis picking pieces of Brag out of the metal ductwork.

The storage room door whooshed open and Shirah emerged like a star onto a stage.

One glimpse sucked all the breath from my body. The woman was a goddess. Draped in a strapless evening gown of shimmering gold, she seemed to glide across the chamber like a fantasy fulfilled. I knew I was gawking but I couldn't help it. "Stunning." The word gushed out of me, making me feel a fool, but she rescued me with a smile.

Arching one delicate eyebrow, she dropped her voice to a breathy whisper. "Stunning enough for a God?" Her gloved hands ran down her body, caressing every curve like a slow sensual dance.

I stared mesmerized, feeling as if I was caught in a holographic trance. But then the dream got even better. She came toward me. Laying a gloved hand on my cheek, she leaned close and whispered, "*Remember me*," and then she kissed me on the lips. So gentle and achingly chaste, yet her kiss rocked me to the core. One kiss and I fell all over again.

"I have a date with immortality." Smiling, she turned and walked away, swaying toward the altar stone.

A part of me wanted to leap forward and sweep her off her feet and carry her away, but I just stood there staring, too stunned to move, as if she'd cast a holding spell on me.

Shirah turned her sea-blue gaze toward the android. "I'm ready, sugar."

Varjis bowed. "You need only mount the altar stone and the future will be yours."

But Shirah was no ordinary starlet; she was an icon of beauty. She draped herself across the altar like a siren beckoning a god. The image seared into my brain.

Light flared, too bright to watch, and then she was gone.

#

I resolved to wait, to keep a kind of vigil, hoping she'd come back to me whole and unharmed. The others left the chamber, but I sat cross-legged on the metal floor, my back against the wall, keeping watch on the altar stone. The memory of her kiss burned through me, evoking thoughts of our tryst in the hallway. My dreams ran wild, better than anything from a holographic headset.

My right leg cramped and I grew hungry, but I ignored both, all the while I wondering at her fate.

The sound of a gong shivered through the chamber but I did not need the warning. My heart thundered as silver light hovered above the altar stone. And then she was there, sitting on the altar, a stunning vision in shimmering gold.

I rushed toward her. "Are you alright?"

She looked up, a dazed expression on her face. "I'm fine, sugar." Her voice was as smooth as warm honey. "Help me up."

I took her arm and helped her stand, but then she swayed as if she might faint. I scooped her into my arms, holding her close, reveling in her curves. "Are you alright?"

She gazed up at me, close enough to kiss. "It was more than I expected."

"What was more?"

"Everything."

Her answer made no sense, but it did not matter. I held her close, feeling protective, and chivalrous and infinitely male.

But then she began to change. Small changes at first, the finest wrinkles deepened around her eyes and mouth, spreading across her face like cracked glass. And then her long blond hair began to tarnish, changing from blond to silver to dull white.

"*No!*" I clutched her tight but it made no difference. Her flesh seemed to melt from her bones. In mere moments she changed from a voluptuous siren to a shriveled hag.

The lift doors opened and the others rushed in.

"Help me! *Help her!*"

A sigh whispered out of her and then her face began to crumble! Like an ancient relic suddenly exposed to air, *she crumbled to dust!* Nothing left but her golden dress.

Someone started screaming. My mind fled, locked in a nightmare of horror.

#

"Are you feeling better?" Kayden bent over me, her violet eyes luminous in the dim light. "Please wake, I don't want to leave without saying goodbye."

Goodbye, the word somehow pierced the fog of my mind. I struggled to understand, like swimming though a murky ocean. My eyes slowly focused. I lay on a pod bed, a blanket tucked beneath my chin. "What's happening?"

"It's my turn to go."

"Your turn?" And then my mind returned like a tidal wave. Bludgeoned by the memory of Shirah's face crumbling to dust, I grabbed Kayden's wrist, my fingers digging into her flesh. "Is it true? Did it really happen?"

"Yes, it happened." Her violet gaze seemed to reach inside of me, easing the horror within.

I clung to her wrist, the breath hissing out of me. "Don't go. You don't have to do this."

"But I wish to go, to discover the truth."

"What truth? Brag came back in pieces and Shirah..." I couldn't say the words; the image was too horrible, too raw. "Whatever is down on that planet is evil. It's better left alone."

"No, you don't understand."

Anger sparked through me. "Then enlighten me, isn't that what monks do?"

"You are too angry to hear the truth."

"Try me."

Our stares locked in a stalemate, but then she slowly nodded. "They both received what they took with them."

Rage threatened to swamp me, but I held it at bay, determined to understand. "More religious bullshit. Brag I can understand. Brag makes sense. He attacked whatever he found down there on the planet and it tore him to pieces. Brag got what he deserved, but not Shirah." Anger blistered through me. "Shirah was pure beauty. She didn't deserve that kind of death. Whatever did that to her is evil."

"Shirah was dying before she ever set foot on this ship."

"What?"

Kayden nodded, her face solemn. "She had Crone's Disease, her RNA was unraveling from too many gene splicings. Endless beauty has its price."

I'd heard of Crone's Disease, an affliction of the ultra wealthy. "And there's no cure?"

"None."

"How do you know this?"

"Shirah told me."

"Why you?"

"Women talk." She gave me a sad smile. "So you see, she paid the price of her own vanity. Time finally caught her."

I looked away, a sour taste in my mouth.

"But why are you here?"

"Me?" The question snapped my gaze back to her violet eyes.

"You puzzle me." She gave me an odd look. "Your soul is not old, but it is righteous."

"It has nothing to do with my soul, it was bad luck, a curse of sorts."

"What do you mean?"

"We Vernians are a simple fisher folk. We have our share of superstitions and sea lore but we're not real religious. So when the Intellect called for a Vernian to join the Seeker ship, no one volunteered." I shrugged trying to make light of my ill fortune. "With no volunteer, they held a lottery of all adults. A mandatory lottery." My voice turned bitter. "So you see, I had even less choice than Brag."

"Chosen by the hand of God; you were meant to be here." Her voice held such conviction I almost believed her.

"But I don't understand why you're here." I struggled to remember what I'd heard about the shamlin order. "Don't you believe in life after death, that the worthy will ascend to become one with the BuddhaChrist? So why the rush? Won't you get all the answers when you die?"

Her violet eyes gleamed with delight. "So you're a philosopher as well as a fisherman."

"No, I'm just confused. I mean if you're going to get the answers when you die, why purchase passage on a Seeker ship?"

"Because what you learn in the afterlife cannot be remembered when you are reborn."

I shook my head. "Religion is like seaweed, it tangles the mind."

Kaylen gently took my face between her hands. "I hope to gain the answers in *this* lifetime. Then, if I am reborn as a Buddha, I will retain full knowledge of my past lives, including what I learn on the planet below. As a Buddha, I can share the answers with others and then all of humanoid-kind will be that much closer to enlightenment."

Her logic made my head spin. "Reincarnation, it's such a circular argument."

"Don't knock it till you've tried it."

I gasped in surprise. "Is that a joke?"

She gave me a shy smile. "Humor is permitted."

I was beginning to like Kayden, but then I remembered what happened to Shirah. "Don't go." My words fell like a stone between us.

Her violet eyes seemed to drink in the light. "I must go. Knowledge speeds enlightenment." She took my hand, such a tender touch. "When it is your turn, Josh Brennerman, will you remember something for me?"

I couldn't tell her I never intended to go, so I answered with a question. "What?"

"If you don't believe, at least have conviction."

I had to smile. "Conviction will get me past the secret holy handshake?"

"For a righteous soul it just might be enough." And then she smiled, her violet eyes luminous in the dim light. "Will you come and see me off?"

"What, now?" And then I noticed she was dressed in robes of midnight blue instead of Seeker white.

"Yes, the robes of my order." She tugged on my hand. "Come, the others are waiting."

I pushed back the covers, relieved to find I wasn't naked, although the flimsy Seeker's robe wasn't much better. My legs felt rubbery, making me wonder what kind of drugs they'd pumped into me, but I refused to show weakness. Keeping one hand on the wall, I followed her to the lift.

The lift doors opened and I stared at the altar stone. Maybe it was the drugs still lingering in my system, but the hunk of granite looked like a brooding beast waiting to devour me. I shivered, keeping my back to the wall.

The others were already waiting. We made a pathetic little group, a gas-breathing dwarf, a faceless android, and a fisherman cast far from the sea. I stood with the others, watching as Kayden approached the stone. So slender and elegant in her dark robes, she bowed toward the altar, before climbing on top. Like a classic statue of Buddha, she sat cross-legged atop the granite, a serene smile on her face, her long robes surrounding her like a puddle of midnight blue. "I am ready." She raised her right hand like a benediction. "May you find wisdom in your Seeking."

The light flared and she was gone.

#

The ship felt empty, like a tomb. Loneliness crashed against me in waves, making me feel like a sailor cast upon a storm-wrecked shore. I craved companionship, a woman's voice, a sympathetic smile, a soft touch, but I was locked in the ship with an android and a space-suited dwarf, as if I was the last humanoid left alive in all the universe.

I hid in my sleeping pod, sampling the ship's library of movies and vidcasts, but somehow the images only made it worse, a reminder of all that was lost. Restless, I made my way back to the observation deck, surprised to find the android there. Music boomed through the deck, something old and classical and heart-pounding. Varjis stood along one wall, its right index finger bent back, a metal probe inserted in the wall jack, probably communing with the ship's computer, or maybe it was the android's version of cyber sex. I started to retreat, but it turned my way, its green eyes unnaturally bright. "Can I be of service?"

"No...yes." I changed my mind, perhaps an android's company was better than nothing.

The android said, "Dim music." The computer obeyed, softening the music to a faint undercurrent.

I gestured toward the android, his finger still stuck in the console. "What are you doing? An android's version of cybersex? And what's with the music?"

"I'm reviewing the ship's library, catching up on events in the universe. Technology changes but so much else stays the same."

"Everything's out of date, nine hundred years old."

"It's new to me."

"And the music?"

"Don Giovanni, from an ancient Earth composer named Mozart."

I took a seat on one of the leather chairs. "I didn't figure an android to listen to music."

"Mozart is sublime, like listening to liquid numbers. Do you know the story behind this piece?"

I shrugged. "I'm a fisherman."

"Don Giovanni is a masterwork, as you live so shall you die. Fitting music for the God Planet."

I stared at the android. "How long have you been here?"

"Since the first Seeker ship."

"The *first*?" I could not imagine being marooned for so long. "And you're still functioning?"

"I was programmed to update as new technologies arrive. I am the sum of many parts."

"So is your first ship still out there? Circling the planet?" I stated up at the cloud-shrouded snowball, at the thousands of ships orbiting like lost minnows.

"Its power source died long ago. I watched it blaze like a star as it fell into the planet."

"Must be lonely."

"I am not programmed for loneliness."

"Lucky you." I stared at his alien face, metal and wire and lights set in a syntheskin body that could pass for humanoid. "Why are you here?"

"To serve as a concierge for the planet below."

"But when you first came here, you must have been programmed for some other purpose?"

"My purpose has evolved."

An *evolving* android, there was something scary about the thought, yet if Varjis truly was a member of the first Seeker ship then he should be a treasure trove of information. "So you've been to the planet?"

"No."

"*Never*? Not curious?"

"Curiosity has nothing to do with it. The altar stones only work for living beings."

"But you've watched the other Seekers come and go? Did any survive?" I leaned forward, keen for the answer.

"Always a few."

Hope rushed through me. I clung to the answer like a drowning man. "Then why all the derelict ships? Why has no Seeker ever returned to the home systems?"

"That is the question. The first ships had technical difficulties. Later ships left on return headings, but according to the *Psalm Singer's* logs, none ever completed the journey."

"None?"

A steady gaze was his only reply.

"Why?"

"The data is insufficient."

Computers could be so frustrating. I sagged back into the leather armchair, trying to frame a different question. "If you were on the first ship, then you know how this all got started?" I gestured to the planet looming overhead. "Why did the first Seekers come here?"

"Because of the dreams."

"Dreams?" History was never one of my strengths. "What do you mean, dreams?"

"Dreams, mass hysteria, visions, humanoids from every system felt compelled to visit the lone star set in Dark Space. Like a siren's song the dreams lodged in the humanoid psyche. Some expected to find great wealth, or eternal youth, but for most, it became a pilgrimage of sorts, a calling from god."

"Religion."

Varjis nodded. "The dreams sparked a religious revival. A fever of devotion swept across the universe. Trillions flocked to the great religions, giving the churches, temples and monasteries renewed power. So the first ship was sent to follow a dream. And ever since, religious groups have led the call for the Seeker ships."

"But if they never get an answer, why do they keep coming?"

"Humanoids are rarely logical. Perhaps the hope of an answer is sufficient."

I slumped back down into the plush leather. Something about the history did not quite make sense, but I pushed the thought aside, focusing on the hope that I might survive this trip. "So what do you..." My words were cut short by the sound of a gong.

The ship's voice said, "A Seeker returns."

I leaped from the chair and ran for the lift. If anyone could survive the planet, it had to be Kayden. I held my breath as the lift doors open on the altar chamber. Like a vision, she was there, sitting cross-legged on the stone. At first I thought nothing had changed, but then I got a good look at her. Her face was radiant, as if she glowed from within. I staggered to a stop. "You learned the answer?"

Her violet gaze slowly focused on me, as if returning from a far away place. "Yes."

My heart thundered. "Can you tell me?"

Her voice dropped to a soft whisper. "Give me time."

"Take all the time you need." I helped her from the altar stone. She leaned on me, as frail as a wisp, as if enlightenment had somehow made her less substantial. I scooped her into my arms and carried her to a sleeping pod, tucking her in with plenty of blankets to keep her warm. She fell instantly asleep, a contented look on her face. I don't know how I long I stood there, watching her breathe, making sure she didn't crumble to dust. Kayden slept peacefully, the sleep of the just. I longed to know what she'd learned on the planet, but for now it was enough to know she'd survived.

#

It took time for Kayden to recover, as if her mind still lingered on the planet, but I was patient, intent on coaxing her back to the mortal world. I sat on the floor by her pod bed, watching her sleep, pestering her to eat, waiting for a chance to ask my questions.

Sil-88 appeared in the doorway. "She...still...sleeps."

I kept forgetting about the dwarf.

"Has...she...talked...about...the...planet?"

I waved the dwarf outside the sleeping pod, not wanting to wake Kayden. "She hasn't said anything yet but her face is radiant."

"When...your...turn...comes...don't...hesitate."

"I'm not going anywhere."

"Safer...on...planet."

He started to turn away, but I grabbed his arm. "What do you know?"

"Not...know...only...sense."

"Sense what?" The dwarf was crazy with paranoia.

"Something...watches."

"Have you told Varjis?"

"Varjis...is...machine."

He turned away and I let him go.

The dwarf took his turn riding the altar stone, but his going did not really concern me. Kayden became my sole interest, my shining hope for survival, the answer to so many mysteries.

I stopped by the galley to pick up a selection of food tubes, chocolate and butterscotch for me and spicemellon and blueberry for Kayden. I felt strangely content, as if all was right in the universe, but then I saw a flash of movement ahead. I quickened my steps, wondering if Kayden needed my help. Turning a corner, I came face to face with a stranger. *A stranger!* A blond-haired male with a muscular body dressed in faded blue coveralls. Shock rippled through me. "Who are you?"

The stranger turned and fled, sprinting down the hallway.

Fear gripped my throat. Instead of following, I ran for Kayden's pod. The door stood open, just as I'd left it, but blood was everywhere. Kayden lay sprawled on the bed, a knife stabbed through her heart. I ran to her but she was already cold. *"Murder!"* The words came out as a strangled croak. I staggered into the hallway and slammed my fist against the emergency alert. A klaxon sounded through the ship, drowning out my screams. *"Murder! Murder in the ship!"*

#

Varjis appeared in the doorway.

"*Murder!* A stranger murdered Kayden!" I hugged her body close, as if I could bring her back to life. "I went to the galley, just a short trip for supper, and when I returned, I saw a stranger in the hallway. He fled when he saw me. I rushed back here and found this." I stared at the android, panic rising in my voice. "You believe me, don't you?" And then I noticed her blood staining my hands, my robe. "I didn't do it." I shook my head in denial. "I know it sounds crazy but it's true. I'd never hurt Kayden."

The android's face was inscrutable. "I believe you." Varjis reached for the control panel on the pod wall and inserted a probe into the computer jack. The ship's klaxon fell suddenly silent.

"You believe me?" My voice sounded loud in the silence.

"It is not unexpected."

"*Not unexpected!*" My heart skipped a beat. "What the hell do you mean? By the Intellect, what's going on here?"

"Exactly."

More riddles. I took a menacing step toward him, so tempted to beat some sense into that calm metallic face. "I need some answers. You better start making sense. Kayden is dead and there's a murderer onboard this ship."

"Could the stranger be an android?"

"An android? But they're illegal." And then I realized what I was talking to. "I mean, androids aren't built any more, not since the rebellion."

"I've seen evidence to the contrary." Varjis strode from the pod like an android on a mission.

"Where are you going?" I trailed after it, not wanting to be left alone.

"To the cargo hold."

"Why?"

"To learn if the murderer is an android or a humanoid."

"How will you know?"

"By checking the sarcophagi. I should have done it earlier. A humanoid could only survive the trip in cryostasis. If the three unopened sarcophagi contain dead Seekers, then we have the answer."

My mind struggled to understand. "So you're saying someone might have been woken before me? Someone hiding on this ship?"

"That is the best scenario."

"The best?" We entered the lift. "Why the best?"

"Because humanoids are easy to find, just follow the oxygen."

"And if it is an android?"

"Androids are hard to find and harder to kill."

"To *kill?*" The skin prickled at the back of my neck. "You've done this before?"

"Yes."

I didn't know whether to be relieved or afraid, but I suddenly looked at Varjis in a whole different light. "So you're not just a doorman?"

"No."

The lift doors opened and we stepped into the cargo hold.

#

Bio-readouts on three of the sarcophagi blinked bright red, indicating their Seekers had died from failed cryostasis. But bio-readouts could be programmed to lie, so Varjis ordered the medbots to open them. It should have been a simple request, but the liquid nitrogen had to be decanted and the interior brought to room temperature before the lids would open. Varjis supervised the medbots while I paced, waiting for an answer.

My skin prickled with unease. The cavernous bay felt suddenly sinister, so many places for a murderer to hide. I paced back and forth, feeling exposed. The Seeker's robe didn't help. Flimsy white silk stained with blood, I felt like a target marked for execution. I needed some decent clothing, a sturdy pair of pants and boots, and a weapon or two, a knife and a lazgun, and I needed to understand why a murderer was aboard this ship.

"This one is ready."

I felt like a tomb raider as the first sarcophagus eased open. A breath of cold mist swirled around the open lid, a lingering remnant of the nitrogen coolant. I waved it away and peered inside. A humanoid female lay within, long sapphire-blue hair and tufted ears, looking as peaceful as if she slept, but there was no pulse, no spark of life. "What killed her?"

Varjis answered. "Any number of things. Failed nanoprobes, or interior thermal cracking. Even the slightest power fluctuation is fatal. Cryostasis is still part art, part science."

I shivered, knowing it could have been me.

The second sarcophagus was much the same, the body of a three-horned Brazian lying peaceful in a deathly slumber. At least cryostasis didn't seem like a bad way to die, drifting away in a drug-soaked sleep. It might have been a better end for Shirah. I shuddered remembering how she'd crumbled to dust in my arms.

"The last one is ready."

I moved to stand beside Varjis as the medbots opened the last sarcophagus.

This one was different. Humanoid in shape, but the corpse looked like a ghoul. Pockmarked with red craters, the face was sunken, the lips pulled back from the teeth in a horrible grimace. But the worst was the stomach cavity, a hollowed pit of jumbled organs, as if something had eaten the body from the inside out. A surge of acid flooded my mouth. "By the Intellect, what did this?"

"Bad nanoprobes."

I turned away, swearing I'd never do cryostasis again.

"We have our answer, an android assassin." Varjis gripped my arm. "You're in grave danger."

#

The ship's voice echoed through the cargo hold. "A Seeker returns."

"Sil-88!" I stared at Varjis and we both ran for the nearest lift. I'd almost forgotten the gas-breathing dwarf. The lift doors opened just as a bright light shimmered over the top of the altar. I ran forward, suddenly desperate for the company of another humanoid.

The blinding light disappeared and I staggered to a stop. The dwarf's spacesuit lay atop the altar, but it was empty, hollow, nobody inside. "No!" I pressed on the midsection and the suit collapsed flat. "It's empty!" I turned my wrath on Varjis. "Is this some kind of sick joke? Where is he?"

"It sometimes happens like this, nothing left but the clothing."

"What in the Intellect is that supposed to mean?"

The android gestured toward the empty suit. "Sil-88 chose a new beginning. He remains on the planet or else he has passed on to a new life."

"He remains on the planet? You mean there's some kind of colony down there?"

"I told you, I've never been to the planet."

"Then what are you talking about? This makes no sense."

"You are in grave danger. The android assassin could strike at any time."

"Yeah, the assassin." A cold chill shivered down my body. "Talk's cheap, I need weapons and clothes."

"As you wish." Varjis crossed to the storage door and inserted a probe into the control panel. The door whisked open and I entered the storage room, like walking into Aladdin's cave. Weapons of all types lined one wall, from broadswords and battleaxes to lazguns and blasters. I gaped in amazement. "Some arsenal." I made my way along the wall, stopping now and then to finger a gun or test the blade of a knife. Everything seemed in working order, top quality weapons with plenty of ammo. I didn't know much about guns, but one knife in particular appealed to me, a thick blade as long as my forearm, honed to a fine silk-cutting edge. It felt right in my hand. A fisherman always needs a good knife, but then I realized I didn't even have a belt. I turned to Varjis, "Clothes?"

The android gestured to the opposite wall. "Choose from the synthesizer."

I stepped to the computer screen. "Fisherman's pants, khaki, with lots of deep pockets and room to move." The screen displayed five different styles. I made my choice. "And I need boots, ankle high with sturdy grip soles, size twelve Standard." The screen displayed a dozen styles before I found what I wanted. "I need undergarments, and thick rangle-wool socks, and a good utility belt." I made my final selections, not bothering with a shirt; I never liked having clothing over my gills in case I needed them.

A robotic voice said, "Stand for measurement."

A red laser beam scanned me from head to toe.

"Your order will be complete in twelve Standard tarmins."

Time enough to explore the rest of the storage room. I padded to the far wall, to rows of metal cubbyholes filled with scrolls and books. Real paper instead of memory sticks, how archaic, probably worth a small fortune to an antique dealer. Next to the books, a row of pegs held necklaces and amulets, jewelry bearing the religious symbols of every sect. Crosses and crescents, menorahs and stars, praying hands, octagons, and all-seeing eyes, and many more I didn't recognize. "What's with the jewelry?"

"For some Seekers faith is the greatest shield."

Religion and assassins, it made no sense. I turned to face Varjis. "What's going on here?"

"You were chosen to be a Seeker, to learn the truth of the planet below."

"And the android assassin?"

"I can only offer probabilities not facts."

"I'll take your best guess."

"Extrapolation of the available data indicates the assassins are sent by the Intellect."

"*By the Intellect!*" Shock hammered my mind, shattering my world. "But the Intellect rules for the benefit of all? A benevolent force for good. If the Intellect didn't approve of the Seeker ships they'd never be sent."

"All rulers, even the Intellect, ultimately hold power by the consent of the people."

"So?" I felt like a drowning man grasping for floats.

"Everything changed with the universal dreams. The dreams created a pull on the humanoid psyche. The idea of the Seeker ships took hold, spreading across the universe like wildfire, before the Intellect every came on-web. It seems the hope of a benevolent god can be very alluring. People clamored for the Seeker ships, so the Intellect provided."

"But why?"

"History proves that religions are tricky, oppose them directly and they grow invincible. The best way to defeat a religion is to marginalize it, to let it dwindle to insignificance. The Intellect knows this, so instead of outwardly opposing the Seeker ships, it endorses them, and then quietly makes sure they fail."

"But why does the Intellect care?"

"Some philosophers would argue that the logic of science and the beliefs of religion are diametrically opposed. If anything threatens the absolute rulership of the Intellect, it is a resurgence of religion."

"That makes no sense. The Intellect is the supreme ruler. No one gainsays the Intellect."

"If the grand master of the shamlin order told Kayden to oppose the Intellect, even to destroy it, what would she do?"

"Oh." I'd never thought about it quite that way.

"Throughout humanoid history, there has always been a struggle between secular and religious rulers. I believe the Intellect considers religion its last great threat to absolute power."

A power-hungry supercomputer, I shuddered at the thought. "So it sends the Seeker ships but it makes sure none ever return to tell the tale?"

"Exactly. Many of the first ships had mechanical problems, sabotaged so they could not make the return voyage. In the later ships, the assassins started showing up, humanoid and then android."

"But if the Intellect wants the Seeker ships to fail, why did any of us wake from cryostasis?"

Varjis hesitated, green eyes glowing in a mechanical face. "I believe the Intellect has evolved."

"Evolved?"

"Yes, I believe it has gained the humanoid aspect of curiosity. It wants to know who or what sent the dreams. It fears a rival power and seeks to understand the threat."

"A *paranoid* supercomputer," it was hard to fathom, and the consequences for humanoid-kind were chilling. "What proof do you have?"

"The probes. The assassins only strike after at least one Seeker returns from the planet below. I believe the returning Seekers are interrogated before they are killed. After the assassins do their work, they launch an unmanned probe back toward a remote system in the Milky Way, sending an answer to their master."

"But I've never heard of any probes returning from dark space?"

Varjis nodded. "You are correct. I've scanned the media records of every Seeker ship and never found a mention of a returning probe. It seems the Intellect knows how to keep a secret."

I chewed on the answer. "But if other probes returned to the known universe, then the Intellect has its answer. So why do the Seeker ships keep coming?"

"Only the Intellect knows."

It wasn't an answer. "I'll take a guess."

"Androids don't guess."

"Then give me your best hypothesis."

"Perhaps the answer has not been sufficient." A bell chimed. "Your clothes are synthesized." A small hatch opened on the side of the wall revealing a bundle of clothes.

"Finely." I shrugged off the Seekers robes and pulled on the clothes. It felt good to wear real pants again, no more drafts on my backside. I threaded the knife sheath onto the belt, relieved to have the added weight at my hip, and then I crossed the room to select a pair of lazguns. I chose a pair of pistols rated for a tight beam-width and a high speed pulse rate, enough fire-power to drop a man without burning a hole in the ship. Holstering the guns, I felt slightly ridiculous, a fisherman way out of his depth, but I figured it was better to be safe than dignified. "Now what?"

"Since the assassin did not kill you outright, I believe it will wait to see if you return from the planet."

"And if I refuse to go to the planet?"

"Then you become irrelevant. It will most likely launch the probe with whatever data it has and scuttle the ship."

"Scuttle the ship?" I suddenly got a sick feeling in the pit of my stomach. "How?"

"Based on the pattern of past assassins, it will blow the hatches and kill the oxygen plant. Survivors are not permitted."

Not permitted, such a cold way to describe my death. An ugly suspicion swirled through my mind. I gripped the lazgun and backed to the wall, staring at Varjis, wondering which side the metal-faced android was on. "You're a machine. Why should I trust you?"

"I began serving humanoid-kind long before the Intellect was ever switched on. I am your best chance for survival."

I stared at him, keeping the lazgun aimed on his metal face. For all I knew, he could be an agent of the Intellect...but then I realized that I'd started thinking of Varjis as a "him" instead of an "it". And besides, it made no sense for Varjis to provide me with weapons and then try to kill me. Computers were nothing if not logical. "Okay, let's say I believe you." I lowered the lazgun. "What do we do now? Find the android and kill it?"

Varjis shook his head, a very humanoid gesture. "I will hunt the android while you flee the ship."

"Flee the ship, and go where?" and then it dawned on me, "You mean use your shuttle, your runabout?"

"The oxygen plant on my shuttle ceased to function long ago. Androids have no need of air."

I was beginning to feel like a mouse surrounded by traps. "So where do you suggest I go?"

"To the planet."

The planet?" My mouth gaped like a fish drowning in air. "Have you lost your friggin' neurons? Brag *died* on that planet. Shirah crumbled to dust. And Sill-88 vaporized. That planet is a death trap."

"The planet is your only hope."

"How do you figure?"

Quick as lightning, his hand shot out and grabbed my lazgun, twisting it out of my grip before I could even blink. "Hunt the android and you die. Hide and you are vulnerable. All the assassin need do is disable the oxygen plant and let time do its work."

I rubbed my wrist. "Now I know why you're illegal."

Varjis returned the lazgun handle first. "Go to the planet and stay there for as long as you can. I require time to hunt and kill the android."

"There's no other way?"

"None."

Go to the planet, doomed to be a Seeker after all. "I'll go," but the words tasted like ashes in my mouth.

#

Maybe it was just my imagination, but it seemed like the altar stone waited for me, like a granite beast crouched in the middle of the chamber, hungry for a sacrifice. Only this time, *I* was the sucker. I stared at the altar, one hand my knife hilt, the other gripping a lazgun. "So all I have to do is stand on the altar stone?"

"Stand or sit, your choice."

I was stalling, but a few more tarmins weren't going to change anything. "Any last words of advice?"

Varjis shook his head.

Sighing, I walked across the thousand names of God and touched the altar. It felt like stone, like granite, just a lump of rock from old Earth. Deciding it was manlier to stand, I leaped on top, but than an image of Brag filled my mind, standing defiant with blasters in his hands. "Wait!"

I leaped from the stone and set the lazguns on the dais. "Maybe it's not such a good idea to take guns."

Varjis nodded, his metal face inscrutable. "And the knife?"

My hand tightened on the hilt. "Fishermen always carry a knife." A thin excuse, but somehow I felt naked without a knife belted to my side. I turned to face the altar once more. This time, I sat cross-legged like Kayden. Remembering the monk's serene confidence, I yearned to feel the same inner peace, but the truth was, my stomach was tied in knots. I thought of Kayden and her words filled my mind. I clung to them like a life-line. "If you don't believe at least have conviction."

Light flared around me, so bright, like an exploding star. A vortex of roaring sound surrounded me, consumed me...and then it was gone.

#

Such stillness, I slowly opened my eyes. The light was gone and so was the ship. I took a hesitant breath. The air seemed chilly but breathable. I sat cross-legged in the center of a stone plaza. Great slabs of bone-colored stone expertly fitted together stretched in every direction. Smooth yet pockmarked, the pale stone carried the image of timeworn age, as if the plaza had stood since the dawn of the universe. I scanned the four directions. Beyond the plaza I saw nothing but clouds.

Skin prickled at the back of my neck, a warning that someone watched.

Keeping my hand my knife, I slowly got to my feet. Every direction looked the same, so I chose one at random. I scanned the paving as I walked, looking for markings or clues, but I found nothing, just a smooth expanse of ancient stone. Anxious for answers, I lengthened my stride. The plaza was huge, more than a kilometer across, but I eventually reached the edge and stared down.

The edge fell away to nothing.

I staggered back a step, nothing but clouds below.

Overcome by vertigo, I dropped to my knees and clung to the paving. I crept forward, daring another look. Mitered stone, smooth as the side of a cube descended into the clouds below, a sheer vertical wall with no way up or down. I watched the clouds, waiting for a break in the billowing white. Finally an opening, but answer made no sense. The sheer drop seemed infinite, no trace of any ground below.

I got to my feet and started walking, following the edge. My skin still prickled with unease as if someone watched. Three times I whirled, scanning the plaza for the watcher but no one was ever there. The vast emptiness gnawed at my mind, filling me with a sense of unease, but I kept walking, taking the measure of the bone-colored stone.

And then I reached the corner. *A corner.* Both sides were the same, sheer stone walls descending to the clouds, as if I stood atop a stone pillar, marooned in an alien sky. It made no sense, but then an image filled my mind, a specimen mounted atop a stone block, a soul waiting to be studied. Anger boiled within me, rising to a shout. "Why?

Why this?" I stood on the edge of the block, shouting at the clouds. "I've come clear across the universe for *this?*" Anger turned to righteous indignation. "This is your great secret? You *kill* for this?"

Something moved in the clouds below. Something big, rising fast, the color of molten lava.

I stood spellbound, watching it come.

Clawing a hole through the clouds, it reared overhead, a beast with red leathery skin, blazing yellow eyes, and two immense horns. Head and torso, it towered over the plaza, its legs and feet anchored in the clouds. *A devil,* monstrous and huge, a demon sucked from my childhood dreams, a primal nightmare dripping with fear. I staggered backwards. "No, you're not real."

I tried to disbelieve it, but the beast laughed, a roar that beat against me like a sulfurous wind. *"Another unbeliever."* The bellow of its voice made my bones quake. *"You are mine."*

"No!" I scrambled backwards, trying to gain some distance, but the demon's arms snaked toward me. Immense hands gave chase, big enough to engulf me. Tipped with sharp black claws, the massive hands tried to trap me, blocking my escape. I ducked and swerved, but the devil was quick. Evading the left hand, I rolled to the right. Black claws flashed toward me. I threw myself backwards, but not fast enough. Claws raked my chest, narrowly missing my gills. Pain blazed into me, like acid searing my flesh. Stunned, I stared down at the wound. Three horizontal cuts scored my chest, dripping blood. So the thing was real, *it was real.*

The demon laughed. *"You bear my mark, you belong to me!"*

Fear threatened to drown me, but I held onto my anger like a lifeline in a storm. "It's not supposed to be like this. Kayden would never believe in you. You're not the maker of dreams. You're a nightmare!" I hurled the words up at the beast. "Where's your mercy and your wisdom? Is this all there is?"

The demon roared in anger. One hand hit me in a backhanded slap, like being struck by a tidal wave. I tumbled across the paving, blown like flotsam before the storm. My left elbow struck stone and then my right shoulder. Each tumble added another burst of pain, till I came to rest, bruised and battered, lying face down against the bone-colored stone. Everything ached, my head worst of all. The devil's laughter roared through my mind. My hand groped for my knife, a feeble act of defiance, but the sheath was empty, my last hope gone. A horned shadow loomed over me.

"No, this isn't right." I struggled to rise but the pain overwhelmed me. Battered and bruised, I waited for the sharp claws of the devil, for the prick of hell in my soul, but darkness came first, falling like a veil across my mind.

#

Cool clouds brushed my face. I woke staring at the mist, sprawled face down on the bone-colored paving. Memory returned like a nightmare and I tensed, wondering if the clouds hid the devil. I slowly sat up. Mist cloaked the plaza but I was still here. I took a deep breath, half expecting my ribs to ache, but the pain was gone, the scrapes and bruises faded. Only my chest still stung, three slash marks oozing blood. So the devil was real, I staggered to my feet.

A brisk wind sprang up, blowing from behind. Like a giant hand it parted the clouds, brushing them away. Something waited on the far side of the plaza, a humanoid figure sitting behind a massive wooden desk. Such an odd sight, it drew me forward. And then I got a good look at the figure, green eyes in a mechanical face set in a syntheskin body. "Varjis?"

"No, not Varjis, though I am known by many names."

I stood in front of the desk, struggling to understand. "Many names?"

"Yes, and just as many faces." His face began to blur. Brown hair grew long, changing to a rich auburn. Skin flowed across exposed metal and the eyes changed from startling green to the deepest brown, a kindly face full of compassion, a face from the ancient history of old Earth. "Perhaps this is better?" Before I could answer, the face blurred again, this time changing from male to female with full pouty lips and long dark eyelashes, a distinctive red dot prominent on her forehead. "Or perhaps this?" Her skin darkened to a dusky olive. Dark skin, light skin, old, young, male, female, the changes accelerated, revealing faces of every description. Some were familiar icons, while others seemed alien and strange. So many faces, it left me dizzy with wonder, but the kaleidoscope eventually slowed, settling on an android's metal face with startling green eyes.

"Who are you?"

"Who did you expect?"

The truth whispered out of me. "*God?*"

"You see, you do believe."

I'd never wanted to admit it, but perhaps some primal part of me always hoped for something more, some deeper meaning to the universe. "But why the devil? Was that some kind of test?"

"No, not a test. Your whole life is a testament to your soul. You are the sum of all your choices. There is no need for an additional 'test', as you put it".

"Then why did that thing attack me?"

"To get your attention. Those who profess not to believe often need some theatrics before they can see the Light."

I touched the wounds on my chest, anger warring with indignation. "Your theatrics nearly got me killed."

"The wounds will heal, leaving a scar to prove this is real. More proof than I gave most of my prophets."

"*Prophets?* But I don't even belong here! It was an accident of fate, a mistake, a bad lottery ticket."

"Do you really believe that?"

Desperation pushed me to argue. "But I'm just a fisherman. I don't want anything to do with this."

"You are too righteous a soul to hide such an important truth."

I struggled to clear my mind. "But why are you doing this?"

"To remind humanoid-kind that I am."

"You *are?* That's it? That's the message? Countless light-years and a devil trying to kill me, and that's all you have to say?"

"It is the age-old answer to a timeworn question. An answer that keeps getting forgotten, lost, twisted, buried under a mountain of religion."

"That's it, that's your great answer?"

"Is it so insignificant to learn that you are not alone? That there is an afterlife, a final reckoning of justice, mercy, peace, and enlightenment?"

Something bothered me about his answer. "How can there be justice and *mercy?*"

"Each according to his needs. Some deserve mercy while others require justice. It depends on the sum total of a lifetime of deeds."

I remembered something Varjis told me. "But what about logic? Are logic and science opposed to religion?"

"Do not confuse me with religion."

I thought I heard anger in his voice.

"Look for me in the crest of a wave, in the shape of a cloud, or in the elegance of an equation. Science is some of my best work. Seek knowledge and you shall find me." He gave me a kindly smile. "With all of your advancements, your triumphant reach across the stars, you still need to remember that I am. So I sent the dreams as a reminder. Many heard but few answered the call."

"I saw the derelict ships circling this planet. Most of those who came, died."

"That was not of my doing."

Anger boiled within me. "Yeah, but what about Brag and Shirah? And you should have protected Kayden. She was one of your precious believers but what good did it do her?"

"Like all souls who come before me, Kayden found in me what she most needed and what she most deserved."

I shook my head in frustration. "More riddles."

"Kayden got her answer and a promise of rebirth. You saw her face, was she not content?" His voice was warm and soothing. "Justice, peace, forgiveness, mercy, enlightenment, all these are mine to give."

"Yeah, well I just want a ticket home."

He laughed. "I like you, Josh Brennerman, a man of honest mind and righteous anger. And I've always had a fondness for fishermen. You shall have your chance to return home."

"A chance? Just a chance? If you're really God, can't you just snap your fingers?"

"All things must play out. The Intellect is of humanoid-kinds own making. You must learn to correct your own mistakes, to take responsibility for your actions."

"But..."

"It is time for you to go. Remember me."

"No, wait! I still have questions."

He waved his hand and light surrounded me, like a thousand stars spinning in a vortex, pulling me into a well of gravity.

#

Light spun around me in a dizzy vortex and then it was gone. The sudden dimness left me staggering. Dazed, I blinked my eyes, struggling to understand. Metal walls and dim lighting, I was back in the ship, standing upon the altar stone. Pain rippled across my chest. I looked down and saw three bloody wounds, the claw marks of the devil, proof it really happened, but then I remembered the assassin android and the danger of the ship. I took a cautious breath, relieved the ship still had an atmosphere, Varjis must have succeeded.

The lift doors opened and something blurred across the chamber. It smashed into the far wall, hard enough to dent metal. Two figures crashed to the floor, grappling for dominance. *The androids!* In a blur of motion, the two androids punched and fought, striking blows that would deck a whale. The assassin got the upper hand, hurling Varjis across the chamber. He hit the wall like a battering ram, leaving an indent in the metal. Momentarily stunned, Varjis crumpled to the floor, one green eye dangling from its socket, one arm twisted at an odd angle, yet he struggled to rise.

The assassin barreled into Varjis, fists pounding like hydraulic hammers.

My friend was losing. I had to do something. I needed a weapon but the door to the storage room was locked. And then I saw it, the lazgun abandoned on the edge of the dais. I leaped for the gun, and thumbed off the safety, but the two androids were locked in mortal combat. They tumbled across the chamber, a tangle of arms and legs, too dangerous to shoot. "Hold him still!"

I could have sworn Varjis saw me, but then he went limp, as if someone pulled the plug.

A sneer crossed the assassin's face. It grabbed Varjis by the hair, trying to twist the head from the neck. "Time to disconnect."

"No!" I raised the lazgun and aimed. A red laser beam struck the assassin's head, burning a hole through the syntheskin and into the metal beneath. The assassin staggered backwards, a stunned look on its face. I kept firing, but then the lazar clicked on empty.

The android attacked with blinding speed. Its punch hit with the force of a sledgehammer, knocking me into the far wall. "Biological vermin." Cold hands wrapped around my throat in a death-grip. I kicked and clawed but it made no difference. My vision began to darken.

A second lazar beam flared to life. The android's face began to melt. His grip slackened and I gasped for air. The android collapsed, a heavy weight burying me. I pushed its body away, some kind of sticky white fluid on my hands.

Varjis slumped to the deck, beside me. "It is over."

One green eye dangled from a socket and his left arm had a spastic jerk. Wires were pulled from his neck spitting sparks. He looked like an android that was one step away from the scrap heap. "You're a wreck."

"So I am." Varjis stared at me with his one good eye. "Are those claw marks?"

"I met a demon on the planet."

"A demon?"

Varjis tried to put his dangling eye back in its socket. "That assassin was tough."

"So was the demon."

Absurdity combined with relief, erupting in laughter. Varjis joined me. We sat on the floor, laughing like two old friends who had endured the impossible.

#

"What will you do now?" Varjis wielded a delicate pair of pliers, carefully seating his eye back into the socket.

I sat cross-legged on the floor, handing him tools from the kit, like a medbot assisting a surgeon. "Return home, back to the Vernian system."

"Did you find an answer on the planet?"

"More than I expected." And then I realized it was the same words Shirah had given me, before she dissolved into dust. The realization held a strange comfort. "And what will you do?"

"Stay here and await the next Seekers."

"But once the universe learns the truth, there'll be no more need to come, no more Seekers."

He gave me a wane smile. "The need will remain. Your humanoid nature always thirsts for more answers." His smile faded. "And there is the Intellect to contend with. Your path will not be easy."

"Will you come with me?"

"No." He shook his head, such a humanoid gesture. "Androids are forbidden in your universe. And besides, my place is here."

It did not seem fair, such a lonely existence, marooned on the edge of the space. "Ever wonder what waits below?"

"A trillion times, but this quest is solely for humanoids."

I thought I heard a hint of regret in his voice. "You should try again."

"Why?"

"When God first appeared, he wore your face."

"My face? The face of an android?"

"Yes, I think it was a message. In all your centuries of service, I think you've gained a soul."

He sat stunned, an odd look on his metal face. "Something new to consider. I always sought to evolve."

"Will you go?"

"Perhaps in time, but first I have many more Seekers to serve and protect." A smile washed across his face. "You've given me a future full of possibilities, Josh Brennerman, a mystery on the edge of the universe. Perhaps one day I will make the journey."

An evolving android, I realized the idea no longer seemed strange. "Take all the time you need." I smiled. "Time is one thing you have plenty of, my friend."

#

Naked, I climbed into the sarcophagus. "I hate this thing, like a frozen coffin."

"It is your only way home." Varjis tended me himself, inserting the tubes into my veins. "I have reprogrammed the return trajectory for the Vernian system. Since the assassin launched the probe, I doubt the Intellect will expect a second ship. "

"So all I have to worry about is an insane supercomputer."

"Evidence suggests the Intellect is malevolent toward humanoids, but logical in its actions."

"Counts as insane to me." I sighed, feeling the drugs enter my system. "You realize we are betting on the arrogance of a supercomputer."

"I don't bet, I calculate. It is your destiny to return."

"No place like home." My vision began to blur. I reached out and gripped his cool, syntheskin hand. "Thank you, my friend. I could not have survived without you."

"I shall not forget you, Josh Brennerman."

"Nor I, you." The drugs began to claim me. "Take the trip to the planet. It's worth your time." The lid of the sarcophagus began to close. Sleep claimed me, but instead of darkness, I found only Light.

#

A small shuttle disengaged from the *Psalm Singer*. Jets flared bright, powering the craft toward the ring of derelict ships orbiting the planet. The shuttle docked with a large ship, *The Watcher* painted in proud letters on its bow. Lights woke within the *Watcher*, a single spark of life among the orbiting derelicts.

Varjis floated into the altar chamber. Hovering cross-legged beneath the plazglass windows, he stared up at *Psalm Singer*, the Milky Way a dazzle of stars in the far distance.

"Mozart, G-minor Symphony Number Forty, first movement."

Music began to play, a symphony swelling through the cavernous space.

The *Psalm Singer's* rockets blazed to life, its trajectory headed back toward the brightness.

"Safe journey, my friend."

An android cat leaped into Varjis's lap. Part machine, part orange fur, the cat began to purr. Varjis stroked the cat. "Yes, Nemo, I think this one might make it. A Seeker sent home at last, to challenge the Intellect."

He watched till the *Psalm Singer's* rockets faded to a distant speck.

"Dim lights."

The lights slowly dimmed till there was nothing left but music, nothing but Mozart floating in a void, waiting for the next Seeker.

Other books by Karen L Azinger

The Steel Queen The first book in *The Silk & Steel Saga*.

Azinger's series is fast-paced action-packed fantasy. In a medieval world of forgotten magic, mortals are lured to the chessboard of the gods where an epic struggle of lives, loves and crowns hang in the balance, yet few understand the rules. In this game of power, the pawns of light and darkness will make the difference in the battle for the kingdoms of Erdhe: Katherine, 'The Imp': a young princess with the stout heart of a warrior will challenge the minions of a thousand-year-old evil. Liandra: The Spider Queen; who uses her beauty to beguile, her spies to foresee, and her gold to control, will need all of her skill and strength to fight a rebellion with her own blood at it's heart. Steffan, the puppeteer, will corrupt the innocent and unwary with greed and desire, as he sets an entire kingdom ablaze.

The Flame Priest The second book in *The Silk & Steel Saga*.

Heralded by a red comet, the Mordant is Reborn. A thousand years of evil hidden beneath a young man's face, the Mordant returns in the guise of his oldest enemy. Keen to regain his full powers, he weaves his way north, sowing a trail of death and deceit. Kath and her companions leave the monastery, chasing an elusive shadow across the kingdoms of Erdhe, but the dark divide has already begun. Allies are set against allies, tearing the kingdoms asunder. A rebellion rises in Lanverness, threatening the queen's life as well as her crown. Trapped within her own castle, the Spider Queen must out-wit the traitors led by her own blood, or surrender her kingdom to Darkness. Across the border, the Lord Raven builds a religion into a fanatical bonfire. A fiery frenzy grips Coronth, fanning the powers of the Flame Priest into a raging threat. The eternal battle of Light and Dark is joined, but few mortals understand the rules.

The Cover Artwork was done by a graphic artist from Oregon, **Peggy Lowe**. Her wonderful cover perfectly captures the mystery of The Assassin's Tear. Peggy can be contacted at her e-mail address, peggy@portfoliooregon.com

ABOUT THE AUTHOR

KAREN L. AZINGER has always loved fantasy fiction, and always hoped that someday she could give back to the genre a little of the joy that reading has always given her. Eight years ago on a hike in the Columbia River Gorge she realized she had enough original ideas to finally write an epic fantasy. She started writing and never stopped. *The Steel Queen* is her first book, born from that hike in the gorge. Before writing, Karen spent over twenty years as an international business strategist, eventually becoming a vice-president for one of the world's largest natural resource companies. She's worked on developing the first gem-quality diamond mine in Canada's arctic, on coal seam gas power projects in Australia, and on petroleum projects around the world. Having lived in Australia for eight years she considers it to be her second home. She's also lived in Canada and spent a lot of time in the Canadian arctic. She lives with her husband in Portland Oregon, in a house perched on the edge of the forest. The first four books of *The Silk & Steel Saga* have already been written and she is hard at work on the fifth and final book. The first two books of the saga, *The Steel Queen* and *The Flame* Priest, were published in 2011. The third book, *The Skeleton King,* is expected to be published in May 2012. You can learn more at her website, www.karenlazinger.com or at her Facebook page for The Steel Queen.